Haunting Tessa

A Spirit Hunters Novel

Temperance Dawn

ISBN: 979-8-9858761-7-8 (eBook)

ISBN: 979-8-9858761-8-5, 979-8-9858761-9-2 (paperback)

Cover Images courtesy of: https://www.shutterstock.com/g/Kirichay+D, https://stock.adobe.com/contributor/201565343/dmitry-tsvetkov

Cover design by: Maja Kopunovic

Published by: Daring Light Publishing, LLC

Edited by: Killing It Write

Formatted by: Melissa Smith Homestead Book Services

Trigger Warnings

This book is intended for mature audiences 18 years and older. This book does contain discussions on mental health, mental hospitals, rape and suicide. If these subjects are triggers for you, please do not read this book. This book also contains violence, explicit language, and scenes of sexual content.

To my team, my crew, my dreamers, thank you all for sticking by me. You've helped me through some tough times, and you've shown me that no matter how dark life gets, there's always light at the end of the tunnel. I love you all.

XOXO,
Temperance

Dear Reader,
You deserve to be loved.
~TD

One

E choes pounded the tile floor as they chased Francis Walker.

She ran down the cold, sterile hallway of the top floor that lacked life.

Dark.

Quiet.

She'd only seen this hallway twice before. The rest of the time, she'd been confined to her room.

The halls mirrored the lower levels she remembered from the days prior to being moved to the fifth floor. Except now, every door she tried to open was locked.

Living in a sanitarium, one became used to the constant pleas of others. Being alone felt unnerving. Alone, she was forced to live in solitary confinement, where her screams went unheard. No one knew she had been locked away, and no one knew she was being chased.

But then, it wasn't like the others would be able to help her anyway. They were all under his control.

Francis tried another door and then the next with no luck. She fought against the burn in her muscles—no longer used to moving and being worked. She'd been tied up for months, confined to her room, the restraints only long enough to allow her to use the latrine and basin. Otherwise, she had been restricted to the bed.

She'd only been free of the restraints for the last few days. The doctor was kind enough to free her while she screamed as the pain of labor ripped open her heart. She knew what the doctor had planned, and with every scream, she prayed it wouldn't come true.

Panic surged through her as she came upon yet another locked door, and the echoing footsteps grew closer. She forced her legs to keep moving and find a way out.

She had pushed the nurse who'd come to administer her nightly concoction of drugs. A mix that would send her into a deep sleep—keeping her quiet.

Using all her strength, Francis had slammed the woman's head into the wall. She'd heard the crack of the woman's skull and fleetingly wondered if she'd killed her. It didn't matter, though. Served the woman right for stealing her baby while she was drugged and for hiding the things that happened in that god-awful place.

The sour woman told Francis the following morning, while she screamed in agony at her loss, that the baby had been taken away and placed with a "normal" mother. There was no remorse from the nurse. Just a cold, heartless explanation. Francis felt no pity when the nurse hit the floor. She was already living in hell, so what did it matter?

Every lift of her leg and pump of her arm was excruciating. She wheezed as her lungs struggled to take in more oxygen, forcing herself to keep moving and not look back, even without knowing where she would go or if she'd make it out. But she had to try. They hadn't yet chained her up again. This was her chance. She had to get out. Even if it meant her death, she had to let someone know what was happening behind those walls.

Her heart ached for the child ripped from her arms. She needed to find her baby. She didn't know what the doctor had done with her daughter, but Francis would do whatever it took to find her child.

Her hands slammed against frigid walls, searching for an unlocked door in the darkness. She couldn't go downstairs. The night orderlies would stop her and pump her full of drugs that would fog her brain with confusion, ultimately silencing her. Then, she'd be tied up again, and she couldn't let herself fall back into that state where she had no control—no voice.

"Francis..." His words were mocking and evil. "You won't survive without me." The doctor's voice bounced off of every surface in the hallway, surrounding her as she navigated the dark, musty corridors. The only bit of light streamed through dirty windows from the few streetlights below. They cast gray shadows of the large tree branches from outside over the walls. Only slightly brighter than the blackness of the night that surrounded her, they hovered like dozens of spindly arms reaching for her.

Her nightgown dragged across the floor like a weight behind her while she ran, threatening to pull her down. But Francis fought and willed her legs to keep running.

Nearing the end of the hallway, the next door she tried opened at the twist of the handle, allowing her to fall inward. She softly closed the door behind her and realized that there was no lock. She turned to the empty room and rushed to a broken window. Damp chilly-night air rushed in. She hoped the doctor was far enough down the hallway not to have seen her retreat.

There were no bars outside the glass here, unlike the rest of the hospital, where they covered every window as constant reminders to everyone within. They were more like prisoners than patients.

She scanned the nearby houses, dark and no doubt filled with sleeping occupants, the residents oblivious to the atrocities taking place behind the walls of the sanitarium that stood on their street. The gate surrounding the property provided an adequate boundary between the neighborhood and the hospital that sat at the bottom of a steep hill. Tall cypress trees and a lush lawn leading to the building were aesthetically pleasing. It was a stark contrast to the horrors that took place within.

One doctor.

One hospital.

Countless patients and endless suffering.

And a secret that had the power to put a stop to the doctor's madness. If only she could reach the outside.

Francis lifted the window, carefully inching it up. The remaining broken glass in the frame wobbled, threatening to dislodge and shatter at her feet. She ducked her head and lifted her leg, then stepped out onto the thin ledge of the building. Molding her body to the cold stucco at her back, she put as much distance between herself and the edge as possible before she sidestepped along the narrow ledge.

The drop seemed to go on forever, with nothing but the ground to break her fall. Each movement of her feet sent shock waves of pain through her aching legs. But she couldn't stop. She would use every last bit of strength she had to escape the confines of the hell she'd been trapped in.

She moved along the edge of the building hoping for an escape route around the corner. Maybe an open window she could sneak back into and find a safe way out.

"Get back in here!" the doctor seethed. Francis glanced in the direction of his voice. His dark eyes radiated with hatred.

She inched further away but pressed her question. "Where is my baby?"

He didn't answer and only stepped out onto the ledge too. Francis caught the sharp bobble in his throat when he stood upright against the building and glanced down. Perhaps there was an element of humanity in him after all. She liked seeing him scared.

"You're in no condition to leave the hospital. Certainly, no condition to be out here. You're weak and need medical attention," his voice cut through the wind like ice.

"I don't need your care!" Peeking to her other side, Francis noticed that the ledge wrapped around the building. She could scream for help and hope that someone would hear. She glanced around, seeking the best direction to orient her voice. "Help me!" But the blustery night muffled her cry.

"Go ahead. The police will come. They'll find out you're a patient of mine. I'll tell them the truth, that you tried to escape, but you're not well." The evil in the doctor's eyes convinced her that hell took up residence on these grounds. All of the warmth left in her seeped away when he spoke again. "That's why you're here."

He was evil, but he was right. There was no way to prove that she'd been kept against her will. Her parents had left her in the hands of the hospital ten years earlier. Her depression and anxiety had become too much for them to handle. They dropped her off one day and never returned. She'd been forgotten and now was the property of a madman. Her home was this hospital.

"Please let me go," she pleaded, prepared now to make a deal. "I won't tell anyone." Her vision blurred from the tears pooling in them over the realization that there may not be any escape for her. "You can just forget about me. I'll disappear, and you'll never hear from me. It will be like I never existed."

"I'm afraid I can't do that."

Hands gripped her arm. She pulled away, but they kept their hold, and she was hauled back inside the place of her worst nightmares. Two orderlies lifted her and dragged her into another room through the window she stood closest to.

"Let me go!" she pleaded, looking into the eyes of the men who had her restrained by the arms. But she was met with cold, emotionless stares. "He's mad. I shouldn't be here. He stole my baby," Francis screamed, using all her energy to fight, but she was too weak to fight against them.

Footsteps, slow, deliberate and magnified as his shoes crunched on the dirty floor, alerted her that he was near. Her knees ached from the hard, unforgiving tiles. The chill seeped upward, straight to her bones.

He came close and knelt to look into her bowed face. She struggled, unsuccessful at freeing herself. "Pennington," she bit out with disgust, "you can't keep this secret forever. Someone will find out." Rage worked itself forward as she met his eyes. He stared back, showing no emotion. "In this life or the next, the truth about you will get out."

His lip curled like a wolf ready to attack. "We'll see," he sneered like she was a piece of garbage. "Take her downstairs. I'll shut her up, once and for all."

"No!" Francis screamed. Desperate, her legs entangled in her hospital gown as she flailed against the men's grasps, knowing what would come next. He'd threatened her before but had never followed through. As long as she remained compliant, she was safe from his wrath. But she'd broken the rules by running, and like anyone who broke the rules in the doctor's hospital, she would be punished.

Francis blinked while staring out of the window, haunted by the memories of her life before the hospital. The life that was stolen from her.

She watched endlessly, wishing to be free of her prison. She watched the passersby, envying their existence. They could feel the breeze against their skin. Taste the salt in the city's air. Smell the flowers...

What she wouldn't give to leave these walls and tell the world what went on inside.

Now, only the ghostly echoes of the past vibrated through the empty space. Sounds audible to only herself and the others who remained. Maybe she could figure out a way to leave. Maybe someday.

Decades passed, and Francis still feared the doctor's maliciousness, his tantrums and his control. She didn't dare fight him. No one did.

Could a ghost suffer through death twice? She certainly didn't want to find out. And so, she remained compliant, a puppet under his control.

The one bit of hope she held onto dwindled more as time passed. The prospect of finding out what happened to her long-forgotten child seemed out of reach. Trapped within the walls of the place that held her captive in life still bound her in short, unforgiving chains in death. So, she held on to the memory of the baby with rosy cheeks and wisps of sandy hair. And the intent to find a way to put a stop to the doctor's wrath remained her number one goal. She'd free herself and the others. Somehow. Someway.

Someday, she would be free.

Two

Present Day

C hange is a funny thing. Crucial to life but often never liked.

Most people feared change—tiptoeing around its sharp edges like it would jump out and slice them. Others, like Tessa Brown, embraced it.

The exhilarating excitement of change breathed new ambition into her. Living a mundane life was never her calling. Though that's what her life had been like until recently.

It wasn't until Tessa took that leap and left Seattle that she felt a release of the anxiety that had bogged her down for so long.

She'd never been afraid of change. Change meant growth. It was an expansion of oneself, moving from one place to the next. New experiences were on the horizon, and now that she was free of a home that restricted her progress, she'd promised herself she would jump into any new and uncharted waters that flowed her way.

Living in San Francisco and doing the work she loved were her first steps in taking full charge of her life.

There was nothing to fear when life was trying to move you forward. That was her daily mantra. Except the hourglass blinking and rotating in front of her now awoke tremors so deep she'd swear her bones rattled.

Waiting for the results of the digital pregnancy test was like waiting for a rogue wave to hit. She knew what was coming, and no matter which way her mind pivoted, there was no escaping what she knew to be true. Fear gripped her in ways she didn't think were possible. Not about having a baby. She'd always known she wanted to be a mother someday. The timing was just off. The fear that washed over her involved Luke.

Her secret nights with Luke Collins were always exciting. Time stopped in the hours she spent alone with him. He had a way of washing away any worries that plagued her and those memories that haunted her. Her mind was free to shut out the opinions and noise of the world about her and her life choices and drift to a place where only the two of them existed. Only she caught the little glimpses Luke cast her way while they were around their friends. Those nights out for dinner with the entire group were casual and cool. He was her thrilling secret she held on to tightly.

And now a baby? She didn't know anything about Luke's family. Only that he preferred never to talk about them, and he'd stated many times he wasn't built to be a family man. What would he say? What would he think when she told him?

It wasn't like the word now displayed on the test screen came out of a purposeful encounter. They'd always been careful. Only once had they gotten so carried away that the moments of passion overtook their thinking. Both had brushed off the thought the next morning. What were the odds it would only take that one time?

Pretty good, apparently. That was over two months ago, and she'd been so caught up in work she'd missed the fact that her period was late. It wasn't until fatigue hit her, and then nausea that wouldn't go away, that she checked her calendar.

What if Luke didn't want anything to do with her when she told him? Would his talk about him never wanting a family or being tied down still hold true? Their relationship was based on the two of them remaining free. No strings whatsoever.

No, he wasn't that kind of guy. But there was always the possibility, and she had to consider it. Would Theo let her out of her lease? Would he allow her to continue living there with a baby?

She blinked, her thoughts pulling away when Theo called for her, his voice slightly muffled coming from downstairs. Her one roommate, Theo, who was more of a live-in landlord, was almost never around as he worked nights while finishing his residency and slept like the dead during the day. But Theo was fun, and the two had become good friends since she'd rented her room. It was normal for them to catch up when they were both home.

She put the cap on the end of the stick and slipped it into the pocket of her jeans. Brushing her wavy, chestnut hair back from her face, she took a few deep breaths to ease her nerves and walked out of the bathroom. At the bottom of the stairs, she heard Theo rustling around nearby. With her hands in the pockets of her open-front cardigan, she turned the corner and entered the kitchen.

"Hey, love." His friendly tone always carried a sweet, melodic tune. "Kyle and I are heading out of town this weekend."

"It's about time," she said with a smile. He'd had a crush on a fellow intern at the hospital for a while now. She'd listened to him for months go on and on about how he wanted to go on a date. Finally, she convinced him to ask. Now, the two were almost inseparable when they weren't working. "You two are really hitting it off. Where are you going?" She wiggled her eyebrows.

Theo faced her as he turned from the refrigerator and mimicked her brow motions. His dark glasses framed his hazel eyes. He ran his hand through his dark, slicked-back hair. "Just down to L.A. I'm meeting his family."

"Already?"

"I know. It's so soon."

"No, it's not. If you guys think it's right and you're comfortable, then do it. Have a wonderful trip."

He lifted his backpack and walked to her, wrapping her in a bear hug. "You're a doll." He walked to the front door, looked back, winked, and said, "I won't be home tonight. We're hitting the road as soon as our shifts are over in the morning."

"Okay. Drive safe."

"Tell Luke I said hi."

The door closed behind Theo, and she froze at his words. *Luke.* Theo was the only one who knew the extent of their relationship. He'd come home early one morning and run into the two of them making breakfast. Theo didn't so much as bat an eye. When she asked him later about what his thoughts were on having friends with benefits, he responded, "Honey, the only people who should care are the two of you. And if anyone else is going to have an issue, then they don't deserve to be in your sweet life. Do what makes you happy, and don't let society run your life."

She loved his honesty. And he was right. Deep down, the one thing she questioned the most was keeping Luke a secret from her sister. Lexi would only be concerned for her happiness. But what if things didn't work out between them? She didn't want any hard feelings within the group of friends.

The pregnancy test in her pocket burned hot. She pulled it out and stared at the results again. Her entire body shook. That had been happening more frequently lately. A chill so deep came through the room that her bones ached.

She checked the thermostat. It was set to seventy degrees, like always. Up until recently, that seemed to keep the old Victorian house comfortable.

Tessa was lucky enough to work from home. She'd finished her college courses a few months ago and now worked solely as a graphic designer. She'd worked hard all through college to build up a clientele, and most of them kept her on retainer. Her chosen career gave her the freedom to work from anywhere she wanted and an income that afforded her the opportunity to rent a spacious room in a historic home.

She was alone most days and enjoyed the solitude. She'd always felt safe and comfortable in the house. However, a recent shift in the energy of the place had her uneasy. Still, she brushed it off as being overworked.

She ignored it. Even when the sense of unseen eyes watching her increased over the last few days, she buried her head in work. But now, chills ran down her spine.

The doorbell peeled, and she jumped, releasing a shriek.

Fuck. Get a grip, Tess.

She hurried to the front door and caught the delivery driver pulling away. She picked up the package, then walked down the steps, stopping at the wrought iron gate that separated the sidewalk from the property. An older woman who lived up the street and passed by each day with her dog, a chocolate lab that had arthritis in his rear legs but still had the energy of a puppy, stopped and waited while Tessa walked over. The dog's tail wagged in a frenzy, and his tongue hung out the side of his mouth in a happy pant. She leaned over the low gate, scratched the dog's head and made small talk with the older woman. They were strangers, really, yet paused every time they saw one another to say hi.

When Tessa turned back to the house a few minutes later, her feet halted before she reached the first step. A strange energy pulled at her, coaxing her gaze to the top of the house. The home was magnificent. An old Queen Ann Victorian. Theo's grandparents bought it decades ago, and he was now living there to maintain it.

Her gaze followed the lines of the house as she looked up to where the steep slant of the roof came together at a point. Just below, the attic window sat dark. Only a cream-colored curtain was visible. Though that wasn't what caught Tessa's eye. It was the way the curtain moved, just enough to make her heart race as if someone was behind it, and they'd darted away before anyone could see them.

She squinted, trying to pick up any movement, but as quick as the fabric shifted, it stilled like it had never even happened. Maybe her mind was playing tricks on her. Lack of sleep and the stunning news she'd just confirmed had her senses heightened and her mind seeing things.

Shaking her head, she walked up the steps, crossed the threshold of the front door, and locked it behind her. Rest is what she needed.

In her room, she removed the pregnancy test from her pocket and placed it under the glass top of the jewelry box on the antique dresser. In the mirror, she caught her reflection and sighed at the heavy bags that brought out the exhaustion in her eyes.

Pulling her hair to the side, she twisted the strands into a loose braid. Tying the ends with a hair band, she climbed onto her bed, took some deep breaths, and within minutes, the tiredness that had plagued her for days won over her mind's racing thoughts, and she fell asleep.

Hours later, her eyes fluttered open. She lay on top of her covers, still in her clothes from the day. The room was dark. She shivered from a chill that gripped her. She rolled onto her back and lay still. The feeling that had woken her was apparent.

Her muscles froze, and her heart pounded in her chest. Moving only her eyes, she scanned the room, seeking out what was watching her. Nothing seemed out of the ordinary, but she couldn't shake the feeling that she wasn't alone.

With her arms, she pushed herself into a sitting position halfway on the bed. She swung her legs over the side and listened, her ears straining to hear anything out of the ordinary.

Cold seeped through her feet when they touched the floor. Not even the area rug under the bed could cut the chill that enveloped the room.

She crept toward the door, reached out and turned the knob. The wood creaked as she pulled it open a few inches. Her unsteady breathing was the only other sound.

Tessa opened it further and peeked out into the hallway. Taking a step out of the room, she called, "Theo. Is that you?"

No answer came.

A swirling electrical current stood static in the hall. For the first time ever, Tessa was uncomfortable beyond comprehension. Still standing within the threshold, she flipped the light switch in her room. The ceiling fixture illuminated, and with light now flooding the area, she padded across the space and flipped the switch on the wall in the hallway, casting out the night.

The relief was short-lived, however, as a flickering of the lights drew her attention to the end of the narrow hallway, where a tall man in an old-fashioned three-buttoned suit with disheveled hair stood. An eerie gleam in his eye spoke for his silence. There was nothing kind about him.

Tessa's blood froze, awakening every cautious fiber in her body. A ghastly stench filled the air. When his lips curled into a crooked smile, he took on more of an ominous look.

Is he real? Was he the one in the attic playing with the curtain? How did he get in the house? Who is he?

The words she tried to speak stuck in her throat. She knew the man in front of her was not living. He emanated death as the lights around him continued to flicker. She'd heard tales of the encounters that both her sister Lexi and best friend Emily had with spirits, but never did Tessa think she would have her own run-in with a ghost. Yet, there was no denying what she was witnessing.

His image sparked in and out, and the few seconds that passed felt like an eternity until she finally found her voice. "Who—" She swallowed the lump of fear in her throat and tried again. "Who are you?"

A laugh so chilling echoed like it was traveling through distant chambers. His eyes flashed with malice. Whatever was with her was meant to be feared.

She didn't understand the spirit world—had never dealt with it—and she wasn't even sure if she truly believed in ghosts. What she did know was if the devil were real, he stood in front of her now.

"Leave me alone." Her voice shook, but if there was one thing she'd learned growing up, it was to always stand your ground. She had her sister to thank for that.

In slow motion, she watched as the man backed toward the window behind him. In an instant, he was gone, traveling through the glass and wall like wind through a screen.

Frozen in shock, seconds ticked by before she managed to move. Once she reached her room, she slammed the door and turned the lock on the knob. Her hands quaked, but she fumbled for her phone. He answered on the third ring.

"Hey, darlin'." Luke's words were said on a breath that usually sent her head spinning with desire.

She stuttered for a moment before he interrupted. "What's wrong?"

"I need you to come over." She made no attempt to hide her fear.

The sound of keys and rustling came through the phone. "I'm on my way. Tell me what happened?"

"There was someone in the house."

"Call the police."

"No." She swallowed the knot in her throat. "This was different. The police can't help."

"What are you saying?" She heard the engine of his SUV fire up.

There was no denying what she'd seen. Tessa was a realist, but even she couldn't explain what had happened. A human couldn't turn the house into an icy hell. And a human sure as fuck couldn't pass through walls.

"The lights are still flickering," she said, trying to gather the right words to convey what she wanted to say.

"Tess, calm down. I can tell you're scared. I'm heading to you now. Tell me, are you okay?"

She took a quick breath. "Yes."

"Where are you in the house?"

"In my room. The door is locked."

"Good. I'll use the door code for the front lock. I'll let myself in. You stay where you are."

"Okay." She sucked in another breath and willed herself to calm down. "Luke. I don't know what I saw. All I know is it was real. *He* was real, and he was there one second and then gone. He looked so evil." She knew she was rambling but couldn't stop the words from coming.

"It's going to be okay," Luke soothed in his calm, deep voice. "I'm coming."

Three

Luke's fingers punched the code into the keyless lock. He peeked his head in, then entered the house, closing the door behind him but leaving it unlocked.

He spoke loud enough for Tessa to hear him. "Tess, I'm here. I'm going to look around and then come up to you."

"Okay." Her voice was muffled coming from behind her door upstairs, and yet he still caught the uncertainty in it.

He searched the living room and kitchen, turning on the lights as he went. Nothing seemed out of place. He'd been to her house plenty of times. He wouldn't know if the smallest item had been tampered with or moved, but he would notice a significant change.

He looked for footprints on the hardwood and smudges on the light switches, but nothing visible to his eye said that anyone had entered the house. Everything seemed just as it always did when he visited.

It wasn't until he exited the kitchen and entered the formal dining room that the small hairs on the back of his neck stood on end.

Shit. He knew that sensation. That uneasy feeling when energy that isn't your own invades your space. But this wasn't just any kind of energy. He'd been in the field of paranormal investigation long enough to know that whatever was present was no ordinary kind spirit just passing by.

With his stomach in a knot, he stalked out of the dining room and up the dark wooden stairs. The old wood creaked under his weight. The varnish on the banister was worn away in spots. For the first time, he felt the historic house's century-old age.

He'd spent many nights with Tessa and never heard the kind of panic in her voice as he did a few minutes ago. She was clearly frightened on the phone. The confident, soft-spoken woman he'd come to know had been fraught and at a loss for words.

He'd never felt uneasy in her house before. Never questioned the threat of paranormal activity here. Something had changed that, and he needed to find out what.

He knocked on her door. "It's me."

She opened it, and he only had a second to look her over before she threw her trembling body at him. When she pulled away, he placed his hands on her shoulders, taking a moment to scan her delicate features. He'd known her for over a year, and during that time, Luke had never seen fear take over her stunning green eyes the way it had then. "Tell me exactly what happened."

A moment of hesitation flashed over her. She blinked as if she were looking for the right words to speak. "Earlier today, I was out in the front, talking to a neighbor. I thought I saw something in the attic window. The curtain moved just slightly, but I didn't see anyone."

"How long were you outside?"

"Not long. I never opened the gate at the bottom of the steps. I stood behind it the whole time. So no one could have snuck by me. I've been home since yesterday, finishing up projects for clients. So I know no one except Theo and I have been here, and he left this afternoon for his shift. I watched him leave. Shortly after that, I went outside to bring in a package. That's when I stopped to talk to the older woman from up the street. When I was about to walk up the stairs, I looked up at the attic window. I thought I was just tired. I haven't been sleeping much. So I came back inside and up here to lay down." She paused, taking a breath that shook on her exhale.

"I fell asleep, and when I woke up, it felt like someone was in the room with me. I didn't see anyone, but I could feel it. I stepped into the hallway and saw a man standing at the other end. Right by the window." She blew out another shaky breath. Luke didn't miss the tear that traveled down her pale cheek.

"It's okay." He guided her to the bed, where she lowered to the mattress. He knelt in front of her. "Was he solid looking?"

"At first. But then he started to flicker, just like the lights. They were going crazy until right before you got here."

"Anything else strange about him that you remember?"

"He was dressed in an old-fashioned suit, maybe from the 1950s. It looked like the suit Ricky Ricardo often wore on *I Love Lucy*. You know, where the suit jackets and pants are loosely fitted?"

Luke nodded. "I know what you're talking about."

"I told him to leave me alone, and he laughed," she said in a cold tone. "The only way I can describe it is evil. Like he was here for trouble. I felt so vulnerable." She rubbed her upper arms with her hands. Luke continued the gesture for her when she stopped to finish her story. "Then he stepped backward and disappeared through the window. He just vanished as if he wasn't even there."

"This is the first time you've experienced anything in the house? Has Theo ever mentioned anything?"

"No. Never. And he's never said anything strange has ever happened to him. Theo grew up here. His grandparents bought this place decades ago. And I haven't seen anything until today." She paused. Her brows pulled together. "Why would I all of a sudden start seeing things here? It doesn't make any sense."

She was right. Hauntings weren't known to start at random. There was always a reason for the activity to begin—something to wake them up. And the fact that what Tessa saw seemed malicious lent even more confusion to the situation.

"Have you guys made any changes around here? Painted walls, updated fixtures?"

"No." She looked perplexed.

Still in a kneeling position, Luke placed his elbow on his thigh and rubbed his chin. "Hmm... Sometimes, even the smallest changes to a building can wake up activity that has been dormant."

Tessa dropped her head. Her shoulders followed. She played with her fingers in her lap. "We haven't done anything around here. Theo is on shift tonight, and then he's heading to Los Angeles with his boyfriend in the morning."

Sensing her worry, he brought his hands to rest on her hips. He gently massaged them in a circular motion while he studied her. He couldn't help feeling like there was something amiss. A secret that hung like a thick cloud in the room. But he didn't press the matter. He had no intention of leaving her alone for the night, which meant he couldn't run home and grab any of his investigative equipment. So there was time for her to open up and tell him the rest of the story later.

He stood and bent at the waist so his eyes were level with hers. "I'll be right back."

"Will you stay tonight? I don't want to be alone."

"There's not a chance in hell I'm leaving you tonight." He leaned in, placed his lips on hers and drank in the sweetness of her mouth. When he pulled back, he felt heat in his belly stir at the color that bloomed on her cheeks. "Stay right here."

He went straight downstairs. When he reached the door, he locked it and did one last sweep of the first level just to be sure he hadn't missed anything.

Tessa's description of her encounter, along with his own uneasiness from earlier, was enough to convince him that a spirit was present. He'd need his teammates to help him figure out what was going on.

He pulled his cell phone from his back pocket and typed out a text:

Luke: Tessa saw something in the house. Staying here tonight.

We need to talk first thing in the morning.

Liam: Do you need me to come by now?

Trey: What did she see?

Luke: I don't think so, but I'll let you know if anything else happens. She saw an apparition, and from the sounds of it, it isn't friendly. Her roommate is out tonight, and I'm not leaving her alone.

Trey: Is she okay?

Luke: Yeah. Just shaken up. She hasn't experienced anything since living here and said her roommate hasn't ever mentioned anything. When I got here, the place was charged. I didn't have anything on me to document what I felt. But something is going on here.

Liam: Stay with her. We'll meet at headquarters first thing tomorrow. If you need anything, I can be there fast. Something sparked the activity, and we'll get to the bottom of it.

Trey: You expect me to keep this all from Lexi, don't you? That woman can sniff out a secret like a bloodhound. She's gonna lose her shit when she finds out Tessa called you and not her.

Liam: You're a tough guy, man. You can handle it.

Luke chuckled. His friends always had a way of diffusing a stressful situation while staying alert. They both knew about his and Tessa's relationship. He tried to play it cool when they cornered him while investigating the forest at Lexi's old job in Spring River, but they knew Luke better than anybody. And Luke knew they'd honor his and Tessa's wishes by keeping quiet. This was the first conversation the three friends had had about Tessa since that night.

Luke: I'll see you both in the morning.

He put his phone back in his pocket and headed up to Tessa, where he found her curled on her bed under the covers. He closed and locked her bedroom door behind him. In the corner, he removed his shoes, pulled his sweatshirt over his head, and unzipped his jeans. He stepped out of them and placed them over the desk chair by the window. He left the bedside lamp on and pulled the covers back.

He noticed she'd changed into an oversized, flannel shirt. The sight of her bare legs woke every inch of him. He stood silent, taking in her curves. Her hips rounded in the perfect proportion to her petite frame. He savored the sight and the feeling of his heart racing that sent heated blood rushing through him. Breathing deeply, he climbed into bed, pulled her to him, and pressed her back to his front. She took his hand, placing it between her full breasts the way she always did when they lay together. Her fingers intertwined with his. He inhaled her warm, sweet scent.

"Would you rather leave? Go to my place?"

Her head rotated. Emerald eyes locked on him, gripping him in a powerful gaze that he had no capability to pull away from. They were fierce, but behind them, hesitation lingered, and the longer he stared, the more the stormy, uncertain seas grew. In a flash, the fury was back. "No. I'm not letting it run me out of here."

He pulled her closer, feeling his dick twitch once again. "If anything else happens, you're coming home with me."

Her lips curved into a small smile, revealing a dimple on her cheek. She nodded.

"Sleep. I'm right here."

She shifted to her original position. The movement brushed against his throbbing cock.

"Lexi's going to lose her shit when she finds out what happened," Tessa said.

He chuckled softly. She was right. Her sister would. But he couldn't worry about what Lexi was going to think when she found out that the house Tessa was living in had an active haunting. His only concern at the moment was figuring out why the apparition made itself known to Tessa? Why now?

And most importantly, he needed to figure out what the hell it wanted?

Four

Her legs burned from the morning jog. Tessa had been an avid runner since high school, but her trained body was no match for the steep rolling hills of San Francisco. Now that she'd finished her college courses, she had time to run more frequently but decided an easy jog would be the better option that morning until she saw her doctor and asked about the safety of running during pregnancy.

She enjoyed the feeling of her muscles growing used to the intense terrain over the past year. Still, at the end of her runs, her legs screamed to rest just before the last incline that led to her house. These times usually cleared her thoughts, almost producing a meditative state for her. But not this morning. Nothing had since last night.

The image of the man standing in her hallway played on repeat in her mind. His laughter stayed with her as a distant echo. It tormented her. And for the first time since moving here, she didn't want to return home.

She could call Luke. He'd come to pick her up. It was a plan she'd use if the day got any worse. He'd left that morning, but not without urging her to come with him. She insisted on staying to do some work. Work that she barely got through because her mind refused to focus. Only by some miracle she finished and sent the last of her files for the day to her client. Then, she changed into her running clothes and left the house.

She slowed and came to a stop to rest, bracing her hands on her hips and allowing the cool air to enter her lungs deeply. Puffs of vapor formed at her lips as her breaths escaped.

Towering in front of her was an old, abandoned structure. It was a historic hospital that once served the city. It was massive and eerie but somehow fascinating. The old stucco was peeling in spots on its façade, some gouges deep enough that the webs of metal reinforcement underneath were visible. She'd heard that the current owners were in the process of remodeling. It was rumored to be haunted. Luke had mentioned he and his team had been working for years to get in and investigate, but the condition of the structure in years prior had halted the former owners from allowing any investigations.

Her eyes scanned the property. Tessa stared at one of the windows on the top floor. A faint image of what looked like a man stood behind the glass. Chin to his chest, he seemed to rock side to side. Odd. She saw no construction vehicles parked in front, and all seemed quiet. Could it be a worker?

Tessa leaned forward, squinting and straining to see clearly, but it was like looking through a fishbowl. The image was distorted, even though it was there. She fought to make sense of it and gasped when realization struck. Her blood ran cold as what he was wearing became visible. The suit jacket matched the color worn by the man she'd seen the night before. Dark gray, loose fitting and a striped tie. *What the fuck is going on?*

She straightened. When the man's head lifted and his gaze met hers, Tessa took a step back. His glare cut right through her, just like before. Icy and sharp.

Once again, he dissipated, evaporating into thin air as if he were never there. She turned and ran up the hill toward her house, all the while feeling for her phone in the thigh pocket of her running pants. But it wasn't there. She must have left it at the house. *Shit!*

Her arms pumped, and her feet carried her as fast as possible up the hill. With shaking hands, she punched in the code to the electronic lock. Once inside the house, she slammed the door behind her, turning the deadbolt.

With her back against the large wooden door, Tessa caught her breath and made her way to the kitchen on shaky legs. Her phone lay on the counter, even though she was certain she'd placed it in her pocket before leaving.

She pressed the screen with her thumb and cursed when she saw the low battery indicator light up. There wasn't even enough juice to display the home screen.

She rushed up the stairs to her bedroom and plugged in the charging cable. She'd give it a few minutes, then call Luke to come and get her.

After tossing a duffle bag on her bed, she paused when creaking sounds came from the hallway.

Frozen by panic, her mind raced as she thought of what to do. She was alone in a haunted house and, at the moment, had no way of reaching anybody for help.

Peeking out into the hallway, she scanned the area, half-prepared to see what had appeared to her the night before. When she saw nothing, she turned back to her room, and at that same moment, a gentle breeze floated by.

Already in a heightened state of awareness, she strained to catch any sounds over the continuous pounding of her heart but soon regretted the idea when a soft whisper came from the direction of the attic door.

Her eyes moved first, then her head followed their path, and when she met the gaze of the woman whose blonde hair fell in whisps, the only sound Tessa could muster was a soft whimper.

"Come," the woman whispered with a wave of her hand. She was transparent, not like the solid figure of the man Tessa had seen before. And though fear gripped every inch of her, unlike last night and a few moments ago in front of the hospital, where hostility fell heavily, Tessa felt a sense of urgency from the woman, and her voice was gentle.

Before Tessa could even blink, the woman walked through the closed attic door.

"Wait!" Tessa looked around, unsure of what to do. First, she was seeing them, and now she was communicating with ghosts too?

With hesitant steps, she inched toward the attic door. Light streamed in the window where the horrid apparition had vanished through last night. It was a stark contrast to the warm light filtering in, hitting the hardwood floor and causing the lacquer that coated the boards to glisten.

Tessa reached out and turned the knob, exposing her view to the rough steps. She'd never been to the top of the home before. It was dark and drafty and smelled of time, slightly musty from the damp city air.

As she ascended the steps, her heart pounded, sending her hearing into a frenzy. The rhythmic thud in her ears was amplified by the blood rushing through her head.

In the attic, she spotted a long string hanging from a wooden beam. She pulled, and a lone lightbulb illuminated. The dim yellow light cast an ominous glow over the surroundings. Though it should have been sufficient, the sun's rays shining through the sheer curtain in the window were barely enough to light the space.

She looked around in awe at the sight of beams jutting up to the exposed triangular-shaped rafters in all directions. Joists attached to the rough floor rose up, connecting to others, giving away their secrets to the steeply angled roof observed from the outside. For a moment, Tessa found herself in wonder. It wasn't every day that the skeletal structure of a home could be seen.

The room itself was filled to the brim with what looked to be countless antiques. Mostly furniture. An old bed sat near the window, with clothing piled on the worn mattress. Boxes were tucked away between supports on the floor, and a narrow walkway lay clear, stretching from the window at one end to the darkness where the light couldn't quite reach on the other.

Tessa looked around, but the woman was nowhere in sight.

Great. Could she be hallucinating now?

A nagging pull broke her train of thought, and she turned toward the dark area. In a corner, where beams came together, crisscrossing low, she ducked and passed under them. A large, black chest sat caked in dust. She knelt and lifted the latch, then opened the top. She didn't understand why she did it, only that something deep inside told her to open it.

Old papers, yellowed by the years, were spread around. She lifted one, and it crumpled in her hand. "Shit." She shouldn't be touching them. They were so fragile that any movement put them in danger of disintegrating.

Before touching any more papers, she scanned the contents she could see, choosing carefully what to examine next. A photo laying off to the side of more fragile papers captured her attention. With a shaking hand, she lifted it and froze. The photo of a man in a suit stared back at her. Tessa turned the photo over, hoping there was writing on the back indicating who the man was, but there was nothing except yellow stains. She placed the photo down, searching for clues as to who he was, she picked up a leather-bound book. The strap holding it closed released when she lifted it. Laying it in one of her palms, she opened it. The pages were scrawled with dates and numbers, but no other markings were written. Confused, she closed the book and placed it back in the trunk, and took one more look at the photo. The sight of the man staring back at her produced an intense nauseous feeling that somehow heightened her awareness of the room.

In a sequence of slow-moving images, memories of the last twelve hours played back through her mind. The man who stood in the hallway last night was the same man who had looked down at her from the abandoned hospital that morning. And now, he stared back at her in the photo.

Her frustration grew. Not understanding why she was all of a sudden seeing ghosts prickled her skin. None of it made sense.

"You're the only one who can help."

Tessa bolted to a standing position. The woman who she'd followed into the attic stood just a few feet away in transparent form. Sunlight flooded behind her, giving her an angelic look. "Who are you?" Tessa demanded. "What do you want? Why am I being tormented now? Do you know the man I saw last night and this morning?" The questions streamed out in a steady flow, leaving no room for the woman to answer in between.

"I can't stay." She suddenly looked worried. Her head swiveled from side to side, her focus on the empty rafters above like she was seeing something visible only to her. Then, her distressed eyes locked with Tessa. "He's coming," she said sternly.

"Who? Him?" Tessa held the photo up.

The woman nodded. "You aren't safe here. You have to leave. Now that he knows about you and..." Her eyes drifted to Tessa's stomach.

Instinctively, she brought her hands to rest low on her belly. The photo she held fell from her hand and back into the chest as she did. How the fuck did a ghost know about her baby? And what did her pregnancy have to do with what was suddenly taking place?

"He's attached to you now. I can keep him distracted for a while and give you time to find the truth."

"Attached to me? Why?"

The woman ducked as if something were coming down on her shoulders. "Find the truth. This house. The hospital. They remain cloaked in the shadows of a dark past. Now that he's been awakened by you, you can put a stop to him. Find the truth!" she repeated, ending her plea with a shout.

A blast of icy air shot through Tessa from above, stealing her breath. She stumbled while running toward the blinding light of the woman and banged her head on one of the low beams. She'd forgotten they were there and that she needed to crouch to move under them.

Pressing her hand to her head where the rough wood had caught her, she pulled it away to reveal blood. The burning there confirmed she'd split the skin open above her brow. Her heart hammered in her chest. She needed to get out of the house.

A low exhale caught her attention. Turning, she screamed when the man who'd now become a thing of her nightmares stood off to her side.

Her head spun as blood made its way into her eye. Tessa stumbled for the stairs leading out of the attic. Just as she reached them and placed her hand on the banister, an intense pressure hit her between the shoulder blades. A stinging sensation formed, and Tessa began to fall. There was no time to react.

While in mid-air, she threw her arms out in front of her, preparing for impact, but instead, she floated as if weightless, in slow motion. Her eyes locked on the woman once again, who was just with her in the attic and now stood at the base of the stairs. Tessa's feet hit the floor with barely a thud.

The woman's gaze was stern. "Go. I'll try to hold him off. Go somewhere safe."

Tessa ran down the hallway and the stairs. At the bottom, a growl forced her legs to move faster. Her momentum slammed her into the front door. Panicked, she cursed while struggling with the handle. Once outside, she took a deep breath, wiped more blood from her head with the back of her hand, spun on her feet and ran toward Liam's house, which was a little over a mile away. She'd been there a few times with Lexi and could be there in minutes.

Tessa knew Luke and Trey were there. The guys were working and planned to discuss what she'd experienced last night. She would be safe with them.

She focused on her breathing—it helped the minutes to pass quickly and carry her legs faster—and when she reached the house, she ran up the front steps, praying the front door was open.

When she reached it, she turned the knob and burst through. She caught herself on the large banister. Her legs gave out from under her, and she collapsed on the bottom step. Her lungs burned, but she forced air into them before yelling.

"Luke!"

Five

L uke forced his mind to focus while listening to audio through noise-canceling headphones and simultaneously staring at computer monitors hoping to glimpse any movement that was not from their own shadows.

His eyes burned from lack of sleep. It wasn't unusual for his paranormal investigations team to be on the road a lot. It was, however, unusual for them to have multiple cases lined up back-to-back.

News of their involvement in the Spring River fire from the previous year had sparked a media frenzy, thrusting the team into a level of popularity they had never experienced before. So much so that their online academy, where they taught others the ins and outs of paranormal investigation, had exploded. Now, they were on their way to mentoring and forming teams under them, building a large community of investigators whose number one priority was helping to put a stop to people being haunted. Teaching others what not to do, to take parapsychology seriously, and to respect the paranormal field was their number one goal.

He and his teammates were deep in going over evidence from a recent location and planned on presenting it to the owner of the estate soon. The exhaustion was hitting him hard, but he'd push through and rest later with Tessa.

The moment he heard Tessa's voice on the phone last night, he wasted no time in getting to her. Nor did he sleep a wink while her luscious curves lay pressed up against him.

He used to live with Trey, but his friend moved out and in with Lexi months ago. The two of them turned an old house down the coast into a bed and breakfast. Now, with his place all to himself, it seemed too empty, too quiet. He longed to have Tessa close by much more often.

As tired as he was, and with the amount of work he had in front of him, he couldn't pull his mind away from Tessa's house and what she'd seen. He'd sent her a few text messages, but she hadn't answered yet. She'd told him she'd be fine and would call if anything happened, so he assured himself she was just busy working.

He admired her. She'd worked hard to build up her business in the amount of time she'd done it, all while attending school. But something nagged at him, and he decided he would go over there as soon as he finished this last piece of footage. He'd take his laptop and monitor and set up at her house. Better yet, he'd throw her over his shoulder and take her to his place, then keep her there until things were sorted out. She'd hate him for it, but she'd be safe. And really, that's all that mattered. They'd also be alone, with no roommates' ears dampening the sounds he loved to coax out of her.

A soft voice on the audio he was listening to pulled him out of his thoughts. As he marked the time stamp to take a closer look later after his initial run-through, Liam tapped his shoulder.

His friend, newly married, had a skip in his step as he walked past him and took a seat. He couldn't blame him. Liam had found the love of his life after a century of being separated. Destiny had brought him and Emily together again, reincarnated and still madly in love.

Trey sat just behind him, and he turned in his seat so all three teammates faced one another.

"I got an email from that professor down in Southern California."

"Yeah?" Luke replied.

"The one we spoke with when we were on that case a few months ago?" Trey asked.

"Yep. He wants to talk about bringing us on to one of his studies. It's paid, and he's in the process of talking with a production company and turning it into a documentary."

"What's the study on?"

"Proving that a body transfers its energy after death."

Luke let out a chuckle. It always tickled him that Einstein's law of conservation still needed to be proved. As far as he and his team were concerned, of course, a body transferred its energy. What was really up for debate was whether or not the soul of a person truly existed. And if it did, why did some souls choose to stay earthbound?

Trey leaned forward with his hand out in front of him to emphasize his question. "Has he secured funding for this study?"

"Yes. He's ready to go. We'd have to travel down south every now and again."

Liam's words faded into the distance as Luke watched Trey lift one leg, resting his ankle on his knee. Luke remained in his forward seated position, his entire body tense.

Liam's news confirmed that the scientific community was finally willing to look at the existence of the afterlife. To use some of their evidence to prove the existence of ghosts was one of their ultimate goals. This was, after all, why they'd been working so hard for so long. But he wouldn't be able to relax fully or concentrate on the new venture until he talked to Tessa.

A strange ache fired deep in his chest. Like every emotion within him pooled into one spot, pulling at his attention from all directions. It was unlike anything he'd ever felt before.

As he stared out the window, he heard his friends calling his name, but their voices remained distant. When he looked back at them, both had worried expressions.

"What's wrong, brother?"

Luke shook his head, not sure how to answer. "I have a really bad feeling."

"You think it's Tessa?" Liam asked in haste.

Just as Luke moved to stand, the sound of the front door bursting open reverberated in the office space. A second later, he was running at full speed in the direction of Tessa's voice yelling his name.

Luke's eyes locked on her petite body sitting on the second step that led up to the living space of Liam and Emily's flat. He was barely able to stop his own momentum and used the large banister to halt his hasty steps as he spun to face Tessa.

He crouched down, noting her skin was flushed and a sheen of sweat covered her face and chest. Blood trickled down one cheek from a gash on her brow.

"What happened?" He reached out, taking her face in his hands. He studied the panic in her eyes as she told him. He caught movement out of the corner of his eye. Liam had a first aid kit open and was already sifting through it.

"I went for a jog after I finished some work. I took a shorter route today because I was tired, but I needed to clear my head. I passed by that old hospital. You know the one? I can't remember what everyone calls it."

"I know the one. Bay City Sanitarium." He took some gauze from Liam and pressed it to Tessa's wound. "We need to get you to the hospital. You need stitches."

Her grip on his forearms tightened. "In a minute. I have to tell you this."

He nodded and kept the pressure on her brow.

"I saw him again."

"The apparition?" Luke asked.

"Yes. But he was staring out of the window of the hospital!"

"What?" both Liam and Trey said in unison.

"It scared the shit out of me. I ran back home and found my cell phone. I was sure I'd brought it with me when I left the house, but it was sitting on the kitchen counter, and the battery was dead, so I couldn't call you."

So that's why he hadn't heard back from her. Luke kicked himself for not insisting she come with him that morning. There was no way in hell she was staying in that house now, and he didn't care how much of a fight she put up. If necessary, he'd call Lexi and have her convince her sister to leave.

Tessa finished telling her story. It left them all with many more questions. Including why the spirit of a woman was now being seen in the house. It was clear the woman knew the man and knew he was dangerous. Why the male apparition was now seen by Tessa in two different locations was what bewildered Luke the most. It wasn't unheard of for a spirit to travel between locations, but it was rare. Usually, a spirit was tied to a place they knew best or where they had spent a significant amount of time. So, why was this man tied to both her property and the hospital?

Trey asked, "Did he look the same as when you saw him in your house?"

"Yes. Down to the suit jacket he wore." She looked back at Luke. "I had the same awful feeling when he looked at me. It felt like he's latched onto me somehow and for some reason. It's hard to explain, but it was like he was looking straight into my soul. And when the woman in the attic said he is attached to me..." She hiccupped.

Luke soothed her, though he was having a hard time keeping his own raging emotions in check.

"Tess, we want to get into the house as soon as possible and see what we can find out," Trey announced.

She nodded.

Luke looked at his friends. "Theo, the owner and her roommate, is out of town. He'll be back in a few days."

"As soon as we get permission from him, we'll be there," Trey assured him. "In the meantime, we'll start digging up the history of the place from public records. We'll look at the land and the home. We'll also look into the hospital. See if anything suspicious pops up."

Liam spoke up. "I'll get on the phone and try to talk to the new owners of the place. See if we can get in there. I know they're working on renovations. Hopefully, they've fixed things to the point where they feel it's safe to let people in to investigate."

"That can wake shit up," Luke bit out. "I want to know why the fuck it's traveling up the street to her house?" His anger wasn't directed at his friends, but he couldn't help the snap in his tone.

"Abso-fucking-lutly," his friend agreed, Liam's tone matching Luke's. "Trey and I will do everything we can to get this research started."

"What the fuck does he want with me?" Tessa whispered, drawing their attention back to her.

It killed Luke that her voice sounded defeated. She was even paler now and looked as exhausted as he'd felt only minutes ago.

"I don't know." Luke shifted to the side and placed an arm under her knees. His other cradled her back as he lifted her effortlessly into his arms and stalked through the door that Liam held open for him. "But I'm going to find out. And put a stop to it."

Six

The throbbing in Tessa's head churned her stomach. Each pulsing sensation hit her with another wave of intense nausea. She pressed her head to Luke's neck while he carried her, trying to block the light from her eyes. Most of the adrenaline had seeped away, and now that it had, she felt the full effects of the gash on her head.

Luke settled her into the passenger seat of his SUV and buckled her in. Seconds later, the vibration of the engine roared to life, sending more pain pulsing through her. He drove, all the while holding her hand and caressing her skin with his thumb.

"Stay awake for me, okay?"

"My head is killing me."

"Yeah. That's quite a bump you have there. We'll get you checked out. I don't want you to worry. We're going to figure everything out."

As hazy as her thoughts were, a realization sparked another wave of panic in her. "Please don't call Lexi. She's going to worry and drive me nuts."

Luke chuckled. "Darlin', you know damn well if I keep this from her, she'll have my ass."

He had a point. She'd have to tell her sister at some point about her and Luke and explain that's the reason why she called him last night. "I hate hospitals. I don't want to stay overnight. Do you think I'll have to?"

"Depends on what the doctor thinks. If you have a concussion, you might."

He brought her hand up to meet his lips. Through her squinted eyes, she watched his golden hair sparkle in the light. The stubble of his mustache prickled her skin in the most delicious way that sent shivers through her. The movement worked his toned arm, and she felt the strength in his grip, yet his touch was gentle. How could she be so turned on in a time like this?

Only Luke Collins could stir such emotions in her during a chaotic time such as this one.

Only he could distract her from the worrisome thoughts that coursed through her.

"Tell me what the woman looked like again and what she said."

Tessa laid her head against the seat with a sigh. "She was in a dress, I want to say, fifties style, I think or maybe a little earlier. A white collar and buttons down the front. She wore her hair swept to the side, and she had those big curls." Tessa brought her opposite hand to her head, pressing her palm against her skull to try and relieve the ache.

"You're doing good. Keep going."

She blew out a breath and tried to remember everything about the next set of events. "There was an old chest in the attic. For some reason, I opened it, and there was a picture inside. I picked it up, and the air changed. It got really cold."

Luke was patient and continued to stroke her hand. "Did you feel like you were being watched again?"

Tessa spoke without opening her eyes. "Yes. It was so strange. When I turned around, she was standing there. She said I was the only one who could help. I asked her what that meant, but she didn't answer. The feeling in the attic changed. She looked like she was scared. Something was there, but I couldn't see it. I started to run but forgot to duck under the beam. That's how I hit my head. I wanted to get out of there fast. When I got to the stairs..." she hesitated, wondering if the details she remembered were real or not. "I must have lost my footing."

"You fell down the attic stairs?" His voice switched from calm to distressed in a fraction of a second. His hand squeezed hers, and she felt the punch of acceleration as the SUV picked up speed. "And then you ran to Liam's? Does anything else besides your head hurt?" he asked in a half-growl.

She thought for a second. Not feeling any pain besides the aching in her head, she shrugged. Then again, her brain felt foggy, and she couldn't be sure. "Luke, she stopped my fall. She's not bad. I know this all sounds crazy, but I'd prepared myself to hit the steps and tumble down, but I didn't. I...floated. When I landed on my feet at the bottom, she told me to run. I didn't question her and came straight to you."

Muttering a steady stream of profanity, Luke shifted in his seat and brought the SUV to a stop at a light.

She sat quietly, debating and deciding that he now had enough to worry about and let him drive the rest of the way to the hospital in silence.

Once there, he carried her into the emergency waiting room and sat her in a chair. She watched as he went up to the window and heard him tell the nurse she'd hit her head and needed stitches.

With a worried look, the nurse came around. Luke helped her sit in a wheelchair and walked back with her. After she was settled into a room, it wasn't long before the nurse asked Luke to leave. He put up a fight, but Tessa convinced him to wait outside while she explained the situation.

An hour passed, and after a lengthy chat with the female doctor and nurses, she'd convinced everyone that Luke was not the reason for the gash on her head. It wasn't so much the cut on her brow as it was the large bruise on her back between her shoulder blades. She remembered the moment she received that mark, but she couldn't tell them a ghost had imprinted it on her. She eventually convinced the staff she'd run to Luke for help when she couldn't use her phone, and they finally allowed him back into her room.

Feeling drained and confused, she wanted nothing more than to return home. But home was the reason she was in her current predicament. Frustration soon took over, and it was compounded by the anxiety of the doctor confirming her pregnancy before Luke returned to the room. The only news that bought her relief was being told everything looked good and she didn't have a concussion. But her mind reeled, trying to think of a way to tell Luke he was going to be a father. At her request, the doctor agreed not to mention her pregnancy again while she was there. She'd take time to come up with the right words to tell him.

"I'm going to fill Liam and Trey in on what you told me in the car," he said after a long moment of silence. He hadn't said much since returning to her side. His face clearly shone his state of concern.

Tessa looked into his heated eyes. How could the color blue look so intense? She swore every emotion possible fluttered in them, shifting between anger and worry. He hadn't let go of her hand since he walked back in.

"That bruise on your back is ugly. As pissed off as I was when the nurse asked me to step out of the room, I understand why she did."

"What do you mean?"

"Tess, that mark on your back is in the shape of a handprint."

"What?" The nurse had asked how she'd gotten the bruise. She said she didn't know.

Luke nodded. "Clear as day. A purple mark in the shape of a large hand. You're positive no one was in the house with you?"

His gray-blue eyes, which seemed to change color with the light, almost looked green at that moment. The thin line of brown surrounding his pupil was visible in the bright light. Too bright for her head, but according to the nurse, they couldn't turn the lights off. "I'm positive. There's more to the story, though."

His eyes held questions, and she could see fury igniting deep within them while he waited. His jaw ticked.

"In the attic. The picture I said I found? It was a photo of the same man I saw last night in the hallway. And in the hospital window. When I realized what I was looking at, that's when the air changed, and I didn't feel safe. I didn't lose my footing." She lowered her voice more, and Luke moved his face closer to hers. "I saw him standing in the attic with me. And when I turned toward the stairs, I felt a hand on my back smack me and shove. When the woman broke my fall, he let out a growl. It was hideous."

Luke brought her hands to his mouth and pressed them tight to his lips. A mix of emotions washed over his face. "I'll figure out who he is and put a stop to it."

"How?" Tessa asked. She knew he hunted ghosts. Knew what he did for a living. But she never thought in a million years she'd be the center of one of his jobs.

Over the last few months, they'd gotten closer, their secret time together slowly becoming more than just fun between the sheets. And every moment they shared together carved out a deeper bond between them. He'd even mentioned that they should break the news to Lexi because he had no intention of letting her go. Only problem was she loved keeping Luke to herself. She'd spent her entire life under the microscope of her mother back in Seattle. To finally have the freedom to do what she wanted and not be questioned by anyone was liberating. But Luke was right. Especially now. She'd have to tell Lexi.

The doctor came through the door then and informed her she could be released but to take it easy and not to let the gash on her head, now covered with suture tape, get wet for a few days and to come back if her headaches didn't subside or got worse.

Luke turned back to Tessa and continued. "This is what I do. What the team does. Don't forget that we helped Emily and your sister."

"I know. It's just surreal. Everything was normal until yesterday. How can things change so drastically and so quickly?"

"I don't have the answers to that," he told her. "Not yet. But I can promise you we'll figure out what's going on. Still, we have to tell Lex."

"I know. I'll tell her soon."

He shook his head. "No. You're telling her tonight."

She'd never heard Luke's tone as serious as it was in that moment. Aside from the bedroom, where she enjoyed him taking control, he never gave her orders.

Stunned, she propped herself up, ignoring the pulsing in her head as she did. "Why the hell is that?"

A twinkle in his eye accompanied a stern stare. It sent a shockwave of arousal through her. From the moment she met him, Tessa knew he would be her undoing. He'd be the one who would break her down and keep all her secrets. She craved his authority and gentleness.

"Because." He stood, bringing his mouth close to hers. He stole her lips in a deep kiss that melted her insides. Had she been standing, she was sure her knees would have buckled under her. When he pulled back, his voice was rough and wrapped in silk that cloaked her in warmth. "You're not staying at that fucking house one more night. You're coming home with me."

Seven

"T he fuck!"

Lexi's temper flared. Luke expected as much, but it still startled him to see her all fired up. He sat next to Tessa, who kept her calm composure, yet she didn't back down. That was his girl. She was tough as nails, even if she didn't always believe it.

"Lex. I'm staying with Luke. You can be pissed off all you want. I'm sorry I kept our relationship from you, but it was my decision."

"Oh hell, Tess. I know you two have been seeing each other since the night of Liam and Emily's wedding. You're a grown woman—you can do what you want. I'm pissed that you won't come stay with me. I'm worried about you. I'm even more ticked off that this is happening to you."

Tessa's eyes were like saucers. "You knew, and you didn't say anything?"

"Yes!" Lexi returned.

"And you never mentioned anything to me?" Trey asked in disbelief.

Luke watched Lexi raise an eyebrow at his friend. "You're the one who opened my eyes to it all that night of the wedding," she turned back to her sister. "It's your life and your business. If I had an issue with it, I would have brought it up, but I wanted you to be the one to tell me. The only problem I have is the fact that you've been dealing with this for more than a day, and I had no idea." She shot an annoyed glare at Trey.

Luke sat quietly, absorbing the news that Lexi knew about him seeing her sister. Knowing that Lex wasn't about to claw his eyes out lifted the weight off of his shoulders. He hated keeping their relationship from her but wanted to let Tessa make the decision to tell her.

Lexi stopped her pacing and came to stand in front of her sister. Luke stood, allowing the two women to sit next to each other. He motioned to the kitchen, and his friends followed behind him.

He grabbed a beer from the refrigerator, picking up two more for Liam and Trey. There were only two things that could keep him calm tonight. Tessa being in his presence, and a cold beer to put out the fire that consumed his nerves.

"You okay?" Liam asked while taking the bottle.

He leaned against the old, tiled counter. The harsh fluorescents above hurt his eyes. He unscrewed the cap, flicked it into the trash nearby, and took a long drink. He wasn't okay, though he didn't know how to admit it. Silent, he shook his head.

"You know we've already started on the case?" Trey told him.

He figured they would. They probably jumped on the phone right after he left with Tessa in his arms.

"It followed her," Luke finally said out loud. It was more of an admittance to himself. One he hated but needed to face.

Liam pulled out a chair at the kitchen table. "Fill us in. We only know what you told us this morning and the little she was able to get out on the stairs."

Trey followed suit. "We know there's more to the story."

Luke filled the team in on the details that Tessa gave him in the car and at the hospital. All the while, he was surprised at how much emotion filled him. Tessa meant a lot to him, and he was only now realizing just how much.

It had been months of sneaking around, and if he was honest with himself, he knew from the beginning she was going to be different. Truth be told, the budding relationship was exactly what he wanted. He just never expected his feelings for her to be so strong.

"To answer your question, no, I'm not okay. The only thing holding me back from going over there and enticing the son of a bitch for answers is the fact that I know it's not the right tactic right now. We need to find out who he possibly is."

"I'm already on that," Trey assured him. "I've left messages for the owners of the old hospital. I know it was purchased a while back. They have plans to turn it into a historical venue for events. I'll be seeing if we can get clearance to get in there ASAP."

"What about the house? Nothing had happened there until yesterday. Why the hell is it picking on her all of a sudden?"

"We'll investigate the house soon," Liam said. "Maybe it followed her from one of her previous runs, and she didn't know it. If it followed her from there, and she's certain it's the same man, we might be able to get some answers by doing some digging into the history of the hospital. I don't want to stir anything else up at her place with an investigation if we can help it."

Luke nodded in agreement. "We need to figure out who the woman is. Tessa said she stopped her fall down the attic stairs. If it wasn't for her, Tessa would have been really hurt."

"Fuck," Trey growled. "Did she give you a description? We can comb through some old photos of the place. Maybe she was a patient?"

"Maybe." Luke took a long sip of his beer and gave his team the description that Tessa had. He joined his friends at the table, then sat in silence for a moment.

Trey reached across the table and gave him a playful shove with his fist. "Welcome to the club. I told you that night we investigated the woods when we were trying to figure out what was after Lexi that love-struck look is good on you."

He chuckled and ran his hand through his hair.

Liam laughed too. "I never thought we'd see the day. Our boy has fallen head over heels, Trey."

"Alright." Luke stood and backed away from the kitchen table. He loved his friends, but he wasn't in the mood to be the subject of their amusement. "Out with you before I pound you both for stating the obvious."

In the living room, Lexi seemed to have calmed down. She and Tessa spoke in soft voices. When Tessa noticed him standing in the doorway and her large, almond eyes sparked with desire, his heart skipped a beat. He caught the subtle catch in her breath too. The slight pause of her chest on her inhale made his dick twitch. Maybe it made him an asshole, but he didn't care. The woman was a goddess. No one had ever come close to stealing his heart before, and he would gladly hand his over to Tessa if she asked for it.

"You ready to go, sweetheart?" Trey asked Lexi. She hesitated, then reached to give Tessa a hug before standing and going to Trey's side.

Fiery daggers burned their way into Luke's neck. He turned to face Lexi, who stared him down. She shrugged on her jacket and huffed out a breath, giving the impression she was ready for a fight. But her demeanor shifted at the last second. Dropping her shoulders, her gaze softened. "Take care of her."

It was a demand.

He nodded, his eyes never wavering from Lexi's. "I will."

She dropped her eyes, and after Trey gave Tessa a hug, Lexi let him lead her out the front door. Liam stopped in front of Luke and placed a hand on his shoulder. "Call me if anything happens. No matter what time it is."

"I will. Thanks."

Liam turned to Tessa and said goodnight.

Alone now, the quiet was welcoming. Luke locked the front door and turned to the only woman with the power to shift his life's course and set him in a direction he swore he'd never travel.

For the first time all day, he had Tessa all to himself. No nurses or doctors. No friends or relatives. Just the two of them and the underlying sensation that he needed to care for her. He wanted to do everything he could to make her feel safe.

When he turned to face her, the pounding in his chest erupted in his ears. She still sat on the large sofa, her small body all but swallowed by the oversized piece of furniture. Her beauty diffused the anxiety he'd been feeling.

He walked to her. Her head lifted as he came closer. Her high cheekbones flushed brighter the closer he got. When she stood and threw herself at him, he caught her, lifting her and pressing her to his body. He needed her in his arms. Her mouth crashing into his sent waves of thrills through his entire body.

She sealed her mouth over his and barely moved as he walked them both to his bedroom. He wanted nothing more than to take her to bed. To make the sweetest love to her. To hear her moans and feel her come apart around him.

He set her down near his bed and walked to his dresser, where he pulled a long sleeve t-shirt out of a drawer. Back at her side, he gathered the hem of her shirt and lifted. She raised her arms and let him pull the garment over her head. He moved to her leggings and pushed them down, leaving her panties in place. His mouth watered, seeing her bare breasts, nipples tight, begging for his attention.

Lowering his head, he rested his mouth on the top of her shoulder, placing soft kisses from the top, trailing up her neck where he stopped at her ear. She exhaled.

"I would love nothing more than to make love to you." He gave her earlobe a flick of his tongue. A little something to keep her thinking. "But not tonight. You need to heal." He pulled the shirt he held over her head, careful of her brow, and helped her guide her arms through. "Go to the bathroom, darlin'. You can use my toothbrush. Then come back and lay in my arms. I'll go to your house tomorrow and get your things."

"Luke." She whispered and ran her hand over his cheek. "I'm okay."

"Damn right, you are. And I'm going to make sure it stays that way."

"I know you will." She walked into the bathroom and emerged a few minutes later. When he finished his own nightly routine, he settled under the covers behind her. "How's your head?"

"It's okay. Not as bad as earlier."

"Good. If it gets worse, wake me."

"I will. Luke?"

With a tug, he brought her closer. "Yes?"

"Thank you."

"You never have to thank me. I'm here for you."

She snuggled into him, fitting her body perfectly against his. A bolt of electricity struck him when her breathing settled to a steady rhythm moments later. How the universe thought he deserved a woman as perfect as Tessa was beyond him.

The shadows of his own past crept into the forefront of his mind, reminding him why he'd chosen a life free of commitment. But maybe it was time to sever those strings. He spent his life searching for reasons why, not always finding the answers. Some things weren't meant to be understood. He knew that. It was a painful lesson at times. Everything happens for a reason, and whatever lesson he was supposed to learn with the introduction of Tessa into his life, he was going to take note. And he sure as hell didn't want to give her up.

The bite of the cold, damp floor seeped through the soles of Tessa's bare feet, numbing her. Fear radiated and quaked through her. Muffled voices surrounded her, and with each step she took, the feeling of dread grew.

People sat in the hallways, some in wheelchairs, others on the ground, each one dressed in a dirty white gown. Her senses were overwhelmed with questions and anxiety. The most pressing one, why was she there?

The long hallway seemed to go on forever, and the steady footsteps of the woman in front of her kept Tessa's attention. But she didn't understand why she followed the woman. An unknown source pulled her toward the end of the hallway.

Through a set of double doors, they entered a room lit with lights so bright it felt sterile. Other bodies stood around, all busy, surrounding an area in the center, but Tessa couldn't see what drew their attention.

At first, she kept to the back, away from the people in white. Eventually, she gave in to her curiosity and stepped away from the wall.

Inching closer to the center where the focus of everyone's attention was, her feet still bare, she tentatively moved. Each step quickened her heart. Men stood shoulder to shoulder while nurses rushed around in a dizzying haze. The words spoken by everyone were slurred and unintelligible. Instruments spread out on a table came into view when the person in front of her shifted. She didn't know what they were or what they were used for, but they horrified her all the same.

Tessa backed away, no longer wanting any part of whatever was going on. She knew she was dreaming but didn't know how to wake up.

The woman she had followed into the room walked passed her in a flash, and Tessa could only see the back of her as she floated away. Tessa followed. Something told her the woman had the answers to why she was there. "What's happening?" Tessa's voice drifted and echoed, but the woman kept moving in silence.

Walking toward the group of people once again, Tessa forced her feet to carry her closer. Soon, she was inches from the group and managed to gain a view through the gaps between them. To her horror, a person lay face up on an operating table. Covered in a white sheet, only their head was exposed.

Tessa watched as a man wearing a surgical mask took an instrument and placed it on the person's temples. Seconds later, the patient convulsed, and her stomach sank at the sight. She refused to watch any longer. Turning, she ran through the double doors. The earlier whispers that came from the people still gathered in the hallways were replaced with shouting as they flailed about.

She ran as fast as her feet would carry her, but the place was a maze. Every door she tried was locked, and there was no elevator or stairwell in sight. What kind of place was she in?

She ran through another set of doors at the opposite end of the hallway that led to another set of halls that branched out. Finally, an open door, and she entered.

It was quiet, but the silence was just as frightening as the chaos she'd come from. With only the sound of her heart pounding in her ears and her heavy breaths, she tried the windows, desperate for a way out. But each one was locked and covered in bars.

As panic rose, Tessa began banging against the glass. It rattled under her pounding fists, but still, it didn't crack, didn't even make a sound that said it was under any strain. She looked around for an object to break the panes, but the room was bare.

A shadow moved across the opaque glass on the door she'd just entered through, and when the door moved, Tessa froze.

The woman who she'd followed earlier walked in. Her head hung low until she lifted her gaze just enough to meet Tessa's eyes. And when she did, Tessa was met with the gaze of the woman she'd seen in her attic.

"He's coming."

"Wh–who?" Tessa asked, confused. "What do you want from me? What does *he* want from me?"

"You have to help us." The woman's voice shook.

"Am I dreaming?" How was she supposed to help when she didn't know where she was or what was going on?

Her vision blurred with tears as she became gripped with fear. "Help you how?" Tessa bit out, fed up with whatever it was that was happening. "Let me out of this place. I don't belong here. Tell me what's going on. Why am I being haunted?"

The woman spun around. Something had caught her attention, but Tessa didn't know what. Before she could ask, a heaviness descended on the room. The woman ran to her, taking her hand. The woman's were like ice.

"My name is Francis. I don't know if I'll be able to contact you again. There are secrets that must be known. It's the only way we can be set free. Please find a way to help us." Her words were hurried in desperation. Tessa heard it in her voice and saw it in her eyes.

"What is happening?" Just as Tessa opened her mouth to ask another question, a growl tore through the air. She barely heard her own scream over the deafening noise.

Francis placed her hands on Tessa's shoulders and spoke, "Go now."

"How? I don't know how to wake up."

The doors burst open, revealing a man hiding his identity behind a surgical mask and dressed in a medical gown. His eyes were fierce, and Tessa swore she was looking into pure evil.

Francis pushed her.

Tessa braced herself for impact against the wall behind her. Instead, she fell and continued to fall through the darkness that surrounded her until she was once again sound asleep.

Eight

H e was never supposed to fall in love. The idea always sat wrong with him. He wasn't meant to love anyone. Didn't grow up knowing how. His father sure as hell never showed him love, let alone any affection to his mother. It was the reason she was no longer with them. The reason Luke had gone through the last of his teenage years without a home or a family. His mom had been the only person who showed him any affection. Fuck he missed her.

Without Liam and Trey, he didn't know where he'd be. All he knew for sure was if it hadn't been for his two best friends, he'd for sure have ended up in a dark place. It was a thought he avoided at all costs but one that crept up from time to time. A subtle reminder of how lucky he was.

After Trey's and Liam's comments the night before and the emotions that overtook him while in bed with Tessa, Luke couldn't let go of the thought or the idea of letting go of the darkness that gripped his memories.

He lifted his head to the spray of the shower. It was just hot enough to remind him he was alive. He rolled his shoulders, loosening the tension and easing the ache.

Tessa still lay asleep in his bed. He'd stayed awake most of the night, and when he did sleep, he woke to every sound and whimper that escaped her. Sometime in the early morning hours, he drifted off, but his mind was inundated with memories of his mom, wondering what he could have done to stop the events that had taken her away from him.

He wasn't like Trey. Luke didn't consider himself sensitive, but he did believe messages could come through in a person's dreams, just like with Liam and Emily, whose dreams were connected not only to each other but to their past lives. He knew whenever his mom came to him in his dreams, something drastic was about to happen in his life. And lately, she'd been making more frequent appearances while he slept.

Now, with Tessa undoubtedly cemented in his life, the feeling scared the shit out of him. He knew he was falling in love—had felt it months ago.

Maybe that's why his mother had come to him, letting him know that he needed to accept fate. He couldn't be sure. The dreams were always the same. She never said much. Only taking his hand and walking by his side on a sandy beach like they did when he was a little boy after one of his father's drinking binges. It was her way of letting him know it would all be okay. That even though their home life was in chaos, there was still beauty in the world. He just needed to be open to seeing it.

Before Tessa called the night before last, it had been weeks since they'd seen each other. Between his traveling for work and her busy schedule, they hadn't found a chance to see one another. He hated that she was now laid up with a wound on her head. It was a painful reminder of what happened to her the day before, and he hadn't been there to stop it.

Anger bubbled up from deep within him. He never quite understood the protectiveness that Liam and Trey felt toward Emily and Lexi. Now, he knew exactly what they felt when their women were in danger.

Tessa had come into his life like a beacon of light. When she walked into the room at Liam and Emily's rehearsal dinner, the world around him stopped. Her beauty was all he could see, and he knew from that moment he was in trouble.

He turned the shower off and reached for a towel. After drying his hair, he wrapped it around his waist and stepped in front of the mirror. He wiped the condensation away and watched as the lingering humidity in the bathroom masked the glass with fog again.

He rubbed his chin and examined his short beard. His eyes were like his mom's deep blue when the light was dim, becoming more crystal and gray in bright light. He didn't look a damn thing like his father, and he was thankful for that. It was bad enough he had to live each day with the painful mcmories of growing up with the asshole. He wasn't sure what he'd do if he had to stare back at him every day in his reflection.

He picked up his electric beard trimmer and ran it over the short stubble, keeping it at the length he liked.

He cleaned up the edges and switched the trimmer off, then paused, thinking he heard Tessa.

His hand was barely on the doorknob when he heard her shout. Yanking the door open, he thought it would come free of its hinges with the force he used.

It took only three strides for his long legs to get from the hallway to his bedroom door. Once inside, he found Tessa tossing and thrashing, the whimpers on her lips calling for help.

"Tessa." He sat next to her, placed his hands on her shoulders and gave them a gentle shake. He didn't want to startle her, but he needed her to wake up. When that didn't work, he shook harder. "Tess!"

Her eyes shot open, and she went stiff. For a moment, he wasn't sure she recognized him. He breathed a sigh of relief when her gaze softened.

"Oh, my God."

"Bad dream?"

"I don't know. I was in a hospital."

"What hospital?"

Her hands were in her hair, and her breathing was still ragged. "The one near my house, I think. The one I passed by yesterday. I don't know for sure, but that's the feeling I got. Everything felt so real."

He scooted further onto the mattress and pulled her close. "What happened in the dream?"

She stared at him, silent, hesitation written all over her face. Whatever she'd dreamed about had instilled a lingering fear in her, and he used all of his energy to tamp down the fury that burned inside.

"You know you can tell me. We're already on this case, so anything that happens, you need to let me know."

Tessa rubbed her face and brought her knees to her chest. "The same woman was there. I was following her, but I didn't know why. She led me to a room where there were people surrounding a patient. They were about to do some kind of procedure, and I didn't want to watch. I ran, but I couldn't find my way out. She found me and asked for help again. She seemed desperate and terrified. She said her name was Francis."

"That's good." He began rubbing circles over her cheek with his thumb. "We can use that name in searches. What else happened?" He didn't need to guess that something more terrifying had taken place. Someone asking for help in a dream would be an unlikely cause to make a person shout and thrash around in their sleep.

"There was something dark with us. The doctor that was working on that patient came into the room. But there was something evil about him. I could physically feel it. I was so scared."

"It's okay," he murmured. "Tell me more about him so I can understand."

"There was a growl. It was the same one I heard in my house. I think he's the same man I saw in my hallway."

That was the second time she'd heard a growl. Luke's stomach dropped. If he'd learned anything during his years of investigating the paranormal, it was that growls never just happened. They weren't meant to assert authority or scare you. They were accompanied by pure danger. Whatever was latched on to her was not to be underestimated.

"The woman was trying to protect me as much as she was trying to seek help. I could sense it. She asked me again to help her."

"Did she say why?"

"I begged her to tell me, but she didn't have time. She only told me her name. Then she said someone was coming and I needed to leave. But I didn't know how to wake up."

"What do you mean?"

"I couldn't make myself wake up. It was like I was under a spell."

Luke mulled the information over in his head. His jaw ticked, and his molars ground together. Whatever force had made its way into Tessa's mind had taken control of her dream, trapping her, and it was screwing with the wrong people.

"After the doctor came into the room, it was so cold. I know he's evil. I could feel it seeping off of him. I think Francis was talking about him."

"The doctor?"

"Yes. I think she's trying to tell me that he's the reason they—"

Luke held his hand up to slow her down. He needed to make sure he understood all of the details. "'They'?"

"She specifically said *they*. While I was looking for a way out, I saw patients in the hallways. Dozens of them. It was like being in a horror film. They were mumbling to themselves and shouting. Was that place ever an asylum?"

Luke ran a hand down his face and back up into his hair. "It was. It was used for tuberculosis for a time, then turned into a hospital for the mentally ill. Later, it became a retirement home until it closed for good and sat abandoned for a long time."

Everything inside of him screamed with apprehension. It was a feeling he wasn't used to. His thrill-seeking mind always enjoyed the unknown aspects of his job. But this time, every protective instinct in him was heightened.

"Later today, we'll go back to your house. You need to pack some things anyway. Do you think Theo will be okay with us going through the attic?"

"Probably. He thinks the work you guys do is fascinating. I'll call and ask him."

"Good. And I'll have Liam and Trey meet us there. We'll see what else we find."

Tessa shifted. He moved to accommodate her, and she straddled his lap. Her long, loose curls fell around her shoulders and brushed his chest when she leaned close. Her smooth legs rubbed against his. The towel around his waist shifted and loosened. It was now bunched up, and it killed him to know there was barely any barrier between his aching cock and her hot body.

Her mouth fell on his in a desperate kiss. Her breathing picked up, and she panted against his mouth, "I've missed you."

His hands roamed to her back, traveled down and squeezed her ass. He moved his lips to her neck, where he sucked for a moment before giving her a playful nip with his teeth. "You're still healing, Tess. I don't want your headache to come back."

She whimpered and slowed her movements. As much as he wanted her, he knew her body wasn't ready. It had been less than twenty-four hours since she'd slammed her head into a wooden beam. "Does your head still hurt?"

"A little. Not like last night, though."

"You need to take it easy today. Come on. Let's get dressed. We'll eat, and then we'll head to your place."

"Luke?" The sound of his name on her lips always weakened his knees. Even sitting, he felt the pressure lifted from him.

"Yeah, babe?"

"Thank you."

"I told you, you never have to thank me."

"Yes. I do. I know we had an agreement. No strings. Just fun. But things have changed." She paused. When her head dropped, he sensed a hesitation wash over her that stole her attention from him.

"What's wrong?" He squeezed her thighs where the roundness of her ass began.

She shook her head, lifted her gaze, and locked on him. He saw something hidden in the depths, and he ached to know what had her thoughts so tangled. It wasn't just the haunting. There was more, and he hoped she'd let her guard down soon and open up to him--trust him with her deepest secrets.

"I think I'm just still trying to absorb everything that's happened. Everyone knows about us now. I was worried about Lexi finding out, but I should have known she'd be fine."

"She's your sister. She loves you and wants what's best for you. I get that." His hand reached up and brushed some of Tessa's hair away from her face. The morning light ignited her emerald eyes. Her cheeks were still flushed from their kissing.

"When I called the other night, you didn't hesitate. You just came."

"If you need me, I'll be there." She needed to understand that there were no questions for him on the matter. She was his world.

"I know that's hard for you. You've shared a little about your past. You don't want complicated. I just want you to know how much I appreciate you."

Luke brought her closer, so they were nose to nose. "With you, nothing has been hard. Nothing is ever complicated. I wanted to get to you. I...needed to get to you. Hearing your voice shake over the phone almost killed me. Promise me, you'll always call if you need help."

"I promise." She pulled him close to her, pressing his head to her breasts and laying her head on top of his. The sound of her heart beating steadied his breathing, and he relished the feeling of her on top of him. The closeness, the intimacy, it all felt right.

Never in a million years did Luke Collins think he'd meet a woman who would bring him to his knees. And the scariest part was he wasn't fighting it. He was going along for the ride, traveling down that new road, and he wasn't looking back.

Nine

"That house has been in my family for years. Nothing paranormal has ever happened there."

Theo spoke over speakerphone while Trey and Liam sat off to the side in two chairs in Tessa's living room. She and Luke remained on the sofa.

Tessa said, "I understand, Theo. But I know what I saw. I didn't want to believe it, but I can't deny what happened."

Theo sighed. "I believe you. I'm just sorry it happened. And I'm confused as to why all of a sudden something is going on."

"Sometimes," Liam chimed in, "changes in an environment will wake up a spirit. You guys haven't done any renovations on the place lately?"

Trey leaned in and added, "We've even seen activity start up with simple things like painting walls in a room."

Tessa looked at Trey, then at Luke. "I did move some of my bedroom furniture recently. I bought a new desk and needed to rearrange things to accommodate it."

"Is any of the furniture in your room original to the house?" Trey asked.

Tessa nodded, and Theo answered, "Almost all of the furniture in the house was there when my grandparents purchased that place."

"When I moved in, I didn't have much," Tessa explained. "It's why I wanted this place. It was furnished, and I didn't need to spend money on things like a bed." It was also one of the reasons she loved the place. Everything from the wood trim to the furnishings and area rugs was mid-century. Most would scoff at the home's interior design, but she fell in love with the listing the moment she saw it. She may have been young, but the stylistic decor and fashion of the mid-century always called to her.

Theo added, "I've done some painting of the walls and removed old wallpaper over the years. But no heavy renovations. The layout is original. The appliances have been updated. Nothing ever happened when I did any work, and I haven't done anything since before Tess moved in. Is that enough to wake something up?"

"It depends." Luke squeezed Tessa's hand and shifted closer to the phone. "We need to figure out who the spirits are first and why they might have followed Tessa home from the hospital. Would it be okay if we looked around the attic?"

"Of course. All the stuff up there is really old. I don't know why my grandparents never cleared it out. It all came with the house when they purchased it."

"Theo," Tessa began, "there were some papers I moved around inside of a chest to pick up the photograph. The papers crumbled when I lifted them. I'm so sorry."

"It's okay. Whoever put them there should have protected them first. Please feel free to look at anything you need to get to the bottom of this. I'll also go see my grandmother as soon as I'm back in town. I'll ask her if she knows anything. Can you text me a picture of the photo you found? I'll show it to her and see what she knows."

"Of course. Thank you, Theo." Tessa sat back.

Luke and the guys ended the call, then he turned to her. Storms seemed to swirl in his blue eyes. Intense and gentle all at once. "Let's head upstairs. Show us what you found. We won't leave your side."

"Okay." She stood, and the group headed up the mahogany stairs, heavily framed in a substantial banister commanding attention. The floor, trim and wainscotting matched the stair color, but the walls had been painted like Theo had mentioned. They were now a subtle gray tone that brightened the space.

Still, as light as the walls were, an eeriness hung over Tessa's head. Pressure built with each step she took. When they reached the attic door, Liam opened it. Her heart pounded wildly, and she forced herself to take deep breaths.

Warmth pressed against her back. Luke's presence behind her settled the unease. It was replaced with the butterflies that fluttered around in her stomach every time his breath hit her skin and his gruff voice reached her ears.

"I'm right here," he whispered behind her.

Once at the top of the steps, he took her hand, walked in front of her and leaned in close. "If you feel anything strange, tell me right away."

She met his gaze finding it half heated with desire, accompanied by a possessive glint that instantly settled her nerves. "I will."

"This chest here, Tessa?" Liam's question broke their deep stares into each other's eyes.

She moved toward Liam and Trey. "Yes."

Liam lifted the heavy top, the hinges squeaking as it opened. The two men knelt in front of it while Luke stayed by Tessa's side. They both peered down from behind Liam and Trey's shoulders.

"That's it. That's the photo." As Liam lifted the photograph, Tessa leaned in closer, all the while keeping a tight grip on Luke's hand. Trey scooted aside, making room for her and Luke. "And that's the man I saw." She pointed to the stern-looking man in the old black-and-white photo.

Luke reached out. "May I?"

Liam handed him the photograph.

"Let me snap a photo. Tess, is your phone on you?"

She reached into her back pocket, retrieved her phone, unlocked it and handed it to Luke. After he snapped a photo, he placed the phone back in her hand, then wrapped his arm around her waist. "Send that to Theo."

She did, and seconds later, a chime sounded, notifying her of an incoming text. She read out loud:

Theo: Got it. I'll show this to Gram as soon as I see her and let you know what I find out. Go ahead and hang on to that photo. You need it for your research.

Tessa: Thanks. The guys want to do an investigation tonight. Would that be okay?

Theo's approval was immediate, then Luke asked, "Can I ask him something, darlin'?" Tessa handed the phone back to Luke and watched his fingers move over the screen.

Luke: Hey, this is Luke. Just want you to know Tess won't be staying here until we figure out what's going on and put a stop to him attacking her. She got lucky with that fall. It could have been a lot worse.

Theo: Absolutely. Don't blame you. To tell you the truth, I'm a little nervous staying there myself now.

Luke: If anything happens when you return, call us right away.

Theo: Will do. Take care and stay safe.

Luke stared at the photo in his hand. She watched his jaw clench as he rubbed his chin. "So this is the son of a bitch?"

Just the sight of the man in the photo irritated every inch of her. Yes, it was the asshole. And he had the power to come and go. The power to go unseen. The strength to hurt the living and frighten them. And, according to Francis, the power to keep others earthbound and trapped.

The thought produced anger deep within her. She wasn't one to have a temper, but a sickening feeling of fury ignited. Heat radiated up and settled on her cheeks. Suddenly she felt like she could tear up the room in a fit of rage. Instead, she breathed and used all her energy to calm her emotions.

Yesterday had been a whirlwind of confusing events. Now, being back in the attic, in the place that was cur-

75

rently her home, she had time to evaluate the gravity of the situation.

What sick fuck thinks they have the right to attack a person who can't defend themselves? What power was he hoping to have over her?

"Why the hell was he in the hospital window?" she asked, not bothering to mask her irritation.

Luke shook his head. "No idea, but there's definitely a reason for it, and we're going to do everything we can to find out."

"Maybe he worked at the hospital," Trey offered. "If your dream is accurate, we can assume he did."

Liam shifted. "That's a good starting point. It's going to be hard to get much info without a name. We should start by looking to see if any strange deaths or circumstances are on record. Hopefully, Theo can get us some more details soon."

"What's this?" Trey asked. He lifted the leather-bound book in his hand. The same one Tessa had looked through the day before.

"I looked in it yesterday. It's filled with dates and numbers but nothing else." She turned away and listened to the muttering of the guys but didn't care to pay any attention.

Tessa continued working on calming herself, but each second that ticked by proved to be harder. The longer she was in the small, confined space, the more her exasperation grew. She'd moved here to get away from drama, uncertainty and suffocating control. Now, she was living in the middle of a haunting nightmare that wouldn't let go of its grasp on her.

She turned to leave, this time remembering to duck under the beam. Once she cleared the low-lying wood, the heat from anger filling her face was replaced with a wave of nausea. Her balance was off, and her legs turned to Jell-O. The floor seemed to now have a fun house effect. She rushed for the stairs. "I need to get out of here."

Luke's steps followed behind her, but she ignored them and made it to the bathroom just in time. Gentle hands pulled her hair back while she emptied the contents of her stomach. Finally, the sickness eased, and she sat back to catch her breath. The sound of the toilet flushing caught her attention. When she opened her eyes, Luke was running a washcloth under the faucet. He wrung out the excess water and sat next to her on the floor, pressing the cloth to her forehead.

"Talk to me." His words were stern and full of concern. "What happened?"

Tessa cleared her throat. "I started feeling really pissed off. I don't think I've ever felt that mad before. Then when I turned to leave, I got dizzy, and I just needed to get out of there."

"How's your head?"

"It doesn't hurt. Luke, when I say I was angry, I mean, I felt like I could have torn that attic apart. I was raging inside."

He nodded. "I felt something was off. I'm sorry I didn't catch it. Why didn't you say anything?"

"I didn't understand it." She shook her head. "It's not your fault."

"I'm the professional. I'm supposed to pick up on these things." He moved the washcloth to the back of her neck, one palm coming around to rest on her cheek. She leaned into it, the words sitting at the tip of her tongue.

How was she supposed to tell him that it was more than her own life at stake—that her sickness was from the baby growing inside of her? They were never supposed to be as close as they'd become. Their time together had strictly been for fun—a means to release pent-up energy, where they could both let go of the worries and memories that plagued them. When they were together, all was right in the world.

Her heart knew Luke wouldn't push her away. As much as he said he was never going to be the family type, his heart was too big to run from the situation that had arisen. But this wasn't how she wanted him to find out. Not while she sat on the bathroom floor. Not with his two best friends still so close by. She'd wait until they were completely alone.

"I want to get you out of this house. Can you walk?" She nodded and shifted to stand. He helped her, holding her tightly to make sure she was steady before letting go.

"I need to pack my bag." With his nod, she headed straight for her bedroom. Luke followed her to the doorway.

"I'm going to talk to the guys right here in the hallway. Will you be okay?"

"Yes. I'll be fine."

"You need me, you yell." His hand rested on her cheek before moving to the back of her head and pulling her close. The hug settled her some, and when he let go, she instantly missed having him close.

Leaving the door just open enough so she could see a sliver of the hallway, she went to work packing. She pulled a suitcase on wheels out of her closet and set it on the bed. Rummaging through her drawers, she quickly chose random clothes and tossed them inside, then retrieved her computer bag and packed up her laptop and notebooks, along with anything else she would need to work.

Back at her closet, she pulled the door open and gasped when a rush of cold air blew through her. Her hair whipped around, and the chill pulled all the breath from her lungs.

The door to her room, which she'd not closed all the way, swung open violently, then slammed shut. The house shook from the shock wave.

Luke's banging on the other side rattled the wood. She ran to get to him, but another blast of frigid air hit her, this time knocking her back. She stumbled to keep her balance. The growl that had embedded itself in her memory from the other night and in her dream rumbled within the walls.

"Luke!"

"Tess!" he yelled, still hammering on the wood. "Open the door."

"He won't let me!"

The outline of a man took form between her and the door. She watched as the silhouette turned into a translucent image of the man who attacked her in the attic. A figure who would forever be burned into the depths of her memory faced her again.

Her lungs froze, seizing her voice. Luke burst through the door, Trey at his side and Liam behind them. Their eyes went wide at the sight of the man who stood between them. Then, like the flicker of a flame when the wind catches it, he was gone.

Tessa gasped, her lungs finally free. Luke met her halfway across the room. "Are you hurt?"

Not able to find her voice, she shook her head.

His arm wrapped around her shoulders, and he pulled her along with him. "We're out of here."

She watched as Liam closed her suitcase and carried it out of the room. Trey picked up her computer bag and followed behind her and Luke. Her blood ran cold as a soft chuckle drifted through the air as they made their way to the main level of the house.

Luke stood in the center of the living room. His face red, eyes ablaze, he looked like he was ready to go to war. But how can you fight a monster you can't always see?

"What do you want?" he bellowed. "Stay away from her."

Tessa moved to stand in front of him. Placing her hands on either side of his face, she did her best to soothe him. "I'm okay. Just get me out of here."

They made their way outside, his teammates following behind.

As they rushed down the front steps, Luke turned to his team. His arm around Tessa held her in a tight, protective grasp. "He's fucking with the wrong people."

"Sure is," Trey answered. "Stay calm. You know this is exactly what he wants. To push your buttons so you can't think clearly."

Liam spoke up. "Right before you two arrived, we heard from the new owners of the hospital building. I didn't want to mention anything while talking with Theo, but they want to meet with us ASAP. Apparently, they've had strange things happening over there for a few weeks now, and they've intensified over the last few days. They were happy to hear from us and want us to get in there right away to see if we can figure out what's going on."

"That time frame coincides with when I started seeing things."

Liam nodded in acknowledgment.

"But why?"

"Hopefully, we'll have that answer soon," Trey responded.

Luke tightened his arm around her shoulder. "I'm taking Tessa to my place. Keep me updated, and let me know when we're meeting prior to the investigation. I don't want to leave Tess for too long."

Luke's teammates nodded, answering in unison. "We will."

"We'll meet back here at seven tonight," Liam informed him. "Let's get to work and figure out who this asshole is."

With a nod, he guided her to his waiting SUV a few yards away. After Trey and Liam placed her bags in the trunk, Luke got into the driver's seat. He started the engine, but before pulling away from the curb, he turned to her. His eyes were still on fire, but his face had softened. "He won't hurt you, darlin'. I promise."

"Why does he want to get to me so badly?"

"I don't know. But one thing's for sure. He isn't going to succeed. He can try, but he'll have to get through me, and that sure as hell isn't going to happen."

Ten

T he looming investigation weighed on Luke. The thought of leaving Tessa alone so soon after being attacked again killed him. But it was a necessary action required for him to do his job, and this was one job he wanted to get done right.

Something itched under his skin. Even with Lexi on her way to stay with her sister while he was gone, his nerves felt like rubber bands pulled to their limits, heightening his senses and clouding his judgment. As hard as he tried to keep his mind clear, he couldn't shake the feeling that shit was on the verge of igniting into a foul blaze.

What bothered him more was that Tessa said she felt angry while in the attic. Whatever force had been screwing with her had gotten too close. Any closer, and it could potentially tighten its hold on her, and that pissed him off beyond comprehension.

The entire situation held the anxiety one feels while waiting for an incoming tide. He was wading out in the ocean while the water was pulled back, eyeing the secrets in the exposed sand. Time was of the essence, and he and his team needed to gather what they could and head to higher ground before the waves crept back and washed them away.

He didn't care to ponder too much on the wonder of the case. Usually, his enthusiasm kicked into high gear, and he couldn't wait to gather every piece of evidence he could. His excitement was nonexistent, replaced by a need to confront the sonofabitch who was tormenting Tessa. That was a change in his character, and he knew it.

For years, his career of investigating the supernatural was his number one priority. The search for finding out what happened to a person after their death drove his mission, but not as much as the possibility of communicating with a single spirit on the other side. Not just any spirit. No, he'd communicated with spirits before. Through spirit box sessions, voice recorder sessions, hell, he'd even played around with Ouija boards a few times. Still, he'd yet to make contact with the one person he wanted to talk to just once more. His mother.

Now, with Tessa in danger and having been attacked three times, he funneled all of his energy into her. At night, he held her close, even hating when she needed to get up for anything. In his arms, he knew she was safest.

He dreaded leaving her side. The space surrounding his heart squeezed, magnifying his anxiety. His gut told him they would uncover something that night. He didn't know how, but instincts screamed that whatever was about to be revealed, he wasn't going to like it.

Luke walked into the living room. Tessa sat on the couch, working on a design project for one of her clients.

A blanket draped across her lap covered her petite frame, a body Luke knew very well. He'd memorized the shape of her. Every inch of her creamy flesh was burned into his memory. From her slender neck, where he loved kissing the bones that protruded when she arched into him, to her waist, where her hips rounded, giving way to the glorious curve of her backside. To the contour of her toned legs where her calves met her ankles. Her wavy chestnut hair framed her beautiful, delicate features. Thick, long eyelashes hid her piercing green eyes as she looked down at the screen of her computer.

Luke walked forward. The screen held her attention as she concentrated and worked away. He stepped in front of her, taking a seat on the oversized ottoman that matched the furniture. He reached under the soft throw. His fingers curled around her ankle and pulled, bringing her bare foot to rest in his lap. One of his hands snuck up the inside of her leg, where he ever so softly caressed her upper thigh. The corner of her mouth pulled to one side of her face. A blush bloomed on her neck, traveled up, and washed over her cheeks. With his other hand, he massaged the soft skin on her foot, his thumb pressing into the arch. She relaxed into his touch, and it was then that her lashes lifted, giving him the satisfaction of seeing her warm gaze.

Her mischievous smirk woke his insides and stirred sensations that tempted him to throw her over his shoulder and march toward the bedroom.

"What are you doing?"

"Just giving you a foot rub," he said with a grin. "Your toes are cold." He also noticed she looked tired. "Are you sure you're feeling alright?"

"I'm okay. Just tired. It's probably the stress."

The rosy hue of her cheeks faded into a paler tone. She'd insisted on not going back to the hospital but promised she would if she had another dizzy spell. "I've been feeling...off."

"How so?"

"I don't know. Worried mostly."

A subtle glint in her eyes sparked but was gone as soon as it manifested. He wondered what else was pressing on her thoughts, deciding not to push the issue. They'd always had an agreement not to delve too far into the other's feelings. Though the situation had changed, it was probably best to not push too fast. He'd let it go for the time being and see if she'd open up to him on her own.

With her gaze still locked on him, Luke pushed her laptop closed, and she allowed him to move it to the side. He placed his knees on the floor and knelt in front of her. Tessa placed both feet on either side of him and scooted forward.

"I'm going to find out who that asshole is," he told her. "I don't want you to worry."

Luke reached around and rested his palm on the back of her neck. He nudged her, and she gave into his motion, inching toward him. Her lips met his, bursting with passion. He gave her what she silently asked for, and he deepened the kiss, letting his hands roam under her shirt. The soft flesh of her back was silky against his hands. The kiss went on for minutes. He kept them on the brink of crossing into that next phase of passion. He ignored the pulsing of his dick in his pants for a bit, but eventually, the ache grew. Before he crossed the point of hoisting her into his arms, taking her to his bed and stripping her naked, he eased away, moving his mouth to her neck, where he swirled his tongue and tasted the slight saltiness of her skin. It killed him to do it, but he had a job to do. His team waited for him.

He pulled back, her broken breaths heating his skin to an impossible level. "I have to get ready to go. Lexi will be here any minute."

"I know," she said with a heavy breath. "She messaged me a while ago and said she'll be here soon."

"I want you to stay inside. Don't leave. I set my phone to alert me if you call or text. Even if it's on silent, I'll get your message. If anything happens––a dream, a vision, a *feeling*, or you see anything here, I want you to let me know."

"I will."

Luke stood at the chime of the doorbell. He let Lexi inside and left the sisters to chat while he finished gathering his equipment and checking the items off his list. He collected every type of instrument they had and made sure he packed it into the team's work van: devices to capture shadows, voices, heat signatures... Even different light spectrums. He made sure he packed all of it.

Back in the living room, he found Tessa all smiles and laughing with Lexi. She looked more like herself, and he relaxed a bit.

She stood and walked to him. When she reached up, he bent to allow her arms to wrap around the back of his neck. He kissed her, and she kissed him back, seemingly not caring that Lexi, the one person she was afraid of knowing about the two of them, was right there watching.

"I'll be back in the morning. Remember, stay here and don't leave."

"I won't leave."

"I'll stay until you're back in the morning," Lexi said.

Luke gave her a nod and his thanks, keeping Tessa's hand in his until he reached the door. "Lock this behind me." He waited to hear the deadbolt latch before walking down the front steps.

In the team's van, he turned the ignition and sat. The hum of the engine provided a calming, meditative sound. He took a moment to ground himself.

It wasn't often that he felt the need, but with his head not in the state it normally was when he went on investigations, he took the opportunity. He pictured his mother in his mind, holding her hand like they used to when he was a young boy walking with her on the beach. He thought of her blue eyes and imagined she was still living and he could still talk to her.

Then out loud, he said, "Keep her safe, Mom, and help me find the information I need to end this."

Eleven

G lowing in the night fog was the feeling of un-
pleasant uncertainty. Lurking behind the haze
was trouble. Luke could feel it.

Funny, he'd always enjoyed the San Franciscan
fog—loved jogging in the damp, salty air, where he felt
liberated. It was hard to dwell on the past when you
were trying to see through a mist concealing your path
ahead. That was the same reason he loved his job. An invisible veil shielded secrets that lay hidden behind every
corner of a paranormal investigation, and he sought
after them like a shark on the scent of one drop of
blood.

His job was an ocean, and he was its explorer. Only
now, he was being sucked down into the darkest abyss
with no way of turning back to the surface.

He'd spent the last half hour doing a solo EVP session in Tessa's bedroom. It was imprinted with her aura. The smell of her lingered. Her gentle, casual personality was evident in the light-colored bedding and pops of pastels. Every piece and trinket was an extension of her. The ballerina music box next to her jewelry case, with its glass lid, was the perfect comparison to its owner. Tessa was tiny and delicate, but underneath, she was tough as steel. He knew she'd be able to dance around the storm that was headed their way. He'd be right there facing the wind and beating rain with her.

It was a room he hoped she'd consider leaving. An ache he'd felt for the past couple of days bloomed into warmth deep inside at the idea. He'd already known he wanted more than what he'd shared with her these past months. She was now in his house, safe, filling the walls with her beauty, and he wanted her to stay.

As he stared at the trinkets and items on her dresser, there was no hesitation. The thought didn't even frighten him. Instead, the feeling of needing her near, experiencing their relationship go from one level to the next, and letting life lead him where he was meant to go only grew stronger.

His emotions reached their limits after doing the initial walk-through of her bedroom. While he stood in front of her dresser and took in the idea of what Tessa truly meant to him and the future he wanted, he felt the chains he kept tightly bound around himself loosen. Luke still wasn't thinking clearly, but he had his teammates, and he knew his friends would watch his back—help him keep his head on straight.

If there was one thing they did best, it was getting to the bottom of mysteries that begged to stay hidden.

This case would be no different. There sure as shit were no other options. Too much was at stake.

At the window, Luke stared back out at the light fog blanketing the city. The former hospital, visible from Tessa's bedroom, stood off in the distance, just downhill from the house. The structure's large facade stood foreboding as if waiting. For what, Luke wasn't yet sure. What he did know was that the spirit who'd shown himself to her was running out of time. His mind was made up. He didn't care about her lease. He'd help pay the remainder of her rent if he had to. She wasn't coming back to this house. Her home was with him.

He tapped his knuckles on the wooden windowsill. As he turned away from the glass and walked the length of Tessa's bedroom, he passed her dresser again, filled with all of her feminine trinkets. He chuckled, thinking he couldn't wait to have all of her belongings strewn around his house.

He doubled checked the camera's position in the corner of her room. It was a wide shot that would hopefully capture anything taking place. Multiple pieces of equipment were positioned around since it was where she was last attacked. He wanted to be sure they could document the slightest change in the natural environment.

The blaring tone of one of the motion detectors at the doorway prompted him to spin around. Both Liam and Trey stood there.

"Ready to get back to it?" Liam asked.

It was well into the night, and the group had taken a break to eat. They hadn't gotten any activity yet and hoped that after pausing in the investigation, they'd pick up on some activity.

Luke nodded and waved an arm over the REM pod that he'd placed on Tessa's bed. The device emitted its own electromagnetic field and would alarm them if the area around it was disturbed. He pulled his hand away when the test proved it was working.

"You're on edge."

He half scoffed at Trey's comment. He was more than on edge. It was like every emotion in existence rose to the surface. "I'm a little tense, yeah," he admitted. "This thing was here earlier. Now it's hiding. It's fucking with us."

"You know you need to keep your cool. Don't let whatever this is get into your head."

"I know." Luke turned back to the window. "I just can't stop wondering what the hell was in that place," he murmured, motioning toward the window at the hospital. "What would make itself seen to Tess and then follow her here. Attack her?"

"A ghost with a sick mind," Liam answered.

"Fuck." Luke ran a hand over his head and squeezed the muscles in the back of his neck. He knew that much, but hearing it spoken out loud boiled his blood.

"We've got your back, man. Both you and Tessa."

"Thanks." He made his way to his team. "I think we should head to the attic."

"I agree." Trey moved to the side, and Liam followed, making room for Luke to exit. "It's where Tessa was physically attacked. Something is attached to that chest. Why else would she have been drawn to it?"

Luke nodded. "I brought the new portal box. I put it upstairs. I wanna start with it and see if anything comes through."

"Sounds good," Liam said. "I want to test it out, get a feel for it."

The three of them headed for the attic door. On the top floor of the house, the unfinished wood creaked with every step they took. The smell of time tickled Luke's nose even more than the dust that floated around. Shadows were brought to life by the dim light filtering in from outside through the one window.

It was an attic, and he'd been in many just like it over the years. Like most, it was filled with forgotten items. Nothing special stood out about it except that this one seemed to hold secrets that threatened the woman he cared about most.

"Baseline was normal earlier," Liam pointed out. "Nothing outstanding. I think we should open the chest. Use it as a trigger object and see what comes through."

Luke watched on the night vision camera as his teammate opened the case.

"Switching on the portal," Luke announced. He turned the knob on the device that resembled an old-fashioned radio. Unlike the spirit box they'd used in the past, this one eliminated the hiss of white noise, allowing them to have a quieter, easier conversation with the spirit. He crouched, for some reason feeling like he needed to be closer to the open chest. He reached inside, feeling the old papers, and carefully lifted a small stack.

"Did this belong to you?"

Silence ensued.

"We want to talk to you. You can speak to us through this," he pointed to the portal. "Can you tell us who you are?" Luke stood, shaking off a shiver that coursed through him. "Whatever is here doesn't want to talk."

"Yeah. I could have sworn I saw a shadow move in and out of the camera frame. Just off to the side near you."

Trey had a lens pointed at him. Luke couldn't see it in the dark, but he knew both of his teammates were recording while he conducted the conversation with the portal.

"It's really cold right here. Like someone is looming over my back." His temper started to boil. He'd be damned if anything was going to harm Tessa and try to keep quiet about it.

"I know you're here. I can feel you. So stop hiding and speak to us. Don't be a coward."

He often provoked spirits to get them to communicate. Especially with the malicious ones. The ones who had an affinity for tormenting the living. There was nothing Luke despised more than a spirit afflicting a person. No one deserved to be abused, in the living realm or otherwise.

"Why did you follow the woman who lives here to this house?"

"It...was me," a far-off voice said through the portal, echoing through the layers of dimensions. It was deep. Lacking kindness. Its coldness reached through the device's speakers, filling Luke with a dread that quickly turned to anger. He had his answer. The ghost did follow her from the hospital.

"Why?" Luke demanded. "Why did you follow her. Why did you push her down the stairs?

A disturbing chuckle came through next. Then the room went silcnt.

"Have you guys been able to come up with clues about past owners? Any deeds or titles show up yet?" Luke asked. "The man Tess saw in the hospital window has to be tied to this house somehow."

"Not yet," Liam answered. "Couldn't with everything closed for the weekend. First thing tomorrow morning, one of us will get down to the county office and put in a request to pull the records."

Luke opened the viewing screen to the camera he held, more so to have a visual on his friends while the conversation carried on.

"But why come back now?" Trey asked. "Or why become active now? Tessa's been living here for nearly a year. What was so different about the other day?"

"Maybe he always hangs out in the window over there," Liam suggested. "This time, he saw her passing by while she was on a run and decided to follow her?"

"No," Luke interjected. "There has to be more to it. We all know spirits don't just latch on to the living for no reason. There's always a reason behind it."

His friends nodded in agreement. "And we can't forget the dream that she had."

Luke had filled his team in on the disturbing dream Tessa had the night before. "She said it felt like the woman was trying to warn her. Protect her from him. Why would she reach out to Tessa here in the house and visit in her dream when initially she only saw the man in the hallway downstairs? There has to be a reason why the woman's spirit felt the need to make contact with Tess."

"This is becoming more complicated by the day," Trey stated.

"I know." Luke huffed out a breath. "And it's taking a toll on her. She hasn't said anything, but I can see it."

Liam lowered his camera. "Let's head downstairs and see what else we can gather for the night. Trey's been working on contacting someone who used to work at the hospital. If we can talk to them, maybe we can get more answers—"

"Shhh." Luke held his hand out. "Do you hear that?" he whispered. The three men each had their own cameras on to see. Even in the dark, Luke was able to communicate. He held his hand up and motioned with two fingers while mouthing the word *walking*. The men fell silent, and a moment later, definite footsteps could be heard. They were heavy, and the sound of the wooden floorboards bending with the movement echoed.

"Let's go." Luke hurried down the attic steps with his team on his heels. One by one, he took the stairs, convinced he'd find someone roaming the second floor. The sounds were so loud and precise, they had to be coming from a person.

Luke aimed his flashlight toward the bottom of the steps. The hallway was pitch-black. "Theo?" he called out, wondering if Tessa's housemate had come home early. "Is anyone here?"

The only answer sounded from a REM pod down the hall. *Tessa's room.*

Luke was in motion in the direction of the sound before his brain could register that his feet were moving. When he walked into Tessa's bedroom, the device that lay on top of her bed sounded continuously. The lights on top were illuminated, indicating that something was definitely breaking the small magnetic field it emitted around it.

He held his voice recorder in front of him. "What's your obsession with Tessa?" He fought to keep the fury out of his tone, but he wasn't doing a great job.

He noticed Liam leaning against the wall, head down. He spoke before anyone could ask him what was wrong. "I just got queasy all of a sudden."

It didn't happen often, but when Liam felt sick on an investigation, it always meant that whatever they were dealing with was about to get a whole lot worse.

Luke admitted, "My head went all cloudy when we walked in here. Like something lured us in and wants to disorient us."

"Sick fuck," Trey uttered.

Luke had had enough. He pressed record on the voice recorder, but the indicator light went off. "Shit! This battery is dead. It was fully charged right before we started."

"Here," Liam held his recorder out but stopped short of handing it to Luke. "This one's been drained too, but it's got a little juice left."

"I'm sick of this asshole playing games." Luke took the device from Liam and held it out. "Listen. Either you tell us who you are, or we find out in the next few days on our own. Either way, we're going to know eventually. So quit screwing around. What's your deal? You just some lonely ghost who saw a woman and decided to follow her home like a lost puppy. That's pathetic, don't you think?" He looked to Liam, who was now bracing his hands on his knees. "Are you affecting my friend? This isn't your house. Get the hell out."

Luke played back the recorder. Adrenaline pumped through him. He felt like he'd just finished a good run. The thrill faded as the voice he played back spoke.

"Play it again," Liam prompted.

The men huddled close and listened to the grainy message on the recorder.

Trey asked, "Does that say, 'fuck you'?"

"Sure sounds like it."

The sound of a door slamming caused all three men to jump. In the hallway, it was evident that the sound came from the attic door.

"I left that door open," Trey insisted.

Luke's head pulsed in pain. His fingers went to his forehead. "I feel like there's an icepick in my eyes!"

"Oh shit!"

The men followed Trey's gaze as he stared down the hall. "Did you see that?"

"No. What is it?"

"There was a shadow. Darker than the hallway. It moved right to left."

A crashing sound came from the ground floor.

"What the fuck is going on?" Liam shouted.

Once downstairs on the first floor, a vase lay shattered in the living room. "How the hell did that happen?"

"I don't know," Luke admitted. "But I sure do feel better down here than I did upstairs. That was so weird. I've never felt pain like that before."

Liam nodded. "Trey, did you get the shadow on your camera?"

"I'll have to play it back to see. My battery died as we came downstairs. We do have a camera set up there. It's a wide shot of the entire hallway. It should have picked us up as well as the shadow."

"As soon as we mentioned its connection to the hospital, things really picked up. I think we're on to something." Luke worked on tamping down his anger.

Liam nodded. "Alright. Look, I think we should pack it up before anything else in Theo's house is destroyed."

"We'll hit the research really hard starting tomorrow," Trey agreed. "Let's see if we can get some good evidence to link this guy to this house, the hospital or both. Should we call Dave?"

Their psychic friend had worked with them on countless cases, including the one that involved Liam and Emily. He was gifted with being able to communicate with spirits, as well as cross them over into the next realm.

Liam answered, "Probably a good idea. He'll be able to pick up on things and maybe connect with the woman spirit and find out why she's visiting Tessa."

Luke grunted his dissatisfaction with the evening. "This place is full of secrets. I can feel it. It's chasing us out."

"I know that's what it feels like, but we got our answer tonight. The hospital is the key. So we keep digging hard in that direction. The next time we come back, we'll be fully prepared with information we can use and have Dave with us," Liam added.

"The next time," Luke corrected, "we put a stop to it. I want Tessa free of this shit."

Twelve

"Tell me what happened last night."

The late morning light flooded Luke's bedroom. Tessa lay pressed against him, her back to his front. His large arms wrapped tighter around her as he moaned a seductive tune into her neck. It was raspy from lack of sleep, and it warmed her insides.

He'd crawled into bed sometime in the middle of the night. She heard him say goodnight as Trey and Lexi left. Her eyes heavy with exhaustion, she'd snuggled close to him, and they fell asleep with their limbs tangled around each other, the way only two lovers can do.

She shifted, turning to her back. Luke propped his head on his palm and looked down at her. He was gorgeous in every way imaginable. Tattoos covered his toned chest and arms that traveled down to his wrists. An angel with wings that spanned across his chest always caught her eye. It was beautiful. She'd asked him about it once, about what it meant, and he responded by saying someday he'd tell her its meaning.

She let her palm rest on the angel. His hand took hers and held it in place. His tanned skin set off the golden tones of his hair and the short beard that framed his strong jaw. His eyes shone all of the different hues of blue in the light.

"We had a run-in with it. But it didn't want to talk. Asshole kept us running around like hamsters on a wheel. Then berated us and slammed a door." Luke scoffed. "Amateur."

"What?"

"He left us a big F you on the recorder. Dickhead doesn't realize we've been cussed out before, and that shit doesn't phase us. He did break a vase, though."

"Seriously?"

"Yeah. It was downstairs in the living room, on one of the end tables. Don't know how it could have happened naturally. Trey thinks we caught it on one of the cameras we had set up. We'll know for sure when we review."

She wasn't sure how paranormal investigations worked and felt her heart sink at the realization that they hadn't gotten any answers as to why the haunting started. "Will we ever know why this is happening?"

The warmth around her hand radiated down her arm when he brought it to his mouth. "I don't know." He kissed her knuckles. "But I do know you're not going back there. Tess, it was in your bedroom again." His gaze was intense. "It made our REM pod go nuts. It was sitting on your bed. You're not safe there."

His words echoed Francis' warning and the knot in her stomach tightened. "I believe you. I don't want to go back there. I'm sure with everything that's happened, Theo will let me out of my lease. I'm staying here for the foreseeable future."

She watched his eyes drift closed and bit her lip. Afraid her statement had been too direct, she added, "I mean...if that's okay."

He cupped her face in his large palm. His thumb stroked her cheek just below her eye. "It's more than okay. There's no way in hell I'm letting you out of my sight."

She swore relief took over his expression. When he looked down on her again, fire and passion erupted between the two of them, dancing between their bodies like twin flames about to come together. She melted under his gaze. Heat rose from deep within, washing over every inch of her skin. She tingled with anticipation, knowing only his touch could soothe the want burning through her.

He turned her palm up and nuzzled his nose in it. He kissed his way down her arm and to her shoulder and nipped the skin of her collarbone with his teeth. She hissed, pulling him closer. He knew exactly how to tease her, and her body always responded instantly.

"You'll stay right here."

She nodded her approval.

"How's your head?"

"Good. I didn't have a headache last night."

"Yeah? Anything else hurt? You did say you fell."

She lifted her head and ran her teeth over his earlobe. "I'm fine."

A low growl escaped him, and he wrapped his arms around her even tighter.

"I need you," she whispered so softly, she wasn't sure the walls could even hear. "Now."

Without a word, he flipped them so he was on his back. There were no instructions needed. Tessa grabbed the hem of the t-shirt she wore, one of his that she'd chosen to sleep in. One he hadn't washed yet. His scent filled the fabric and engulfed her while she slept during the night without him. Now, she pulled it over her head, exposing her nakedness to him.

Luke let out a sound, something between a growl and a moan, and she shivered at the effect she had on him. Nothing was sexier than watching the man under her come undone by the sight of her body.

He ran his hands up her sides, stopping to knead her breasts, then down, where he squeezed the roundness of her ass before pulling her to him.

"Come on up here, baby. You know how I like it."

She obliged, loving the demand in his voice. Knowing exactly where he wanted her, she scooted up and rested her knees on either side of his head. She'd never given up control the way she did with Luke. He was the only man who had ever made her feel comfortable enough to do so. With him, she always knew she was safe. With him, she wanted to turn over the reins, let him steer and control their passion. A passion that always led to pleasure so high, they fell together back to earth in a crashing wave that broke on a shore where only the two of them existed.

Her hands went to his head, then she ran her fingers through his thick hair. She wanted his mouth on her. Had missed his touch. The ache between her legs pulsed so intensely, she thought she'd come before he even touched her.

When he slipped his thumb between her folds, she let out a sharp gasp. Her head went back, her eyes closed, and she sunk down, pressing herself against him. He stroked her clit so lightly she was sure she'd die from the teasing pleasure.

He used two fingers to separate her lips, and when he gently blew on her bundle of nerves, her hand left his head and gripped the top of the headboard. Her whole body shook with debilitating desire.

"This is all for me."

From the tone in his voice, she couldn't tell if it was a question or a statement.

"Only for you," she panted in a whisper.

He moaned. "You're so wet, and I've barely touched you." He flicked his tongue, and she jolted in response.

When he reached behind with his opposite hand and inched two fingers inside of her, she tensed as the waves of pleasure grew.

He pulled away, and she whimpered at the loss. "I'm going to make you come hard and fast. Don't you dare hold back. I want to hear you scream," he commanded.

With his fingers inside of her, he pumped and swirled, stroking every inch that he could reach. Then, he latched his mouth over her impossibly aching clit. His other hand went to her breast and played with her nipple.

Her body was pure electricity. Rushing blood in her ears caused them to ring while she turned into a conduit, both of them exchanging their energetic fervor.

He teased her with his tongue. Little flicks and suctioning, alternating between back-and-forth motions and circles. Just when she thought he was going to go back on his word of making her come fast, he suctioned her clit into his mouth, then held it there while his tongue ramped up its pace. She should have known. Luke always kept his promises. If he said he wanted her to come fast, she did. And if he wanted to drag out her pleasure, keep her teetering on an impossible edge, somewhere between agony and bliss, that's what he did.

She gripped the headboard, her hips moving against his face buried between her thighs. She looked down, and a burst of emotion exploded deep inside when she caught him watching her.

His eyes radiated lust and something else. Something she thought she'd only seen a few times in recent weeks but had brushed the thought away. It wasn't possible. Luke Collins was not in love with her. He said himself that he could never love. Said he didn't know how.

He closed his eyes. His features relaxed. Gone was the urgent alpha she'd come to know, replaced by pure satisfaction. She knew he was getting just as much pleasure just by watching her.

He kept a strong hold on her clit as he indulged himself. And when he moaned, releasing vibrations that shot straight through her, the muscles in her lower stomach tightened. Her pussy tightened around his fingers, and remembering his words, she didn't hold back.

His tongue pressed harder, and that was all she needed. Her orgasm exploded through her. Wave after wave of euphoric bliss coaxed moans from her. She was glad they were alone. She'd be embarrassed if anyone heard what he'd done to her—was capable of doing to her. Those sounds were reserved only for the two of them.

She rested her head on the arm still outstretched on the headboard. Her breaths came out in pants, and her heart pounded in her chest. She felt his eyes on her and smiled, looking down at him. His mouth glistened with the remnants of her.

He helped her scoot down. She paused when wetness slicked her thighs. The wide smile on his face confirmed her suspicion.

"I'm not embarrassed in the least. It's been too long, darlin'. You bring me to my knees."

She leaned down, kissing him, tasting herself on his lips. "You have no idea what that does to me. You came, and I didn't even touch you," she whispered.

"Oh, you touched me." His tone was deeper than she'd ever heard before. He pulled her tight as if he were trying to merge their bodies together. "You touched me more than you'll ever know."

Emotions pooled in her eyes, and she fought to keep them at bay. The prospect of a real relationship with Luke Collins burned deep within her. But true love didn't exist. Women in her family never found love. Lexi was the exception. But if it happened for her sister, why not for her too?

Their mother's statements hung in the back of Tessa's head like heavy curtains waiting to shut out the light that tried to flood in. Instead of putting herself in danger of heartache, she did what she'd been doing recently. She shut out her feelings--pushed all of her emotions to the side, and focused on her reality. She wasn't meant to be loved. That only existed in fairy tales. She didn't dare wish for it.

He moved his hands and coaxed her to look at him.

"Something is happening between us, Tess."

She nodded while she fought to find her voice. "I feel it."

"I'm not running from this. I don't know what wicked spell you've put on me. Frankly, I don't care. All I know is I need to be near you. It scared me before, but not anymore. The thought of not being around you is too much to even think about."

"Luke," she cooed.

"I hope this isn't scaring you. I'm just letting you know you've done something to me, and I want to see where it takes us. I'm not going anywhere. You can trust me."

All of a sudden, the reality she'd convinced herself was her only option seemed wrong. Her heart picked up its pace from the emotions rushing through her. Her mind screamed to tell him about the baby. To tell him what she most desperately craved.

Him. All of him.

She closed her eyes, contemplating the words to start with, when her phone buzzed on the nightstand. She saw the name pop up on the screen.

"It's Theo," she said as Luke handed her the phone, somewhat relieved that the news she needed to tell him was postponed for a bit. She'd take a little time to come up with the right words. If the right words even existed.

Focusing on the screen, she said, "He says he wants us to meet him at the house. His grandmother will be with him. She wants to talk to all of us."

Thirteen

Fear makes the wolf seem bigger than he is.

But how do you ignore the dark forces of another world once it punches into your realm of existence? How do you brave the unknown? What was once invisible and mysterious is now a reality with no guidance on how to handle it. How do you stand up to an enemy you don't understand and one that has the higher ground?

It was an unfair and ugly characteristic in a world that held so much beauty. Tessa's frustration grew with each passing moment. She repeated the phrase to herself over and over, wishing the fierce beast that lurked within the walls of the house she called home would return to its lair.

She kept her thoughts silent, careful not to let Luke know she was feeling apprehensive. Her hand rested in his. He didn't speak, but she didn't need him to. The tense muscles in his jaw and the white-knuckled grip he had on the steering wheel all told her he was just as anxious about going back to the house as she was. Yet, the hand he lay on her lap, the one stroking her skin with his thumb, remained relaxed. The contradiction helped ease her fears. No matter what happened, he'd be by her side.

She never dreamed she'd be under the wings of any man. Now she was living with the most gorgeous and protective man she'd ever come across, and she welcomed his alpha nature. It began the moment his intense blue eyes fell on her at Liam and Emily's rehearsal dinner. He captured her in a spellbinding grasp, and in that moment, something deep within told her he wasn't going to break the magical hold. As scared as she was to admit it, she knew she didn't want him to.

As anxious as she was about returning to the house, Luke was far from pleased. She'd never seen him brood the way she had after calling Theo that morning to ask that they meet at another location. But Theo's grandmother insisted that they meet at the house to talk.

Luke parked around the corner in the only space available on the street when they pulled up to the house. As soon as Tessa stepped through the threshold, a pounding erupted in her head. She kept quiet, not wanting to alarm him, but she counted the seconds that ticked by waiting for Trey and Liam to arrive. Now they were all gathered in the home's front sitting room. An empty space on the end table was left where the broken vase previously sat. It unnerved Tessa.

Theo's grandmother, Lettie, spoke after Liam and the guys filled both her and Theo in on the happenings the previous night. "Well, you boys sure had an eventful night."

Her voice was aged, and though her features showed the years she'd lived through, she was still a beautiful woman, her eyes full of warm compassion. "I can't say that I've ever experienced anything here in the house. Ben, Theo's grandfather and I bought this house when our children were still young. We raised them here, and nothing strange ever happened. Although, there was one instance..." She stared into the hallway beyond the room they sat in as a memory appeared to replay in her mind's eye. She blinked, looking back at them. "It was a very long time ago." She sighed, dropping her head, and her hands fidgeted in her lap.

"What is it, Gram?" Theo asked, placing a hand on her shoulder.

Luke sat forward. His voice dropped to a soft tone. "Lettie, any information you share could help us figure out what's going on. Believe me, there's nothing you can tell us that will make us doubt you. We've seen some crazy things over the years."

"When we first moved in, a neighbor came by," she began. "She was a nice woman. She sat right here in this room with me and had a cup of tea. She was amazed that we'd purchased the home with all of the original furniture. I told her we didn't mind. It was all in great condition, and we had put all of our savings into pur-chasing this place. Having it furnished was a big bonus for us. That was the only other time I'd been asked if anything strange had happened here. I asked her why she would ask such a thing? She told me there'd been strange things that occurred with the previous couple that lived here. The woman who lived here had taken a major fall and died."

"Oh my God," Tessa breathed.

"Apparently, it was rumored that the place was haunted, and she and her husband had been experiencing strange things. But we were never made aware of it when we bought the house."

"And you say your family never witnessed anything strange while living here?" Liam asked.

"No, never."

"What happened to the neighbor, Gram?" Theo asked.

"Well, she and her family moved away around the time your mother left for college. We stayed in touch for a long time, then she passed away a while ago."

"All of the stuff in the attic?" Tessa broke the silence. "Is that from your family, or was that already here?"

"Oh, all of that. That was all here. We just didn't feel right messing with any of it. It felt too personal. So we just left it alone. We never went up there anyway, and the kids never liked being in the attic. Over the years, we just forgot about it, honestly. When my husband passed away, and I moved to the assisted living community, I took our personal belongings, leaving behind everything that was here when we first got the keys."

Trey asked, "Is there anyone else you know of who may be able to provide us with more history?"

"Maybe her daughter can help. I haven't spoken to her since she called to tell me her mother had passed. That was a few years ago. When Theo takes me back home, I'll look for her phone number so he can pass it on to you. Hopefully, she's still at the same location."

"That would be greatly appreciated." Luke sat back.

Lettie looked straight into Tessa's eyes before asking, "Are you okay, dear? Theo told me what happened. I'm so sorry you've been frightened here."

"I'm okay, ma'am. Got a bump on the head, but other than that, I'm just fine." She didn't dare mention the mark it left on her back when it pushed her down the stairs. Or the fact that the woman's spirit saved her life.

"I have to say, I wanted to meet here today to see the house again, and I didn't think I'd walk in and feel any different, but there is definitely something strange about being here now. The air has changed."

"I feel it, too," Theo confirmed.

Lettie looked to each of them before landing on Tessa, and asked, "Why on earth would a spirit follow you here and attack you?"

"The bigger question is, what connection does the spirit have to this house," Liam said. "The picture Tessa found in that trunk was of the same man she saw here and at the hospital. That can only mean that he's connected to both places somehow."

"Will you be able to figure out what's going on?" Lettie asked.

Trey assured her, "We're going to do everything we can to find out and try to put a stop to it."

Then Luke leaned forward. "Until then, Theo, like I mentioned before, Tessa won't be staying here. It's attacked her multiple times, and she isn't safe here."

A wave of nausea came over Tessa as the guys spoke. Luke moved in close and whispered, "You okay?"

All eyes were on her. She felt so small in the crowded room. The ringing in her ears started up again. Unease crept in, along with a heat that moved up her body and settled in her face. "I need to get some fresh air." She stood but was halted when her head spun, throwing her off balance. She landed in Luke's lap.

Before she knew what was happening, she became weightless, just like when Luke had carried her to his car a few days before.

"We're going back to the hospital."

"It's this house," she told him weakly.

"I'm sure it is, but I want to be a hundred percent sure it's not from you hitting your head."

He hurried her to his SUV, carrying her like she weighed no more than a five-pound bag of sugar. And once again, placed her in the passenger seat. When he pulled the door closed on the driver's side, Tessa turned to him. "Luke, listen to me. We need to talk."

"We'll talk on the way."

Irritation gripped her. She normally loved his dominance, but enough had happened over the last few days. It was time she came clean and told him everything. The nausea faded as soon as he sat her in the car. Her head was now clearer. "There's something I need to tell you."

"I know you said it's the house," he started as he put the key into the ignition, "and I don't doubt that. But with your head—"

"Luke, would you fucking listen to me for a damn minute! Put your alpha ego on the back burner, and let me talk."

He stared at her with a mixture of confusion and worry on his face. His eyes radiated with an intense glare. "My alpha ego?" he quipped. "You are my number one priority. This has nothing to do with egos."

"I don't want to argue with you. I'm asking you, please, tell the guys we aren't going to the hospital. I don't want Lexi worrying. I don't want her questioning anything."

"Questioning us about what? She knows about us."

Tears burned the back of Tessa's eyes. She fought hard not to let them fall. The words were on the tip of her tongue. They screamed in her mind. She'd fought the urge to tell him numerous times over the past few days, not knowing the right way to say them. Three words that held the power to destroy what they had, to scare him to the point of no return. But there was no getting around what had to be said.

"What aren't you telling me, Tess?" His tone gentled. In the stillness of the car, he reached out for her, both of his hands cupping her face. He leaned closer, and the feel of his breath on her lips melted the last bits of restraint she had. A tear fell, burning its way down her cheek. His thumb brushed it away.

"Darlin', I promise you, there's nothing in this world you can tell me that will make me change how I feel about you."

She shook her head, wanting to believe he was right. That he wouldn't abandon her like her own father, who she had never met. That he'd prove her mother wrong and stay. Not all men were selfish. She could find love and happiness.

But the next words he spoke almost stilled her heart. Everything came to a standstill. Not the sound of whooshing cars nor the hustle and bustle of the world outside made its way to her ears. Only the sound of his voice and the words he uttered echoed in the closed, confined space. Freezing time.

"I know about the baby."

Fourteen

Only the sound of his own heart beating in his ears could be heard while he drove. There was no destination in his mind. He just knew the two of them needed to be somewhere that would drown out the static of the world.

After he uttered what he knew she was trying to tell him, it was like a rubber band had snapped. All of the tension surrounding her, at last, seemed to have broken. But the shock of saying the words out loud for both of them to hear hung in the stillness of the air. They needed to reconnect. Nothing had been right since the night she'd called him. They'd existed in each other's presence, but the link between them had stalled. It was time to revive that bond and show her he wasn't going anywhere.

He pulled the car off the highway. Tessa hadn't asked why he overshot the direction of the hospital. He did hear the sigh of relief escape her. As hard as he was sure she tried, she hadn't been able to mask the sound entirely. He'd put the car in gear and started driving moments after she insisted she was feeling better. Holding her hand the entire drive, she didn't fight his grasp, but he felt the tension in her body. They needed to go somewhere they could relax and talk.

Once parked, he stepped out and walked around to open her door. The wind caught her hair, flipping it around her face as she exited the SUV. Her hands caught it, and she twisted the locks with her fingers and held the ends.

He retrieved a blanket from the trunk, one he always kept there for days like this when he needed to escape and clear his head. He put his arm around her shoulders after locking the doors and walked her to his favorite spot.

They were the only two around on that particular part of the beach. Except for a couple of dogs playing with their owner off in the distance, they were alone.

Tessa still hadn't spoken, and it killed him knowing that she felt she couldn't tell him.

That she struggled with telling him.

He had no one to blame. He'd planted that seed in her head at the beginning, making it clear he wasn't boyfriend material, wasn't the family type, and certainly never wanted any children. But that was before he'd taken the time to explore his heart's deepest desires.

What he wanted most in the world was what he feared the most. He'd been fooling himself for years. The truth was, he loved the idea of having a family. He just didn't trust himself—didn't know what it took to be the person someone could rely on. But he wanted to be. He was determined to be. He was going to rip those toxic ideas from their roots and make sure they never grew back.

He dropped the blanket to the sand, took her face in his palms once more, dropped his head and captured her lips. There was no teasing.

No softness.

No waiting.

He took her mouth and devoured her. Poured his soul into the kiss, wanting her to feel nothing but his need for her. He didn't slow down until she gripped his forearms, and her moans pooled into his mouth. It was only then that he pulled back, leaving his hands where they were on her hips to steady her.

"How did you know?"

"Let's sit."

Luke picked up the blanket and unfolded it. He guided Tessa to sit in front of him. With her back pressed against his chest, he draped the blanket around the both of them. Their body heat instantly soared under the heavy material.

"I saw the pregnancy test in your jewelry box last night."

He caught her squeezing her eyes shut at the realization of her mishap. The test lay face up in full view through the glass lid of the jewelry box.

"But honestly, the day you were in the ER, I had my suspicions."

"I thought they kicked you out of the ER."

"They didn't. They just asked me to step out of your room while they examined you. As soon as I did, there was a trauma page, and all of the available nurses were called to assist. I slipped into one of the hallways and just hung around for a bit. That's when I saw another nurse take the machine into your room. I watched her wheel it back out a while later, and not long after, she saw me hanging around and told me I could go back in and be with you."

"You knew what that machine was?"

"Doesn't take a rocket scientist to know what it's for." He kissed the top of her head. "The wand thing and gel were attached to it. I watch those medical shows on TV. I figured it out."

"Why didn't you say anything then?"

"I wanted to give you a chance to tell me. Honestly, when you didn't bring it up, I figured it was nothing and maybe they were just doing a routine exam. But then, last night, I saw the test. It was positive."

Her eyes fluttered closed. "I forgot I'd left it there. I was sure it was going to be negative, just a fluke that my period was late. That's happened before when I've been stressed. But I hadn't felt any pressure since moving here, so I thought it was odd."

Luke wrapped his arms tightly around her. "Why didn't you tell me at any time while you've been staying with me?"

She let out a huff.

"Don't answer that," he said and urged her to lift up. He repositioned her so she straddled his lap. "Tess, I know what I said in the beginning. Last year, when we first met, I was still in that stage of my life where there was no changing my mind about the future I was going to have. The future I convinced myself I deserved. I come from a fucked-up background. A father who never showed affection to anything except the bottle he held in his hand every night."

"You're not your father." Her words were stern. They washed over him, and he breathed them in. "I'm so sorry I didn't tell you sooner. I just didn't know how."

"Don't be sorry. It's not your fault. I planted ideas in your head, and I'm sorry for that. Those were my own insecurities. Me not wanting to face my own demons. But I'm not running from those demons anymore. I'm here, and I'm not going anywhere."

She rested her head against his. They sat silent, but he drank in her presence. "Listen, we're going to still take one day at a time. I meant what I said. I want you near me. This doesn't change how I feel. If anything, I need you more. I'm not leaving you, Tessa. I'm not running."

He waited a beat before asking her the most important question of all. "How do you feel?"

"Tired. Nauseous."

He made a mental note to look up everything that could make her feel better and ease her sickness.

"How do you feel about...?"

"Being pregnant?" she finished. "I'm scared."

He sat quiet, wanting to give her all the space she needed to talk freely.

"But I'm happy."

"Yeah?"

"Yeah. You?"

"I'm still in shock. The guys couldn't understand what was wrong with me last night. I saw the test on your dresser, and it was like a caged beast tore itself out of me. Don't worry, I didn't tell them."

"Lexi can't know yet. I want this time for the two of us. There's so much going on—"

He placed a finger to her lips. "No need to worry. This is our secret for the time being. But I will say, I might have to go into hiding when you tell your sister."

Tessa giggled. "She's going to be surprised, but she'll be okay. I know once she gets over the initial shock, she'll be ecstatic."

"Okay, now for the million-dollar question."

"What's that?"

He flashed her the biggest grin he could muster. "How did this happen?"

She slammed her palm into his chest, pushing him back. He took advantage and let himself fall to the sand, but he took her with him. He let his hands rest on her hips.

"You men are all the same. How did this happen? I'll tell you how."

He held her head and pulled her down to meet his waiting lips. When he broke their kiss, he said, "It happened that night on the beach. The last time we were together." He squeezed her ass and kept a hold of the blanket with his other hand at her back. Though they were the only ones in the vicinity, he wanted the intimate moment shielded from all eyes. "When I took you on the sand in the middle of the night."

A rosy hue bloomed on her cheeks.

"In the moonlight, after our swim, and the waves broke around our bodies."

Her breath whooshed out. He watched her eyes close again, and a smile stretched across her face. He knew she was replaying that night just as he was. Remembering those moments as she dared him to follow her into the ocean while they strolled the empty beach at night.

He'd chased after her, the chill of the water no match for the heat radiating off of him, seeing her skin glisten in the night, illuminated by the moon and starry sky. When he caught up to her, they waded in the ocean, tangled in each other, their feet barely planted on the sandy ocean floor as the waves rocked them. They were waist-deep in the water when he lifted her into his arms and carried her back to shore with every intention of making it back to their hotel room that faced the ocean. But the lust that ignited between the two of them said otherwise.

"How long ago was that?" he asked.

"Almost three months ago."

He swallowed, feeling emotion bloom in his chest.

"Are you feeling better now that we left the house? You seem to be worse when you're there."

She nodded. "I don't know why. That morning I went for a run, I had been feeling terrible. It was supposed to just be a walk. I thought the fresh air would help. But I felt so good once I got outside that I decided to just do an easy jog. The moment I stepped back inside, I felt awful again. Now, every time I'm back there, I feel that way. Luke?"

"Yes?"

"I feel like whatever is there wants to harm me because of the baby."

The statement froze his breath.

"It doesn't make sense otherwise. Nothing happened until I started having pregnancy symptoms. And the day I took the test was the same night I saw the man in my hallway. Now that I think of it, it started before I even suspected I was pregnant. Like someone was always watching me, but I didn't understand what it was. And it escalated."

"You aren't setting one foot in that house again." The protectiveness in him came through. It took hold, anchoring itself to the two things that meant the most to him in the world. "I don't care about your lease. I don't care what Theo's grandmother wants. I'll talk to him if I have to. That thing has followed you and attacked you three times."

"Twice."

"No. Today, you were on the verge of passing out. The energy in the room changed right before you said you needed to leave. That was no coincidence. It was gearing up to attack again, and I'm not taking any chances. So, you're not going back there. Ever. You can call me out on my alpha ego all you want, but I'm telling you, for your and the baby's safety, you can't go back there. I'm sorry I took you there today."

Luke ran his hands up and down her body as she straddled him and felt a twinge of excitement when he watched a shiver pass through her. She could never hide her reactions from him, and he fucking loved that. "After seeing the test last night, I wanted to talk to you this morning, but... We had other needs to tend to."

She gasped, squeezing his hips with her legs.

"Are you sure you're feeling better?"

"Yes. As soon as we got into the car, the ringing in my ears and pressure in my head stopped."

"If you start feeling off, tell me the moment it happens. I'm not taking any chances with you. Tell me right away."

"I will."

Luke fought the pulsing in his pants. The weight of Tessa on top of him stirred his need for her. He'd take her right there on the beach, in the sand. It would be a beautiful contrast of sensation, making love under the sun's warm glow with the chill in the air surrounding them.

Making love. Yeah, he wasn't afraid to admit anymore that's what he wanted. But he'd wait. Wait for her to get used to the idea that he was now committed to a real relationship. No more rendezvous meetings and one-night visits. When the mystery of the haunting was solved, he wasn't letting her go. He was opening himself to a world he'd promised he'd never set foot in. It was scary as hell, but it was what he wanted. And with Tessa, he knew it was worth it.

Fifteen

"So you were the one to finally break Luke."

Tessa stared, stunned at Emily's comment. Her sister's best friend had always been like a sister to her too. She knew Emily like a book, but she had no way of seeing this conversation coming.

Luke didn't want her alone, even at his house. He was at the abandoned hospital with the team, meeting with the current owners, setting up a time to investigate the location, and trying to get more information on the building's history. It had been three days since the last incident at her house when they'd met with Theo and his grandmother and almost a week since the haunting began, and aside from the usual wave of morning sickness accompanied by constant exhaustion, she was feeling better. Still, Luke insisted she spend the day with Emily in her home office.

Liam had remodeled the downstairs area of the home he inherited from his landlord a couple years prior. The lower level was split into two sections. Liam's open space and meeting area were at the front of the Victorian home. Beyond that, through the small kitchenette, he'd built out a cozy office space for Emily, with its own separate entrance from the outside hallway. It was convenient since Emily assisted the team on occasion with local investigations.

"Don't do it."

Tessa blinked away her thoughts. "Do what?"

Emily walked across the room carrying two mugs of tea. She set one of them on the table in front of Tessa.

"Try to deny what I've seen unfolding right in front of me. I saw you two at my wedding." Emily wiggled her eyebrows as she spoke. "You can hide that shit from your sister, but not from me."

"Lexi knows about Luke and me. I think she's a bit shocked by it, but she's happy."

"I can't believe you two kept it a secret from her for so long."

Tessa giggled. "Honestly, I can't believe it either." She took a sip of the tea. "And apparently, it wasn't really a secret. Lexi knew the whole time and didn't say anything. I just didn't want her worrying, and I wasn't sure what was going to happen between Luke and me. If things didn't work out, I didn't want there to be any weird feelings or awkwardness between anybody. So, I figured it was better to keep it a secret from everyone."

"I get it." Emily sipped from her mug. "Tell me, have you spoken to your mom?"

Tessa had always confided in Emily on the issues with her mother. Though Lexi was her sister, she didn't like adding to the anxiety that Lexi already carried regarding their mother. She had her own issues with the woman, but Tessa had different struggles, many of which Lexi was unaware of. Emily was the only one familiar with how their mom had spiraled downhill since Lexi's move to the Bay Area and what it was like for Tessa living near her during her last few months in Seattle. Emily always offered her support and lent an ear when needed.

"She sent me a message the other day."

Tessa looked at Emily in surprise. Even considering her mother's past behavior, that was a bold and surprising move for Cindy Brown. "What about?"

"Don't worry." Emily patted her hand. "I know how she is. She's fishing for information. I said as far as I knew, you were doing very well, and she should be proud of what you've accomplished in the time that you have."

Tessa scoffed. "The ability to feel delighted for another human being is well outside of the scope of her character. I talked to her a couple of months ago, and she made it very clear that she was still disappointed in me for leaving her. I told her it was time for me to find my own way in the world."

"And that set her off, I'm sure."

Tessa nodded.

"She's jealous, Tess, of both you and Lexi. She was never able to find her own happiness, so she tried to keep you two down. It was her way of feeling superior."

"I know."

"You haven't told Lexi about that last conversation?"

She shook her head. "No reason to. It's always the same conversation. I was hoping that once I moved here, it wouldn't hurt as bad, but it still stings. A lot."

Emily reached out again and took Tessa's hand. "I want you to know that you are always welcome here, and I'm always here for you."

"I know, Em. Thank you." Tessa leaned over and threw her arms around Emily.

They hugged for a moment, then Emily pulled back. She rested her face on her knuckles, her elbow on the table, and her warm brown eyes looking right through to Tessa's soul. A flash of excitement shot across her face before she asked, "Now, another important question."

"Okay?"

"When's the baby due?"

Tessa coughed in surprise. Heat shot to her face. Her heart pounded. "What?"

"Just a feeling I have. You're glowing. And judging from the hue on your face, I'm guessing I'm not wrong."

Tessa stared at her friend in disbelief. She always knew Emily was intuitive, but damn! "I..." She struggled to find words. "You're right."

Emily put her hands to her face and stifled a squeal. Her friend's excitement brought out a deep laugh from Tessa. "When I was in the ER, I was worried because I'd run so hard that day."

"Oh, you're used to running and conditioned for it. I'm sure it's okay," Emily assured her.

"That's what the ER doctor said. But they did an ultrasound anyway and told me I was about twelve weeks. Most likely, I'm due in mid-July, but I have to go for my first appointment to get an official due date. I need to find a doctor. I had planned on doing that today, but Luke insisted I come spend the day with you so I'm not alone. But now that you know, it won't be a big deal if I make a phone call. Em, I'm so scared."

"Why?"

"How am I going to be a mom? I don't know what a mom is supposed to do. I don't have any memories of my mother being motherly."

"I had those same fears. Still have them from time to time. I never had a mother figure, either. You had Lex to look after you." Emily had been abandoned as an infant and grew up in foster care. If anyone understood where Tessa was coming from, it would be Emily. "But, I think we're all born with instinct. It just depends on the person and whether they're willing to listen to their inner voice or not. I have an amazing husband and extended family now. And you have an amazing man and friends who love you both. Look, Liam's mom and dad practically unofficially adopted Luke years ago. Both Trey and Luke are like sons to them. Wait until they find out. The amount of love and support you're going to receive will be wonderful. You'll see."

"Thanks," Tessa sighed.

"Does Luke know?"

"Yes. I told him. Or, actually, he found out without me by accident." Tessa filled Emily in on how Luke found the test in her room and suspected it when she was in the ER.

"Wow. He's okay?"

"Yeah. I was terrified of telling him. I almost died when he said he knew."

"I bet. And Lexi?"

Tessa felt her own eyes go wide as she shook her head. "God, no. Not yet. I'm still letting the fact that I'm officially dating Luke sink in for her. I don't even want to think about what she'll do when she finds out."

"Well…" Emily drew out. "Maybe, it will help if I tell her that I'm pregnant first."

Twice in a span of ten minutes, Tessa felt her heart launch into light speed. "Oh. My. God." Tears ran down her face. "Really?"

"Really," Emily whispered. Liam and I want to keep it a secret for a bit longer, though. You know, that whole twelve weeks mark? I'm just a little behind you. I'm due toward the end of July too. We'll be pregnant together!" Emily choked out with tears in her eyes.

"Oh, Lexi is going to be an aunt twice in the same month. She's going to be so happy."

"She's going to be ecstatic for you and Luke."

"I know she will, but I also know she's going to need some time to absorb it."

"Do you want the number for my doctor? She's great. I think you'll like her."

Tessa accepted. She watched Emily scroll through her phone and write down a name and phone number. She handed it to Tessa. "You're going to be an amazing mom, Tessa. Don't ever forget that you and Luke have a support system. You guys have all of us."

"Will you keep this just between us? Luke and I don't want anyone to know yet."

"Of course, I won't even tell Liam. I'll wait until you two tell him. I think he and Trey should hear it straight from Luke."

Sixteen

It wasn't supposed to end this way. Francis assured herself she had to be dreaming. All of the sorrow and confusion that surrounded her couldn't possibly be real. How could a person subject anyone to the kind of madness she was experiencing?

She was just a young woman, misunderstood, and the people who should have cared about her the most turned their backs on her.

Now, she was a prisoner in the same hospital that had promised to make her better. A once magnificent structure built to house and care for people was now a penitentiary of doom.

No one escaped. No one recovered. No one questioned the diabolical treatment. If they did, their personal hells would become worse and more painful.

That was her mistake. She questioned. No, she didn't stop questioning. He'd warned her to keep quiet—to never ask about the reasoning behind what he did. But she could no longer keep her lips sealed when she found out about the fifth floor. The upper level of the building. The area that was kept secret from everyone below. Only a select few orderlies and nurses had authorization to access that part of the hospital. But Francis' curiosity got the best of her when she heard screaming one night.

Her relationship with the doctor led her to privileges that others didn't have, including her door being unlocked at night and her permission to roam the halls more often than the other patients.

He'd promised to prove she was well. He was going to release her from the hospital one day, he said. He was going to take care of her. He'd even bought her dresses and given her permission to wear them instead of the standard hospital gowns. She didn't know why he'd chosen her, only knew the affection and caring he showed her filled a void of loneliness she'd felt for years.

It was late, far later than she'd ever stayed awake before. The patients in the ward were in their rooms, sleeping soundly after receiving their nightly doses of sedatives. She had begun hiding her pills under her tongue, then stashing them in a cup she kept hidden in a drawer. Her thoughts were clearer when she didn't take her pills, and maybe, if the doctor saw she was more alert, he'd be able to release her sooner.

The screaming on that night sent chills through her. She'd heard shouts and cries before, but nothing like this night.

It was a woman, and agony was all that could be gathered from the horrendous wails that echoed through the night halls.

Francis walked out of her room. There was no nurse in sight. Thinking someone was in need of help, she went to the stairs, where the screams flowed and bounced off of the concrete walls. She climbed the steps. Maybe the orderlies needed assistance. She'd assisted in calming some of the patients before. Since she was also a patient, they tended to trust her more easily and listen to her calming words more readily than the orderlies and nurses.

She passed the fourth level, and the screams still echoed from above. The fifth floor. The doctor had told her never to go there. It was off-limits and dangerous. But what was so secret about the top level? What was causing the terrifying screams coming from there?

Francis took each step with great caution. Both terrified and driven by the now constant screams that she heard. When she reached the top, the air in the empty hallway struck her like a blow.

It was cold, sterile and wrong. There was no nurse's station, only a lonely hallway that led to double doors at the end. She assumed it was a treatment room, as that's where the screams were coming from.

She hurried toward them but didn't go inside. Instead, she peeked in through the glass in the door to glimpse what was happening.

It was a mistake that would cost her. She knew that now. That one decision had thrown her entire life into a whirlwind of a disaster, thrusting her into a reality that was unthinkable.

She sat on the cold, hard floor with her ankles shackled to the radiator. Her fate had been sealed that night she let her curiosity wander too far.

And now, there was no escaping it.

Seventeen

S tucco peeled from the front facade of the building. Luke's emotions burst into a mixture of excitement and a determination to get to the bottom of what was happening to Tessa.

He couldn't help his enthusiasm to investigate a location, especially one as old and packed with history as the old hospital. Having a closer look at the place had him wracking his brain as to what could possibly be lurking within its walls that would also have the ability and need to attach and follow Tessa home.

But also, what was the story with the spirit of the woman who was strong enough to have a conversation with Tessa and insinuate itself into her dreams?

His anxiety grew a little more each day, and now that they saw the place up close and personal, he worried about what the hell he was going to find.

As much as Luke craved answers, if he was being honest with himself, he had to admit he didn't know if he could handle whatever they discovered.

What if he couldn't protect her and the baby? It was one thing guiding others who sought their help and expertise. It was a whole other ball game when you were stuck in the middle of a situation you had no control over. The answers he knew were waiting inside could ease his worry, or they could stir the whirlpool of fear even more. Either way, there was no turning back. If he had it his way, he'd whisk Tessa off to another place, a different city, and start a new life. But he knew that wasn't the answer. It followed her once, and it would certainly do it again. It was a fucked-up predicament that kept his mood on edge.

"We got permission to be here tomorrow night." Trey walked toward him, with Liam following behind. Luke hung back in the parking lot to text Tessa while his friends finished up with the owners of the location. He needed to know she was okay, but also to tell her he'd be late. She agreed not to drive back to his house until later that evening when he was finished with a meeting.

"Tessa okay?" Liam asked.

Luke nodded. Looking up at his friends, he knew they were silently questioning why he'd missed the last few minutes of the meeting after the tour.

Liam's brows knitted. "She's going to be okay. This isn't our first time dealing with a situation like this."

But it was their first time fighting to understand what was after a woman one of them loved who was carrying their baby.

"I know. It's just a lot to handle. Now I know exactly what you two were going through." *More so.* "I didn't know I could feel like this."

"How's that?" Trey asked.

Luke waited a beat. "Knowing that the one you want most desperately in the world is right in front of you, and you don't know how to shut out the noise in the background. That the shit you've been telling yourself for years, that you didn't need it, didn't really want it, didn't deserve it, is all bullshit."

"You deserve it," both Trey and Liam stated together.

Liam put a hand on Luke's shoulder and squeezed. "We're going to figure it all out. You need to keep your head on straight. You know you can't let it affect you. All of the doubt? That's exactly what it wants. You know that. Don't give it any power. Tessa is probably feeling it, too, so you need to make sure she's aware of it. Fight this together. And never forget that we're fighting it right along with you."

He knew his friend was right. One of those demons was still alive, echoes of his past screaming from the depths of his memories. "I need to go meet someone. Trey?"

"Yeah?"

"Can Lex stay with Tessa again while we're here tomorrow?"

"I'm pretty sure she can."

"If not, Emily will stay with her," Liam assured him. "You gonna go see—"

"Yeah," Luke said, cutting his friend off. "I need to do it. I'll keep my cool, I promise."

"You call us if things get heated," Trey scolded.

As much as he wanted to, he couldn't fight all of Tessa's demons at the moment. Whatever went unseen and haunted her, he needed his team by his side. That fight would begin soon. But there was one demon he could face alone and put an end to the torment he'd been burying down deep for years. It was time the links on that chain were destroyed.

"I will. I have to do this. And it has to be now."

A recent rain had moistened the ground. Dust that would usually be kicked up by moving tires remained on the unpaved road.

At night there wasn't shit to look at. The valley lacked streetlights, and unless you were from the area or had updated GPS with you, you wouldn't know that the single dirt road that led to the middle of nowhere across the bay existed. During the day, the drive was nice. One would even say peaceful, depending on who you asked.

As he climbed the hill, cows were visible in the distance, grazing on the lush hillside that was now green from the winter rains. He pulled up to a house that was the definition of a shit hole.

House was a generous word, actually. The state of it now being a broken-down shack that should be condemned, was much more fitting.

He took note of a second car parked in the dirt and pulled up beside it, then turned off his SUV and stepped out. The scent of fresh-cut grass dissipated as the breeze wafted the smell of manure and garbage in his direction. His eyes watered. He dreaded walking inside, knowing what he'd encounter, and practiced breathing through his mouth before he did.

The door squeaked, giving away his presence. A moment later, the floorboards creaked. Someone stumbled out from the bedroom, cursing. Dust cast a haze in the small room as the sun shone through the dingy windows.

"Oh. It's you."

Luke chuckled. It was more an attempt to tamp down the anger already bubbling to the surface. "Good to see you too, Dad." He took a seat in a chair at the small dining table.

A blonde woman strutted out of the bedroom, barely clothed and her makeup smeared. "You didn't say you were expecting company, Billy."

"He ain't staying long. Never does. Ain't that right, boy?"

Luke cocked his head in agreement. He noticed the dilation in her pupils when she came close and leaned in. He wanted to gag with the woman's cleavage in his face. "Too bad. We could have had some fun too. Two Collins' men in the same—"

Billy grabbed her arm—a little too hard for Luke's liking—but he stayed quiet and watched, prepared to step in if his father got too rough. Billy placed money in her hand and shoved her out the door.

Good ol' Bill, still up to his same tactics. The same ones that drove his mother into a pit of despair.

Billy opened the fridge and pulled out two beer bottles. He placed one on the table in front of Luke.

He noticed the evidence of time on his father's face. Too much time for his true age. The lifestyle he'd chosen to live wore him down at a fast pace. His frame was frail now. He was no longer the intimidating, raging beast that Luke remembered when he was a young boy. His father couldn't stand up straight, and his legs were bony. He was wasting away in the hell he'd made for himself, and Luke didn't give two shits.

He'd given him plenty of chances to make things right. Even after his mother's death, Luke told him he didn't blame him, hoping that would make his father see the light and change. It didn't. And now that he was a grown man, he understood the torment his mother went through, and he didn't blame her. Not one bit. But he had lied to his father all those years ago. Luke did blame him.

Luke twisted the top of the beer. It was warm. Billy probably couldn't pay the electric bill. He took a swig anyway, out of politeness.

"What brings you around these parts?" Billy asked and took a seat on the old couch. It was ripped in spots.

"Just wanted to check in on you."

"That's a damn lie."

It was, but he wouldn't admit it out loud. "A son can't come check in on his old man?"

"A son can, but you never do."

Luke nodded in agreement. Who would want to visit this place?

"You still hanging around those friends of yours. Chasin' ghosts?" Billy made a spooky gesture with his hands. "You always had quite the imagination. How's that working out for you?"

"It's going well. Real well, actually." Luke stared him down, wanting Billy to understand that he'd done well and was nothing like what his father swore he'd end up being. "I make a decent living teaching others the ropes. Have a successful podcast."

Billy took a long swig of his beer without any reply.

"I'll be honest with you, Dad. I came here to tell you something."

After another beat of silence, Luke continued. "I met someone, and we're having a baby."

"Passing on the old gene pool." Billy's laugh sent a sick feeling straight to Luke's gut. "See, boy, you've been runnin' your whole life, but what you need to understand is that my blood runs through your veins. You can't change that. You're more like me than you want to admit."

Asshole was talking shit just to get a rise from him, and Luke knew it. He'd heard this speech before. Every time he accomplished anything, Billy's comeback was always meant to punch straight through the gut and knock him down. Too bad for Billy, he knew better now.

"You ever think of Mom?"

"Ah, shit, why you bringing that woman into the conversation. She left us."

"You drove her away!" He couldn't contain the anger in his voice anymore. "I'm not getting into this shit with you again."

"Yeah, you're gonna run again."

Luke stood and faced his father. He felt like a beast had sprung from his body. The small room seemed to shrink with each passing second. He pointed at Billy, who was still seated on the ragged couch. "No. I'm not running. I never ran. I was looking for a way out of this shit hole. And you know what? I'm gonna stay the hell away from you from now on because all you've ever wanted was to bring me down."

Luke seethed inside but forced himself to lower his voice. "I came here to tell you that you're gonna be a granddad." He placed the beer back on the table. "But here's the real kicker. You'll never see me again, and you sure as fuck won't ever see my kid. It's clear all you care about are your one-night stands and your fuckin' beer."

Billy remained silent and took another swig from his bottle. "I've given you chance after chance to come around and see that there's more to life than the hell you've created here." Luke walked to the door. "Now, you'll live the rest of your days knowing that there's family you're missing out on."

Luke put his hand on the doorknob, then turned to stare his father down one last time. "Mom didn't leave us. You drove her to it. And I was too much of a coward to stick around when I saw she needed help. I abandoned her just like you did but under different circumstances. I stayed away too much and ignored the pain. That was selfish of me, and I'm never making that mistake again."

He turned the knob, throwing the door open harder than he needed to. Billy shouted in the background. His frail body made an attempt to intimidate Luke when he finally got to his feet. Cursing him, like he always did.

Luke ignored the man who created him. The person he wished his father would become didn't exist. The demon he'd been running from all those years was nothing more than a coward.

Back in his SUV, Luke turned the key and felt the engine roar to life. As he drove away from the place that had become his living hell growing up, he noticed a lightness settle over him. He always left Billy's fuming and smoldering with anger, like the residue of burning, toxic waste had been smeared all over him.

This time, it felt like a weight had been lifted off of him. The anger he felt inside waned faster.

He'd broken his promise to Tessa about keeping the baby a secret. He'd apologize to her for it, but it didn't matter. Billy was a distant memory. That chapter of his life, the one that kept him at arm's length from the one thing he needed most in the world, was now closed.

A new chapter was beginning, and no one in the living realm or beyond was going to change that.

Eighteen

Tessa drove to Luke's house in the early evening. He'd sent her a text that he was on his way back and would be home soon, so she stopped at the store to pick up some groceries, wanting to make both of them dinner. She wasn't a great cook, but she could manage in the kitchen.

When she'd finished her work for the day and made an appointment with the doctor Emily referred, she surfed the internet for recipes on garlic pasta. She'd found one that made her mouth water. For the first time in weeks, she actually had a craving for food, and she wanted to satisfy it.

The pasta was done, and the chicken cooked. The doorbell had her pause her task of slicing the chicken into strips. Setting the knife down, she wiped her hands on a dish towel and went to the door.

"Who is it?" When no answer came, she raised up on her tiptoes and peeked through the peephole to find the top of a woman's head. Dark brown hair with streaks of gray. Tessa knew that hair. When the woman looked up, Tessa's breath caught. *How did she know where to find me?*

She wrapped her fist against the door. "Open up, Tessa! I know you're in there."

Tessa smoothed her hands over her blouse. Her still flat stomach turned with anxiety. She took a few deep breaths and ran her hands over her head. *It's okay. You know her game. Just don't let anything she says get to you.*

Tessa turned the deadbolt and opened the door a few inches. "Mom?"

"Are you going to let me in?"

Tessa opened the door fully, motioning to Cindy to enter. She did, and in no time, was silently scrutinizing her surroundings. Tessa couldn't imagine what she could possibly find wrong. The house was pristine and a thousand times more comfortable and welcoming than any place Cindy had ever kept while Tessa was growing up.

Her mother turned to face her. "What are you doing here?" The clip in her voice told Tessa this was not going to be a fun visit. And the alcohol drifting off her mother proved Tessa's initial feelings. Cindy's words always held a sharper edge when she was drinking.

"This is a friend's house. Can I ask what *you're* doing here? How did you know to come here looking for me?"

"I went to the address you originally gave me when you arrived here, but you weren't there. I was worried when no one answered the door, so I used my phone to track your location."

Shit! She'd forgotten that Cindy had tricked her into allowing one of those geo-tracking services to monitor her number while she attended college.

"I just worry about you. What if something happens. I just want to always make sure you're safe."

It was a plausible reason for any parent to want to keep track of their child and the only reason Tessa allowed it. But it was clear after her last conversation with Cindy that her wishes for boundaries fell by the waist side. Because for Cindy Brown, boundaries didn't exist. The only thing that mattered was her own needs. And if they weren't met the second she requested them, all hell would break loose.

Tessa made a mental note to change her number soon. "So, you're spying on me?"

"Checking on you. You haven't called or answered my calls in weeks."

"I'm a grown woman, and I told you I've been busy. When you refused to drop the subject, I told you I needed space." Tessa turned to the kitchen. Her mother could follow if she liked, but Tessa was determined to keep complete control. Cindy had a knack for turning a situation around and making herself a victim.

Back at the counter, Tessa resumed cutting the chicken. Once that was done, she placed the pieces into the waiting pan where she'd already prepared a sauce to coat it and the pasta.

She glanced up at her mother. "Had you messaged me ahead of time, I would have made more. But if you insist on staying for dinner, I'm sure I can whip something else up."

"You cook now?" Cindy huffed. "You never cooked for me, even when I was sick and begged for a meal."

"You never cooked for me a day in my life," Tessa muttered under her breath.

"What was that?" Daggers shot out from Cindy's eyes.

"What are you really doing here, Mother? Let's be honest. You aren't here because you were worried about me. You flew down here unannounced, then tracked my phone and showed up here to stand there in judgment for nearly ten minutes now, during which you haven't once asked me if I'm okay or even how my work is going, which proves your story about being concerned is complete crap. So, what's your motive?"

"I have to have a reason to see my own daughter?"

"When it comes to you, yes."

"Fine!" she shouted. Her face turned crimson, eyes lit ablaze, similar to her sister Lexi when she got angry. Except Cindy had not one bit of genuine compassion in her. Lexi's anger always stemmed from pure love.

"I want you to come home."

Tessa straightened and stared her down. *Is she serious?* The idea that her mother would come all the way to San Francisco to demand Tessa move back home was ridiculous. But it was also her mother, and if Tessa had learned anything over the years, it was to never underestimate Cindy Brown.

"I'm sorry you came all the way here to ask that, but it's not going to happen. San Francisco is now my home. I have my work here and good friends here. I'm happy. And I'm not leaving."

"So, you're just going to abandon me? Who are you cooking for anyway?"

"A friend."

"Oh. I see. A man lives here. You came here to shack up with someone. I should have known. You're cooking in his house. Obviously, he isn't here. What kind of arrangement is this? Don't you know that love isn't real?" she scoffed. "You're just like your sister. Thinking you're in love. We aren't lovable, Tessa. It's in our genes. We're destined to not find it."

There it was. Tessa had known it was coming. Cindy was there to start a war. Except Tessa had the upper hand. And she'd win.

Nineteen

Luke walked up the front steps leading to his front door. With his keys in hand, he went to unlock the deadbolt, only there was no resistance when he turned the key. It was already unlocked. He reached and turned the doorknob, pushing the door open. His heart raced when he heard Tessa's raised voice coming from inside. Another woman's words met hers with agitation—one he didn't recognize. It shouted over Tessa. His feet couldn't carry him fast enough.

When he stalked into the brightly lit kitchen, he watched as a woman raised her hand and brought her palm down, hard, on Tessa's beautiful cheek. The sound of skin slapping skin cut through the room like a knife. It happened within a matter of milliseconds, and he had no way of stopping it.

He watched Tessa bring her palm to the side of her face, with shock and pain written on her expression. When she looked up, her eyes locked with his.

He hurried to her, turning his gaze to the other woman, and demanded, "What the hell is going on here?" He took Tessa's hand and guided her to the opposite side of the room.

"So you're the one my daughter is choosing? You over me. Her own mother."

Oh. Mommy Dearest.

He ignored the woman and turned Tessa's back to her mother so she could look at only him. His fingers brushed the redness that had bloomed on her face. As gentle as he was, she still flinched under his touch.

He'd heard bits about her mother, mostly from Trey, who relayed that both Tessa and Lexi had an extremely strained relationship with her. Growing up in an abusive home himself, he knew the hurt Tessa was feeling. But he still couldn't comprehend how anyone could lay a hand on someone so kind and loving. No one had the right to hurt her. No one.

"So, you came here to find yourself a sugar daddy? Someone to take care of you?"

Luke glared at the woman. "Leave. Now." There was no question in his tone. "This is my house. Get out, now."

The woman stood silent, sending him a glare of her own that pissed him off more. Tessa was the spitting image of her, only the woman lacked all kindness. Disgust poured off of her in waves. "You know what? Fine," she said after he returned the stare with even more heat. "Tessa, I gave you everything."

"That's a lie," Tessa countered. "Gram gave me and Lexi everything. All you did was drink and throw guilt at us to get your way. And now, I'm done. I don't want to see you again."

"This is..." The woman waved a hand between him and Tessa, then stopped and looked at Luke in disgust. "He is the worst decision you'll ever make. You think he actually wants you. You think he loves you? No man *wants* a woman hanging around. They just want a roll in the sheets. And that's all you are to him. You'll see. You'll come crying back to me when he—"

"That's enough!" Luke roared when he felt Tessa flinch.

Fuck. No.

He was putting a stop to this shit right now.

Tessa jumped, and he hated himself for scaring her. He stepped in front, shielding her from the vicious looks and any further hate that might spew from her mother's mouth.

"Look, lady. You have no right coming in here and talking to Tessa like that. And you sure as hell have no right laying a hand on her. No one does. Tessa is a grown woman, and she'll make her own decisions. Now, get out of my house." He pointed in the direction of the front door.

"Are you going to let him talk that way to me?"

"Yes," Tessa stated matter-of-factly. She was calm but firm, and he loved her for it. "Don't ever come back here, Cindy. You are not welcome." Tessa's words were flat and decisive.

Before Mommy Dearest could ask another question or make another hateful comment, Luke stalked toward her, keeping plenty of distance but not caring that his size might intimidate her. She didn't argue and turned to walk away.

He followed her down the hallway and to the front door. Holding the door open, he said, "Don't ever come back here again. If you do, I'll have the cops escort you down to city jail and file harassment charges."

He slammed the door in her face just as she opened her mouth to speak and locked it.

Tessa was no longer in the kitchen when he returned. Turning off the oven, he moved the dinner Tessa had cooked to a trivet to cool on the counter.

She'd cooked. His heart melted at the thought, and anger bubbled up again, knowing their evening had been interrupted by a vile, uninvited presence. He put the food in containers and placed it all in the refrigerator. He'd clean up the dishes in the morning.

He went to their bedroom. *Their bedroom.* He loved the sound of it.

On the edge of the bed, Tessa stared out the window. Silent tears poured down her cheeks. He approached and took her hand, pulling her to him. "Come with me."

She followed him to the bathroom, where he closed the door and turned on the water. "I need to shower." He wanted the smell of Billy's house off of him. That day was now a memory that needed to be cleansed away. The only room he had left within him before the night turned into a new day was for Tessa, and he needed to wash the sight of the hurt away. He needed to let her know the only thing that mattered now was the two of them being together.

She looked at him. "Okay."

He pulled his long sleeve t-shirt over his head in one swift motion. "I want you to shower with me." His hands reached out and cupped the back of her head. When he lowered his mouth to hers, she opened for him, and he took her invitation. Gently. Slowly.

His hands undid the buttons of her blouse. He pushed it over her shoulders and let it fall down her arms and off her wrists.

Silky skin met his palms, sending shivers through him as they traveled the length of her back and up to her sides. He cupped her breasts, loving the weight of them.

Tessa undid his jeans and pushed them down his hips. He did the same with her pants.

His dick pulsed with need, but that would have to wait. He was going to tend to her fully before he made love to her.

When all their clothes lay strewn around the tile floor, he pulled the shower curtain back and helped Tessa inside. He followed, pressing her back to the cool tiles. She sighed, and he took advantage by closing his mouth over hers.

She was so fucking sweet. Like rare honey worth its weight in gold. Her scent filled his head, vanilla mixed with something he couldn't put his finger on.

He washed her body, then scrubbed his own. When he felt the last bits of stench from his old home flow down the drain, he pressed himself to her again and kissed her softly.

Luke pulled back and looked down at her. It pained him to see her eyes puffy with tears.

"I'm not looking for you to take care of me, Luke, I swear. I'm independent. I can provide for myself."

"Damn right, you are." His own voice sounded intense under the cascade of water. "And I'm sticking right by you. It's a two-way street, and we're gonna meet each other in the middle.

"She said I was just a fuck for you. She said the women in our family don't find love. We aren't meant to be loved."

Tessa had never opened up to him about her personal life before. That was his fault. He'd set those boundaries in the beginning, and now, he was going to erase them.

He didn't even know her mother's name until that evening. His girl was opening herself to him, and he was going to be there to catch her.

"Everything she said is bullshit. You deserve all of the happiness in the world. And you deserve to be loved."

"She asked me to move back to Seattle."

He stiffened.

"I told her there was no way in hell."

Thank the fucking gods.

"Tess. I never had any intention of falling for you as hard as I have. I saw you that night and—"

"*Shhh.*" She placed a finger to his lips. "I know she was spewing bullshit. We both agreed to the arrangement we had. Don't take what she said and put any blame on yourself."

"You are the most beautiful woman I've ever met, and you're so fucking strong. You're unbreakable. The shit you've gone through. All of the disappointment, abuse, neglect. You could have given in. You could have allowed the situation to cloud your mind and win over what you knew you were capable of accomplishing. But you didn't. You held on to your dreams, your goals stayed in your sight, and you kept moving forward. You deserve respect. You've earned your success and deserve so much more. You deserve to be loved."

He watched her eyes close. The bones of her throat bounced with a swallow. Her lips parted on a deep inhale, revealing the edges of her teeth where he loved to run his tongue when his mouth was sealed to hers. So delicate. She was putty when in his arms, bending to his every desire. It drove him mad, and he couldn't ever get enough of her.

She always demonstrated just how sharp she was. A sea on a calm, clear day, but beyond her horizon, rogue waves waited, ready to release their energy against those who wronged her. Those waves were rushing to the surface now. One already hit. He admired that strength.

With his arms caging her between his heated body and the tiled walls, he shielded her from the pelting water of the shower. The shift in tension was palpable, melting away like ice in a sweltering heat.

"Say it out loud."

"What?" she asked on a whisper of breath.

"Say that you deserve to be loved."

Her eyes fluttered open, locking on him.

She hesitated, so he repeated his plea. "You deserve to be loved. Say it."

In a barely audible whisper, she said the words.

"Louder," he demanded.

"I deserve to be loved."

In a swift move, he bent, taking her lips and devouring every surface when she opened for him. She met him with the same urgency, pressing herself to him while her hands grasped his shoulders. Nails digging into his skin sent sharp tingles down his spine. He deepened the kiss.

Her soft moans vibrated on his lips as he drank in every sound with greed. He already knew the warm, silky interior of her mouth by heart but needed desperately to burn every crevasse and texture, every dip and curve, into his memory again.

Heat surrounded them. The sound of the shower's spray played a melody in harmony with their heavy breaths. Fighting his urge to take them further in that moment, he pulled back.

No more hiding. He'd already started the chain reaction of breaking the links that bound him to his past. With the visit to his father's house, the constraints were slipping away. Now, he needed to confess to her, knowing she'd be the one to help him rid himself of the last rusty pieces of battered metal worn and eroded by the tides of time.

He watched her chest rise and fall. Her eyes remained closed, lips swollen and parted, begging him to continue. He caressed the side of her face and waited for her to look at him. Within a few seconds, her sea-green eyes hit him with storms of passion swirling in them still.

"I saw my dad today." For the first time, he didn't hold his breath while saying the words. They flowed from him effortlessly. "That was the meeting I told you I had to go to. He was drunk, of course. I needed to see him, though. Needed to close that chapter."

"What do you mean?"

The storms in her irises settled into calm seas.

"He's the reason why my mom committed suicide."

"Oh, Luke." She stroked his face. "I didn't know."

"He treated her like garbage. And me. Once I was old enough, I stayed away. Barely ever went home. I even gave my mom the cold shoulder because I couldn't understand how she tolerated him." While Luke stopped to swallow the bile that rose in his throat before continuing, Tessa never took her eyes off his.

"I knew something was wrong. I felt it. I'm the one who found her. She left a note. It was written to me."

"Oh, my God." Tessa wrapped her arms around his waist. She held him tight.

"She said she didn't blame me. She just couldn't live with the way her life was anymore." He let the emotion coat his voice without a care in the world. Tessa deserved all of him. Every single bit. He'd give it to her. "Months after it happened, I told Billy I didn't blame him. Told him we could go on and still be a family, but he didn't want it. He chose his drinking, drugs and women over me. His own son. That's when I left to live with Trey.

"Today, when I went to see him, I told him about the baby. I know we said we wouldn't tell anyone, but I needed him to know that I'm a better man than he is. He accused me of running away when I said he'll never see me again. But that's not true. I'm not running. I'm right here. I'm with the person who I care most about, and I'm not leaving."

Her hands roamed over his chest. "You are not him. You won't end up like him."

"I should have been there for her," he choked out on a sob. He placed his hand over Tessa's that covered the tattooed angel on his chest. "It represents my mom. In memory of her."

She stared at the tattoo before her loving eyes came back to his. He'd never explained its meaning to anyone before. Not even to Liam and Trey, though he was sure they had guessed what it meant to him. She was the only person he'd ever told what the tattoo really meant.

"It's not your fault." Tessa kissed him gently, and her softness instantly eased the sadness coursing through him.

"The moment I saw you, I said to myself, if I ever fall in love, I want it to be her. The one I would fall in love with. Let me love you. Please."

As the water washed over them, Luke felt layers of uncertainty flow down his body, taken away from him and released.

Tessa laced her fingers behind his neck, pulling him to her. Her breath was hot against his face, and she was almost panting. Her chest rose and fell with each intake and exhale.

The movement he made to cup her breasts was a sub-conscious one, done before he knew what was happening. When she threw her head back and leaned into him, he wanted to melt against her. He knew her body well. Knew she was begging him to take what he wanted, what he needed. Her body always responded to him with the slightest touch.

"Only you," she whispered so softly he might not have heard, but her words could never escape his ears.

"You've changed me. I don't know how, but you have. I don't want to ever let you go."

He kissed her neck, nipping the skin with his teeth. A move he knew drove her crazy.

"Then don't." Her words were nectar for his soul. The animal in him, the one that lurked beneath his skin, that liked control, tore at the surface. Tessa's piercing green eyes flickered with flames. They were fiery and full of need, and they drove him mad.

He lifted her wrist over her head and held it there. She brought the other one to join. He loved how she let him have control. He'd give her authority later, but right now, it was his turn, and he was determined to show her just how much she meant to him.

There was no going back for him now. For either of them. From this moment forward, Tessa was his.

Twenty

Her breasts were impossibly tight. With her hands held in place above her head by Luke's grasp, her breasts were rock hard, and if it weren't for the delicious tingling sensation that enveloped them, it would have been uncomfortable. The soreness she'd been feeling in them seemed to dissipate at that moment.

Her stomach swirled with desire. Heat gathered between her legs. A rush of wetness joined it when Luke dipped his head to her nipple. Taking the tight bud in his mouth, he teased her until her legs began to shake.

With his large body caging her against the wall, she felt safe. Even though nothing out of the ordinary happened in his house when it came to the haunting, she'd felt uneasy most of the day, weary when she walked in alone earlier that evening. Now, even despite the run-in with her mother, she was calm. Even when Luke instructed her, he always made her feel that she was still in control.

She whimpered at the loss of his mouth on her. Through heavy lids, she watched him turn off the water and pull a towel from the rack.

After helping her step out, he used brisk motions to wipe away most of the water from their bodies, just like he'd done so many times before. Then, he picked her up, only this time, his hands rested under her bare ass, her legs wrapped around his naked waist. The feel of his length brushing against her as he walked them to the bedroom stirred the anticipation inside of her. She nibbled his ear and flicked her tongue over it. He quickened his pace.

He lay her down on the king-size bed. The dark sheets were cool against her heated skin. Luke didn't waste any time. He was on top of her, kissing his way across her collarbone.

When he kneaded her breasts again, she let out a gasp. He rested his forehead on hers, and his brows pulled together in question.

"They're so sensitive," she quickly explained. His lips pulled into a smile, and his expression lit up with warmth.

"Yeah?" he asked and stoked her nipples gently. "I'll be extra careful."

Tessa nodded.

"I want your hands behind your knees. Hold your legs for me. I need both of my hands for what I'm about to do to you." His tone was deep and filled with lust and sent her anticipation into overdrive.

Tessa felt her face flush.

"You know the rules."

She nodded. There was no domination like what she'd read in books. From their first night together, they fell into a natural rhythm. She submitted, letting him control the pace, and he stopped at the drop of a hat if she said so.

Tessa did as Luke instructed and pulled her knees up. The position multiplied her arousal. He kissed his way down her body, stopping at her lower stomach, where he lingered, nuzzling and breathing deeply. He continued, moving lower, and she realized why he needed both of his hands. He left one palm at her breast, his long arm allowing his fingers to tease the peaks. With his other hand, he dipped into her wetness at the same moment his lips closed over her pulsing clit.

Every inch of her body hummed. It was electrical, fiery, almost too much to bare, as every part of her most sensitive areas were being teased at once.

His hand worked magic between her legs. The orgasm that followed only seconds after he touched her exploded like a dam giving way to the pressure. She cried out. Her hips ground against his hand and head as he continued his ministrations. A second wave of ecstasy followed, and it was then that she released her hands from behind her knees and latched onto his head, her body bucking and shaking from pleasure.

"Do you have any idea what you do to me, darlin'?" Luke was now hovering above her. His impossibly large cock pressed against her entrance. "The sounds you make. The way you move." He pushed inside of her. "Your taste." He lowered his head, and she tasted the essence of herself on his lips. "Your scent."

His rhythm was painfully slow. She needed more. Her heels dug into his back, coaxing him to go deeper, harder. But he resisted.

"I need you now," she begged.

He raised up onto his knees. His hands went behind her hips and lifted her ass to sit on his thighs.

He reached down, placed his thumb in her mouth, and she swirled her tongue around it. When he removed it, his hips thrust at a steady pace. She closed her eyes and arched when the thumb she'd moistened stroked her clit. He moved it in steady circles at first and increased the pressure and pace, pulling a third orgasm from her. She pulsed around his rock-hard cock. When she finally opened her eyes, he was staring at her with a heated flare.

"I'm yours," she told him.

His expression softened.

"All yours. Take what you need." She placed her hands above her head, knowing he loved seeing her on full display to him.

Holding her up to meet his thrusts, his grip on her hips tightened, sending delicious sensations through her. He was now pistoning in and out of her. Her breasts bounced, and she fisted the sheets as another wave of pleasure built inside of her. She teetered on that edge, trying to hold on for as long as she could.

"Come now, Tess. Right now!" he demanded.

Luke planted himself deep inside right as she arched and cried out again. His hot cum emptied into her. With her eyes on him, she watched him shake and his eyes close, his features relaxing with pure bliss. She saw the tension leave him. He looked lighter, even looked like he was glowing. She saw the chains he'd kept bound around himself fall away in a beautiful sight. For the first time, she saw all of him.

He trusted her. He'd let down his guard and shared all of his demons with her. It was time for her to now let go of the demons that plagued her. She'd give herself to him fully because, deep down, she knew she trusted him. Wanted to give her all to him. Wanted to feel the unconditional love she'd been convinced couldn't exist for her. The sight in front of her proved all of those assumptions to be wrong. Only someone who loved another could open themselves up and trust them to hold them together.

Luke stayed there, kept her in that position until his erection softened, and he slipped out of her. "Crawl up to the pillows."

She did and took full delight in the sight of his tight ass when he walked out into the hallway. He returned, still fully naked. His tattoos highlighted the definition of his muscles. His bright eyes took in the sight of her. She'd splayed her body out for him.

"My vixen is asking for trouble."

"Who, me?"

He chuckled, sat on the edge of the bed and wiped between her legs with a washcloth he'd brought back. Warmth radiated through her when his palm rested on her stomach again. She'd never seen his face hold so much emotion before.

"My first appointment is next week," she stated in a soft tone. Her hand went to his.

He looked up at her with pure admiration. "I'm going with you."

She nodded. "I know."

Luke tossed the washcloth to the side and crawled into bed next to her. He pulled the comforter over them.

"Are you cold?"

She snuggled into his side. His hand went around her and rested between her breasts. "No."

"Good. Because the only thing I want touching your body is me." He kissed her shoulder. "Sleep. I'm right here. No one is going to hurt you."

She fell asleep to the sound of his steady breathing. And for the first time in her life, the feeling of unconditional love surrounded her.

Twenty-One

The massive double front doors were a ruse. Outside, stone steps led halfway up a full story. Through the main entrance, another set of stairs ascended to a large foyer where corridors branched off of the rotunda in the center of the building. The real grandeur surrounded the landing of the stairs. Above, a painted glass ceiling framed inside of a dome kept the elements out.

The previous day's distractions prevented Luke from taking in the spectacular sight of the inside. Now, alone and keeping a watch on the monitors, the magnitude of the building struck him. It pulsed with its own heartbeat. As stunning of an architectural feat as it was, it held a mysterious presence that both astonished and weighed down on him, like a breathing organism.

Luke sat at the central command center they'd set up in the rotunda, choosing to use the old receptionist's office—a glass-enclosed chamber with a clear view down the three hallways. With multiple monitors set up in front of him, he had his eyes on Liam and Trey, who had each taken a level alone. Liam, on the second floor, Trey, on the third.

They weren't sure of how active the location would end up being and thought it best for one of them to stay behind and keep an eye on things. Especially after what happened at Tessa's house. If the activity didn't seem to be too dangerous, they would continue with all three of them splitting up and taking a section of the building to investigate.

Luke sat impatiently, wanting to find what had followed Tessa home. He knew the ghost was there. Felt the itch of watchful, icy eyes on him. The same sensation he'd felt in Tessa's dining room that night. It was waiting. And his need for answers grew by the minute.

The hallways were pitch-black, but every now and again, he thought he'd spotted shadows, blacker than black, peeking out from the rooms connected to the halls.

Watching the monitor, he spotted Liam just barely inside the frame. He jumped when his teammate radioed him on the walkie-talkie.

"Want to go down that corridor on the main level? It seems really quiet. Nothing is happening down here. Maybe you'll have better luck."

"Copy that," Luke responded. Then he pressed the walkie's button again. "I keep thinking I'm seeing shadows down that hallway and really want to check it out.

I'll keep you posted on what I find. Trey, how's it going for you?"

"Same down this way. Absolutely nothing. It's eerie but quiet. Be careful."

"Will do. I'll head down the east side of the building and let you know if I get anything."

He clipped his walkie to the waist of his pants, gathered his handheld equipment and placed them in one of the numerous pockets in his cargo pants and tactical vest. With a camera in his hand, he headed down the east wing, the night vision on the viewfinder of his camera as his only guide.

He wasn't afraid of the dark. The darkness always woke a thrill in him, pushing him harder to find what lurked in the blind abyss. With each step, he hoped he got closer to answers.

Tapping into his instincts, Luke headed straight toward a definite pull at the end of the hallway. The closer he got to a set of closed doors, the heavier the air became. He never considered himself as intuitive as Trey, or their psychic friend, Dave, but he did trust his senses to lead him in the direction he needed to go and keep him safe. Something was down there, hiding. And he was going to find it.

He reached for his voice recorder and pressed the button. The lack of light wasn't an issue in using his equipment—he'd memorized each piece meticulously and could work all of it blindfolded.

When the indicator light illuminated, telling him the device was on, he continued, halting at a door with a pane of frosted glass in the top half. Just as he was about to enter, he stopped, turned to his left, and stared at another door identical to the one he stood in front of.

That was it. It reeled him in like a fish on a hook. Three strides to the left, and he turned the knob. He went inside.

A desk was visible through the camera's screen, and he spotted old file cabinets lining the walls.

Smells of damp papers and dust flooded his nose. His eyes burned from the moldy stench. He probably should have brought his mask with him, but his interest was too piqued to go back and grab it.

A sharp pull to one side of the room wouldn't let go of his attention. Taking a few steps in the direction that called to him, he froze at a loud slam that came from the hallway. He jumped, spun around, and hit the cabinets behind him. Searching for his bearings, he righted the camera in his hand, ran toward the door of the room, and checked the area just outside.

"Hello?"

Muffled whispers hit his ears, so faint, they for sure couldn't have been in his own dimension. He couldn't make out what they said. Holding the recorder out in front of him, he asked a series of questions, but no responses imprinted on the device.

From the corner of his eye, Luke thought he spotted movement and turned again, this time keeping the camera pointed straight ahead to capture whatever might materialize. When nothing happened, he resumed his search. Figuring something was trying to get his attention while he was looking for clues in the room, it was best to carry on with what he'd been doing. He was on to something, and he got the sense that someone didn't like it, so he walked back to the cabinet that he'd been standing at when the bang broke his attention.

Reaching out, he pulled a drawer open. It protested with a loud squeak after being closed for so long.

Luke couldn't believe his eyes when he looked into the camera's viewfinder to see files upon files still resting inside. Untouched. Not even locked up, like you'd expect private medical records to be. Instead, they lay in full view to any scrutinizing eyes that happened to come across them.

After all these years, the names of the people who once inhabited the hospital were still there. Their identities etched into the papers that lay strewn in the rotting drawers. But the souls, their spirits? He knew many still roamed these halls. He felt it. Felt the heaviness in the air.

The claustrophobic oppression of invisible bodies crowded around him. He imagined they looked over his shoulder, probably pissed off that he was looking at their records. Then again, maybe they hoped he'd find their identities and help put them to rest, letting them know they were not forgotten inhabitants. They had names. A life. A story.

"These files should have been stored properly," he said aloud to the listening ears he knew were near, even if he couldn't see them.

A beep sounded, causing him to jump again. He pulled the EMF detector from his belt clip. It sounded continuously as he held it out in front of him, lighting up, confirming that something disrupted its electromagnetic field. The place was drafty, but the frigid air that engulfed him as he circled the center of the room couldn't be ignored.

"If anyone is near me, make this device light up again."

He stood still as he gave the instruction. A moment later, the lights lit up, and the beeping echoed again from the equipment. "Thank you. Can you back away so the sound stops?"

Again, whatever was near him, followed his direction. The EMF meter went silent.

He walked back to the open drawers, and following his instinct, he pushed it closed and opened the one below. Something or someone guided him.

Using the EMF device, he moved it around the drawer. It sounded when he moved it to the back. Reaching in with his opposite hand, he closed his grasp around a pile of papers and pulled a stack of files out. He walked to the desk nearby and placed them down. Exchanging the EMF detector for his flashlight, he clicked it on and examined the files.

The files were filled with names, diagnoses, treatment notes and medication lists, along with old photographs of some of the patients. A cool breeze brushed his hand, dragging his attention to a stack he hadn't yet touched. Picking it up, the skin on his arms pebbled. Even with the layers of clothing he wore, they were no match for the electricity and chill in the air.

Laying a single file down on top, Luke opened it. He studied the name, squinting at what he saw, unable to believe what he read. Were doctors admitted to mental hospitals as patients? According to the document he was staring at, they did. But why?

Most of the papers that should have been in the file seemed to be missing. It was much thinner than the others. A single sheet listing Dr. Roy Pennington as a patient. The rest of the page was marked over with black ink.

Luke pulled his phone from his back pocket, turned on the flash, and took a snapshot of the paper. He jumped, a yelp escaping him as the image of a woman stood in his peripheral. As soon as the flash faded, she was gone. He trembled at the fright of the apparition. That's what it was. He was sure of it. Blonde hair, a dress that fell inches below her knees, and eyes full of so much sadness, he felt like he could weep for the woman.

He stood quiet for a few moments while the event sunk in. He'd never witnessed an apparition appear in front of him out of nowhere. He knew the woman meant him no harm, but it was a shock, nonetheless.

Footsteps echoed outside the room. He could tell it was a pair from the rhythmic beat.

"Luke?" a voice asked.

"Yeah. In here."

His friends came running to the door after he answered, his voice guiding them to the room he stood in.

As soon as they walked in, he looked both of them in the eye. "You won't believe what just happened."

"Something exciting?" Liam asked. "Trey heard you yell. When you didn't answer your walkie, we came looking for you. What happened?"

"I took a picture of this page from a file. I felt like I was guided to it. When the flash on my phone went off, I saw a woman standing beside me. It happened so fast."

"You saw her in the flash?" Trey asked.

"Yeah. You know how the flash lasts longer than the shutter when it's dark? I thought I saw her, so I turned my head to be sure, and sure as shit, she was standing there staring right at me." He stepped toward his friends, holding the piece of paper in his hands. "We need to check this out. This is what I was taking a picture of."

The men huddled around, each of them shining their light on the page.

"A doctor admitted as a patient. That's interesting," Trey said.

"I thought the same. The apparition caused the EMF to go crazy. I asked it to make it light up, then back away to make it go off, and it did it on command. Then something told me to check another drawer. When I did, it was like a cold hand guided me to the back of the filing cabinet to a stack where this was laying." He held up the paper. "This means something."

Liam nodded. "Let's get on it first thing in the morning. We've been here all night. I say we pack up soon and pick up here in a few days. Let's hope we can get more information on Dr. Pennington so we can use it when we ask questions again. You alright?" Liam stared him down, concern written all over his face. "You look shaken up."

"Like I've just seen a ghost?"

The group chuckled.

"Yeah. That really caught me off guard, but I'm alright." He ran his hand over the back of his neck. "I think the woman I saw was the same woman Tessa saw in her house and her dream. She fits the description Tess gave me."

Trey said, "Hopefully, the contact Theo gave us can provide some information that will help us."

Luke nodded. The overwhelming itch on his skin told him something big was coming. Bigger than they'd ever dealt with before. "I have a feeling whatever information we find is going to turn this investigation in a whole new direction."

Luke's pulse spiked. Dr. Pennington was behind what had attacked Tessa. He was sure of it.

Before he could say any more, Trey's hand rushed to his back pocket to extract his vibrating phone. They'd all set their phones to do not disturb but had tweaked the settings to allow for only their closest contacts to come through in case of emergencies. Lexi wouldn't be calling unless something was wrong.

Twenty-Two

"I can't believe you cook now."

Tessa stood at the counter while Lexi stirred a pot at the stove. Her sister had never been one to enjoy being in the kitchen, but since she and Trey started running the bed and breakfast down the coast, she'd taken to it with enthusiasm.

"Ella has taught me so much, and she insists on coming by every few days to help," Lexi told her.

Ella was Lexi's assistant manager when she ran the winery before it burned down. Ella and her husband retired soon after and moved down the coast, not too far from Lexi and Trey. "I think she likes to stay busy."

"She's a sweetheart."

"She is," Lexi echoed.

"I tried cooking yesterday. I found a pasta dish that looked good." Tessa set down her water and walked to a chair at the small table in the eating nook.

"How did it turn out?"

"I don't know."

Lexi turned and shot Tessa a curious look.

"Mom showed up."

That stopped Lexi in her tracks. With her head lowered, questions radiated from her sister's piercing blue eyes. Tessa saw the annoyance on her face. "You're kidding?"

Tessa shook her head.

"How the hell did she know you were here?"

"I asked her that same thing. She said she went to my place, and when I wasn't there, she tracked my phone. Remember when she tricked me into letting her add my number to that phone tracking site when I was in school?"

"Oh shit."

"Yeah. I totally forgot about it. Now I need to get a new number because I don't trust her to tell me the truth about which site she used."

Lexi turned back to the pot on the stove, her cheeks pink. She placed her opposite hand on her hip and shook her head. "What did she say?"

Tessa filled Lexi in on the encounter. She paused, bringing her hand to her cheek as she remembered the sting when her mother's hand made contact with her skin. It was a sting of not only hurt but betrayal.

The only good that came out of it was that Tessa finally had validation there could never be any real relationship between them. Her mother didn't know how to love. It was a painful truth Tessa had lived with her whole life. And now, she had to admit it so she could move on.

"Then she slapped me."

It was like slow motion took over. Lexi turned, at a loss for words, as she stood wide-eyed for a beat before rasping, "What?"

"Luke walked in right as it happened."

Lexi's mouth dropped, and a flicker of relief was replaced with curiosity. "What did he do?"

Tessa stood, walked to a cupboard and retrieved two bowls.

"Tess? What did Luke say?"

"He put himself between us, and when I told her I didn't want to see her again, he reiterated that she was never welcome back here. Then he walked her to the door."

Lexi nodded with approval. "How's he holding up?"

Tessa shrugged. "He's being Luke. The tough guy."

Lexi giggled. "Trey's the same way. I always thought that caveman crap was annoying, but on Trey, I don't mind it." In an exaggerated tone, she mocked, "'My woman. Stay away.'"

The women laughed. Lexi spooned a ladle of stew into the bowls. Tessa sliced some bread. After they ate, she fell asleep while watching a chick flick with Lexi. She woke sometime later to find things were different.

She was outside, barefoot. The cold seeped through her bones. The street was deserted, a strange sight for the city, even at the late hour. She walked for a long while. Just ahead, she saw her house but didn't stop. Her feet kept moving past the old Victorian and toward the abandoned hospital that stood a little way down the hill. A woman stood outside one of the windows on the ledge of the building.

Fear wiped the confusion away, and Tessa tried desperately to think clearly. If she turned left, she'd be at her house in minutes. But she didn't want to go home. She wanted to go back to Luke's, where Lexi was. She didn't remember her sister leaving. Didn't understand why she'd left Luke's house herself without putting on shoes or a jacket. Everything seemed wrong. As she thought more about the situation, her anxiety grew.

The woman on the ledge was shouting, but Tessa couldn't make out what she was saying. She moved to walk closer to see if she could help. The woman saw her. Even at a distance, they locked sights on each other, and the faint sounds of the woman's words hit her. "Go back!"

A man leaned out the window. He looked like he was trying to coax the woman back inside. But something was off. Tessa didn't have to be close to him to know that his intentions were not good.

Then, his head turned, and Tessa's lungs stilled.

Pressure yanked her back. Her vision turned fuzzy, and as if waking from a dream, the sounds of the outside world hit her. Loud and jarring.

"Tessa!" a familiar voice yelled, but it was distant.

A caress on her cheek woke her fully from that dream state. With her head in a daze, she tried to understand why she was standing when she'd been dreaming. She looked around, blinking the confusion away.

"Tessa. Look at me." Luke's comforting tone came to her more clearly.

"Luke?"

He bent down, the image of him now in focus. Suddenly feeling unsteady, she grasped his forearms. "What happened?"

"I was hoping you could tell us. Lexi called. Said she stepped out of the room for a minute, and when she came back, you were gone. The front door was open, and she couldn't find you."

Tessa had no recollection of leaving Luke's. She'd fallen asleep and was dreaming. Or so she thought.

"I thought it was all a dream. I—" She blinked and looked at their surroundings, then pointed to the hospital. "There was a woman on the ledge. She was screaming for help."

"We just came from there, darlin'. It was only us three. No one else is there."

"I couldn't say for certain because it was so far away, but I think it was Francis, the woman from my dream. That same man was with her."

"The one who followed you?"

Tessa nodded and realized that Trey and Liam were standing off to the side.

"I don't know what happened. I remember thinking I wanted to wake up, but I couldn't. When I saw the woman, I walked closer to see what was happening. There was no one around to call for help, and the man turned and looked at me from the window. He was leaning out. It looked like he was trying to get her to go back inside. There's something not right about him."

"Okay," Luke stated with a gentle pat on her shoulder. He bent and put one arm around the back of her legs, the other at her back and scooped her up. "You're not wearing shoes." He put her in the passenger seat of the team's work van.

On the short drive back to his house, she asked, "How did you find me?"

"Lexi called Trey in a panic. We hopped in our cars to see if we could find you. Something told me to turn down that street. I never go that way, but I listened to my gut." He took her hand and brought it to his lips. "I saw you walking. You looked like you were in a daze."

Tessa sat silent the rest of the drive. When he parked in the driveway, he answered a text message on his phone. He typed quickly, and when he was done, he turned to her. "Liam and Trey are going to stay at the hospital for a while longer to see if they get anything. They'll pack up the equipment."

She nodded, relieved that she hadn't put a complete end to their night, even if she did interrupt it.

Luke continued. "Liam said his parents are heading out of town in a couple of days. I'm taking you down there tonight. Whatever hold this fucking thing has on you, it knows you're close by. I want to get you as far away from this place as possible."

"What if it follows me again?" she huffed and threw her head back against the seat. "Fuck! I hate this. What did I ever do? All I was doing was living my life, trying to find peace, and then this shit happens." She slapped her hand against her thigh in frustration. Her heavy breathing was the only sound in the truck. She leaned her head back and squeezed her eyes against burning tears.

Luke brushed her face. "I'm going to be with you at all times. Clay and Janet have a really big house. Liam and Trey will come down with Lexi and Emily. We'll all be together. We'll all put our time into figuring this out."

She looked at him, unable to mask her emotions any longer.

"Let me take you away from this place for a while."

She nodded, accepting his invitation.

"I promise you, Tess. We're going to stop him."

Twenty-Three

"You won't believe who lives nearby."

The team, along with Emily and Lexi, had been staying in Carmel since the night Tessa sleepwalked. That's how she preferred to think of it. Luke, however, described it as her being "under the influence" of the spirit. That left a sour taste in her mouth—the thought that anything could control her and put her in danger put her on edge.

Tessa closed her laptop and gave her undivided attention to the group walking into the room. Liam, Emily, Lexi and Trey all rushed in.

Next to her, Luke sat forward. "Who?"

"The contact Theo's grandmother Lettie gave us," Liam answered. "She wants to talk. She says there's a lot we need to know. She also said she's surprised nothing's happened in the house up until now. She wants to meet in person."

"That's good, right?" Tessa turned to Luke. "It sounds like she has a lot to tell us."

He nodded and caressed her knee.

"I made some progress, too," Trey started as he sat on the leather loveseat. "I learned that the hospital was used as a sanitarium only for a short time. That's the time period when things get weird. There's almost no information on the place between the years of 1947 through 1952."

"Why is that?" Lexi asked. "You'd think a hospital would have been overseen by someone official."

Trey turned to her. "The key phrase in this case during those five years is it was a sanitarium. And many, back in the day, were privately funded. They didn't have to answer to anyone. Had it been an asylum, government-run, there would have been more for us to go on. As it wasn't, there was only information that the patients were transferred to other hospitals around California, but no explanation as to why. After that, it was used as a regular hospital for a time. Then as a retirement home until the eighties, when it was shut down due to lack of funding and disrepair."

"And it's just been sitting there ever since?"

Trey nodded, and Liam added, "The current owners are trying to get it designated as a historical sight. It was built in the late 1890s. All the previous owners since then have had bad luck. Every time they would begin a repair, something would happen. The current owners weren't true believers until they bought it and began renovations. It's taken months for them to renovate what areas they managed to so far and complete the indoor pool area. They just finished it a couple weeks ago, but according to them, it was hell getting any construction company to stay and finish the job. Workers kept having strange occurrences happen that scared the hell out of them."

"So it *is* haunted?" Tessa asked.

Lexi acknowledged that with a nod.

"But, what does it want with me? I've never even set foot in there."

Luke turned to her. "Hopefully, that's what we'll find out later today." He looked to his team. "What time do we meet?"

The quaint country home sat just up the road from the ocean. Its pitched roof and inviting porch, along with the eye-catching front garden, calmed Tessa as she walked up the few front steps with Luke and his teammates.

Inside, the home's charm matched its exterior. An old-fashioned wood-burning stove sat on top of a brick floor. Its long, black exhaust tube reached up and disappeared into the ceiling. The bite of the chill outside was extinguished in the room, and the stove radiated its heat throughout the single-story house.

Still, Tessa found her heart beating in her throat as she listened to the woman who Theo's grandmother connected them to. Bonnie sat on one of the two sofas. Luke and Tessa, on the other. Trey and Liam sat in a couple of dinette chairs that Bonnie pulled from the eat-in kitchen. Lexi and Emily had stayed behind to visit with Liam's mother, Janet.

Tessa insisted Lexi not accompany them and was thankful to Emily, who agreed to stay behind as well. She loved her sister but didn't want her stressing herself out with everything going on. Tessa was safe with Luke, and there was nowhere else she'd want to be other than by his side at the moment.

She zoned out as Bonnie described living next door to Theo's grandparents. Her mother, Pearl, had been friends with his grandmother. Tessa brought her attention back to Bonnie when she heard her mention Lettie.

"How is she doing?"

Liam took the lead. "She seems to be doing well. I'll be honest, ma'am, we don't know her very well. She only said you would possibly have some information for us regarding the house they lived in."

"Right. Can I ask what happened that has you all so concerned?"

Luke looked to Trey and Liam, then to Tessa. She opened her mouth to speak but halted.

"Why don't you start by telling Bonnie what happened that night," Luke suggested with a nod.

Tessa's anxiety about telling anyone other than the team heightened. Who on earth would believe her? Then again, they were there for answers, and she was going to help find them, whether people believed her or not.

"I've been living in the house for about a year now. I'm Theo's roommate, Lettie's grandson. Recently, I've been feeling uneasy in the house, like someone is watching me. Even when I'm alone, there's a feeling that I'm not by myself. Last week, I saw a man standing in the upstairs hallway near the attic. He disappeared right in front of me. The next day, I went for a jog. I passed that old, abandoned hospital."

"Yes," Bonnie replied. "I know the one you're talking about."

"I stopped to rest. When I looked up at the building, there was a man staring back at me from one of the windows. It was the same man I saw standing in the hallway at the house." Tessa shivered, remembering the encounter. "I'm sure it was him."

"Go on," Bonnie urged.

"He looked at me. Right at me, and his eyes were so hateful. That's the only way I can describe it. I thought maybe someone was in there since I've seen trucks in and out lately, but as I stared, he disappeared. Just evaporated right in front of me again."

Bonnie stared at Tessa with concern. "Oh, my."

"I ran up the hill to get home. Once inside, I saw another spirit, this time a woman. I followed her into the attic. When I got up there, I saw an old trunk and opened it. That's when I found the picture of a man. The same man I'd seen. The woman in the attic told me she needed help. Later, she came to me in a dream begging me to help her."

"Theo and Lettie sent me a message with the photograph that you found." Bonnie dropped her head. "Mother told me she was afraid someday history would repeat itself, and things would start up again."

"Can you tell us what you mean by that?" Trey asked.

"That home was bought in the mid-1940s by a doctor."

"Roy Pennington?" Luke offered.

"Yes." Her answer held questions as to how Luke knew that information.

"Ma'am, did my friend Liam tell you that we're paranormal investigators?"

Bonnie nodded.

"A few nights ago, we investigated the former hospital building. The current owners are looking for answers as to what's haunting it. They're finding it difficult to complete renovation work because of strange occurrences. While I was in one of the rooms, I came across some old patient files. My equipment started going off like crazy, and I was led to a particular drawer that had a file on Dr. Roy Pennington. Doctors normally aren't listed as being patients in mental hospitals, at least none that we've come across over the years. Is the man in the photo Dr. Pennington?"

"It is." Bonnie's eyes dropped, and sadness took over her features. When she looked up, she began.

"My mother was a nurse at that hospital. She worked there while we kids were in school. She befriended a woman who was also a patient there. Francis Walker."

Tessa held in a gasp and squeezed Luke's hand. Bonnie went on. "Mother called her Franny. She always said that Franny wasn't supposed to be there. That she wasn't sick. But her parents were convinced that she was in need of medical attention because of her moods. Today we would recognize it as depression, but in those days, if a person was off, even just a little bit, they would be put in hospitals. Some, like Franny, were forgotten."

The men nodded, and Bonnie went on. "Dr. Pennington came along after Franny had already been there for quite a few years. He took over as head doctor. He bought the house next door to us. Mother never liked him. She said there was a strangeness about him. I don't remember him, only that I saw him come and go a handful of times while I played out front.

"Anyway, one day, Franny confided in my mother that the doctor had taken a liking to her and promised he'd have her released from the hospital. Mother was concerned, of course. Franny had been put there when she was a young teenager. She had no experience with people telling her lies, let alone men. Mother had heard things about him. She never did tell me what the rumors were that she heard, but I do know that she told Franny to be careful and not to trust anything he said. Franny was not happy about that."

They all listened to Bonnie without interruption. Hearing so much about Francis shook Tessa to the core, filling her with sadness. She moved closer to Luke, soaking in his warmth.

"One day, I remember my mother being so upset. She said Franny had been placed in a ward on the fifth floor reserved for dangerous patients, where my mother was not permitted to go. Mom was assigned to the lower floors and couldn't see Franny anymore."

"Did she say why?" Trey asked.

"I didn't find out until years later. My mother told me she found out that Franny was pregnant."

This time Tessa was unable to hold in her gasp. Luke flinched.

"I take it Pennington was the father," Liam said in disgust.

"That was my mother's conclusion, but she was never able to find out for certain. She also found out that Franny's parents signed papers giving Dr. Pennington custodial rights. Soon after, Mom convinced a fellow nurse to let her upstairs to see Franny. That's when Franny told my mother she was put on that floor because she'd seen something she shouldn't have."

"What did she see?"

"Franny wouldn't say. Refused to. Said if she told her, Mom might then be in danger. So I can't say what it was. I can tell you my mother was let go a couple of days after that visit. I can also tell you that Franny died in that place."

"How?" Luke asked.

"Officially, she died of drowning. Later, I don't know how, but my mother found out—" Bonnie seemed to struggle to get more words out. After a moment, she said, "Pennington performed a lobotomy on her." Those last words were said with pure disgust.

All three of the men dropped their heads.

"That was a standard practice in those days, wasn't it?" Tessa asked, wincing at the thought of the procedure.

Luke turned to her. "Unfortunately, yes, and it was barbaric. People were turned into a shell of themselves, walking around, emotionless, in some cases, no longer able to communicate."

Tessa felt sick all of a sudden but pushed it out of her mind. "You said Francis was pregnant. What happened to the baby?"

"No one knows," Bonnie replied. "My mother never saw Franny again. About a year later, Pennington was removed as head doctor under strange circumstances, but nothing ever hit the news, so I have no idea what happened there. Some speculated for years that he had been working with the local police chief to cover up a horrible crime."

"Any ideas on what exactly?" Liam asked.

"None. However, not long after that, Pennington himself was committed and then died there. Apparently, the patients didn't take kindly to him. They attacked him in the middle of the night. I heard it was gruesome. I never dove into any information on the whole thing. I didn't want to know."

Trey sat forward and asked the next round of questions. "Lettie said your mother, Pearl, came by just after she and her family moved in, wondering if anything strange had happened to her family in that house."

"Yes. I remember that. After Pennington died, a newly married couple bought the house. They were so nice. Until then, the house had sat unoccupied for some time, so when they moved in, my mother was so happy. She hoped to become friends with the woman. The two of them bonded immediately. Her name was Joyce." Bonnie paused and looked right at Trey. "I think my mother knew what had happened."

"What do you mean?" Trey asked.

"I knew my mother very well. I knew she was hiding information. When Joyce shared with her the strange things happening to her in the house, my mother warned her. She tried to convince Joyce to move, but she wouldn't listen. That was her dream home. She and her husband had put everything they had into it. Even when the attacks became more frequent and dangerous, Joyce refused to leave."

"Attacks?" Tessa whispered.

"Joyce told Mom that something was coming after her. Pushing her, throwing things. Even locking her in a room. My mother was convinced it was Pennington's ghost."

Tessa's head spun. The room had gone from still to a dizzying state in seconds.

"One day, I came home from school, and the police were there. My mother was outside and very upset. Joyce's husband was hysterical. I found out later that evening that Joyce had fallen down the attic stairs. She'd broken her neck and died."

All three men let out a sigh of sorrow. Tessa stared at Bonnie, knowing there was more. The two women looked at each other, the heavy weight of anticipation steadying Tessa's head. She had to know the rest of the story. Something told Tessa that Bonnie could sense her fear that the bomb she was about to drop would shift the entire state of the investigation.

Tessa asked, "Why would Pennington attack her? He never knew her, did he?"

"I personally don't have an answer to that. After it happened, my mother was terrified for anyone who moved into that house. That's why I say I think my mother knew exactly what Franny saw. Whatever is there doesn't go after just anybody. It picks its victims carefully. Ones who, in its eyes, are most vulnerable."

"You're referring to Pennington?" Trey asked.

Bonnie nodded in silence.

Luke scooted forward on the sofa next to Tessa. His jaw was clenched, and a reddish hue blanketed his skin. She knew his intuition was on the same page as hers. And like her, he needed to hear it said out loud. Needed confirmation of the worst of their fears. Without it, they couldn't fully protect themselves.

"Why did your mother think he attacked Joyce? What made her so vulnerable compared to someone like Lettie, who lived there and never had a problem?" Luke asked.

"Oh, my dears," Bonnie said, looking down at her hands in her lap. She shook her head. The few moments of silence in the room were loud with apprehension. When she looked up, her eyes went to Luke, then locked on Tessa.

"Joyce was pregnant."

The sting of Bonnie's words was like ice water being poured on Tessa. It stole her breath and froze both time and her in place. Bonnie's sentence hung in the air with a haunting charge that electrified the room, shooting a pulse of energy that shocked Tessa to the depths of horror.

Twenty-Four

Nothing could have prepared Luke for the bomb that Bonnie dropped a few hours ago. On the way back to Carmel, emotion sat heavy in his chest. His lungs ached, like when you free dive and your body is telling you to turn back for the surface. But he couldn't. The answers were now within reach—he just needed to navigate the cold, dark waters a little more before he'd be able to turn back and confront Pennington with the information he held.

He was in Liam's father's study with Trey and Liam. The women needed some time to bond, so Tessa had gone into town with Emily and Lexi, both of whom were heading back to their own homes later that day.

Luke was nose deep in his laptop when the muffled voices of his two friends broke through the haze of anger and anxiety.

"Talk to us, Luke." Trey stared him down. Luke knew this conversation was coming. It was inevitable. With an exhale, he looked up. Silent but giving his friends his attention.

"Is there something we need to know?" Liam asked. "You looked like a war had erupted right when Bonnie told us about Joyce, and Tessa turned paler than white paint."

"You haven't said much lately, either," Trey added. "It's not like you to be this quiet."

Luke leaned back in the computer chair. It squeaked under his size. He pressed the heels of his palms to his eyes. Emotion stirred in them. It was all becoming too much. The news about the baby, the talk with his father. And now, the knowledge that both Tessa and their baby's lives were in danger because some fucked up ghost was an evil son of a bitch in life had a vendetta against pregnant women in death.

"It's always the assholes who stick around. Never the nice ones."

"That's not true," Liam countered. "The nice ones do hang around. They just don't cause a shit show."

Luke leaned forward and focused on the intricate patterns on the area rug that covered the dark wood floors of the room. Elbows on his knees, he laced his fingers together, pressing his thumbs to one another. "I came across some fucked up shit a little while ago. Pennington was a sick bastard."

"I think we found the same info." Liam asked, "Regarding his removal as head doctor at the hospital?"

Luke nodded. "He was impregnating his patients and selling the babies," he seethed.

"What the fuck?" a fourth voice exclaimed, interrupting their conversation.

All three of them looked up to find Liam's father, Clay, standing off to the side in the doorway. "Tell me I didn't just hear what I thought I did."

"You heard correct, Dad," Liam answered. "This so-called doctor was as sick as they come, and he was in real good with the local police department at the time. An anonymous interview revealed that the police chief knew of Pennington's crimes but kept them under wraps because Pennington was paying him to keep his mouth shut."

Clay came the rest of the way into the room and sat in the dark brown leather armchair. "Luke, is this the Pennington you think is tormenting Tessa?"

Luke nodded, still holding onto the secret he knew couldn't remain a secret anymore. The only way he could fully protect the two things he cared for most deeply in the world was by telling the three men in the room, who he trusted the most, what was truly at stake.

Liam sat forward in his seat with his hand on his knees. "Okay. Let's sort this out. We have a doctor who took over a hospital in the late 1940s. He was highly sought after because of claims that he was able to cure the mentally ill." Liam ticked off each point on a finger as he spoke. "Sometime in 1950, he was investigated due to claims that he was using lobotomies unethically, but the investigation dropped off the radar. Now we know that allegedly he got Francis Walker, a patient at the hospital while he was head doctor, pregnant. She saw something, and it was enough for her to tell a nurse, Pearl, who was also a friend, that she'd seen something terrible but wouldn't tell her exactly what it was.

Soon after, she was moved to another ward where she couldn't have visitors, and according to Bonnie, Pearl snuck in and was able to confirm Francis was pregnant, but no one knows what happened to the baby. She died not long after she would have given birth."

"My God," Clay stated in disgust. He ran his hand over his face, then broke the brief silence in the room. "Say these aren't rumors, and it all happened. Why the hell did no one ever come forward. All the people who worked there never said a damn thing?"

"It wouldn't be the first time we've learned of atrocities taking place in hospitals," Liam answered. "In those days, it was unheard of for anyone to speak out. We see it all the time. We'll interview people who worked in hospitals we're getting ready to investigate, and they'll all admit that malpractice and neglect of patients happened. Whistleblowing is still relatively new in our society."

"However, in 1952, Pennington was terminated," Trey added, "and his medical license was revoked." Trey scooted forward in his chair with a stack of printed papers in his hand. "According to this account, Pennington had gone on a rampage at the police department. He was irate and threatened the police, who took him into custody. The only news story I could find was this one."

Trey shuffled through the papers and handed one to Luke. "While in custody, Pennington showed signs of mental illness. He never served any time. Instead, a doctor diagnosed him to be mentally unstable, and he was admitted to the same hospital he was once in charge of."

"I bet that didn't go over too well," Clay huffed.

"Sure didn't," Liam agreed. "The only official document we could find was that Pennington was murdered while a patient, and it was the other patients who attacked him. He was beaten to death."

"My God," Clay said with a shake of his head.

Trey continued. "I was able to corroborate Bonnie's piece of information. Our contact in the records office emailed me. He found a deed on the house linking Pennington. So he did own the place. I also found that they shut the hospital down as a dedicated mental hospital after Pennington's murder. The patients were taken to other hospitals throughout California."

Luke cursed under his breath, and Trey added, "About a year later, a reporter for the local newspaper came forward but insisted on staying anonymous and not saying how they'd gained information. The reporter's article stated there was a cover-up. That Pennington was impregnating the female patients, and the entire top floor of the hospital was where he kept them. He delivered the babies himself and sold them on the black market. Apparently, the funding for the hospital was declining, and he needed the money to keep it open."

Luke kept his head down during the entire conversation, his stomach turning like angry waves on a stormy sea.

"The reporter said they even had evidence that the police chief was in on it, and the two of them were splitting the money, so that's why Pennington was never charged with anything. He even stated it was the police chief who requested Pennington be evaluated by a doctor, who was a friend of Pennington's and also worked at the hospital."

"What a pile of shit," Clay said. "You boys uncovered all this just this afternoon?"

Liam nodded. "After our meeting with Bonnie, we took our research in a different direction, looking for stories and rumors instead of facts."

"So this is all hearsay?"

"For the most part. Although it's the only information we have to go on. Prior to today, we had next to nothing."

Clay asked, "Why was Tessa attacked out of the blue, though? She's been in that house for a while."

"That's a question we were trying to get to the bottom of before you came home," Liam told his father.

Luke felt the burning stares on him. When he didn't answer, Trey continued and filled Clay in on how the attacks began in the house.

"So that was Pennington's residence while he worked at the hospital." Clay rubbed a hand over his chin. "Trey, you said Tessa stated she'd been feeling like she was being watched prior to that evening she saw Pennington in her hallway. So, something was already in play. It just all came to a head that day."

Clay paused, and Luke heard him stand and walk across the study. He glanced up briefly and watched Trey stand too. Clay took Trey's place and moved the chair nearer to Luke. In a hushed tone, the one Clay Wesley was so famous for, he asked, "Luke. There's more, isn't there?"

"So much more," he admitted.

"You know we've all got your back, brother," Trey stated.

Luke knew it. His friends had never let him down. But saying the words out loud somehow made the situation more real. Voicing his theory would bring to light a danger he wasn't sure he was strong enough to face. But he'd have to face it either way.

"What I'm about to tell you guys is strictly between us. No telling your women or anyone. Tessa and I wanted to keep it between us for a bit longer, but this is getting too dangerous. If I'm going to protect her, you guys need to know."

They all looked on. There was no more dragging out the conversation. With a deep breath, he let the words flow from his mouth in a steady stream.

"Tessa and I are having a baby."

A burst of excitement and congratulations erupted from the room. A few loving slaps on his shoulder coaxed him to straighten in his chair. The delight on his friend's faces relaxed him. "Tess really wants this to stay a secret for now. We go for our first appointment next week. She said after we know everything's okay, she'll want to tell everyone."

"It stays between us," Trey agreed. "But I'll be honest, man. If Lexi becomes suspicious, she's gonna go sniffin'."

"You're really afraid of her, aren't you?" Liam quipped.

Trey nodded enthusiastically. "Yes."

The group laughed.

"Besides the haunting, how are you doing, son," Clay asked.

Clay was truly the father Luke never had. The endearing term warmed his chest. It always did. "I was scared to death when I found out." Luke filled them in on how he came to know the information.

"That's why you were acting strange that night."

Luke acknowledged Liam's statement.

"But now...? Shit. I'm excited. I'm also pissed the fuck off that we can't enjoy this time the way we should be able to. I'm a nervous mess and don't want to let her out of my sight."

"Understandable." Clay stood and walked to the bar, where he poured a drink for each of them.

Luke took the glass and a sip of the smooth whiskey. "So now that it's out let's get back to what we do best. Why the fuck is this thing after her?"

"Well, now," Clay began, "I'm no expert in the field, but..."

"Go ahead, Pop," Luke insisted.

"My theory is that people who are terrible in life take that with them into death. So just because this whack-job is dead doesn't mean he's not looking to continue his horrid atrocities in death."

Luke and Clay locked eyes. It was exactly what he'd been thinking but was too fearful to state out loud.

"You might be on to something, Dad." Everyone turned to Liam and listened intently. "Bonnie told us about the couple who moved into the house after Pennington died. She said the wife, Joyce, was pregnant. She said Joyce had visited her mother and told her that strange things had begun happening in the house. She was being physically attacked. Even locked in a room."

"That's exactly what happened to Tessa," Luke reminded everyone. "The bastard pushed her down the stairs, and the day we all met there, she got locked in her bedroom."

"Exactly," Liam confirmed. "The energy had always been there. Joyce was pregnant, so she was naturally a target for this asshole. When Lettie bought the house, she told Bonnie's mom that she wasn't planning on having any more kids, and she never did, so there was no reason for the presence to be active and explains why it wasn't. It stayed dormant all these years. Then Theo rented the room, and Tessa came along. All was quiet for a while. Until…" Liam turned to Luke. "When did Tessa find out she was pregnant?"

"Right before she saw him in the house. Then she saw him again before she took that fall down the attic stairs. Francis!" An epiphany hit Luke. "She knows about the baby somehow! That's why she was there that day. She probably knew Pennington was going to try and hurt Tessa, so she stepped in and saved Tess from falling."

"God damn," Clay shouted.

"I don't think he followed her," Trey interjected. "I think he's always been able to go back and forth. The house is so close to the place where he died. We've seen this before—spirits wandering from one familiar place to another."

"Right," Luke agreed.

"So, he knows when there's a pregnant woman in the house. That's when he shows himself, literally, and tortures them. But why?"

Luke looked at Trey as he spoke. Everything fell into place. Each puzzle piece was now fitting together. It didn't matter that what they had to go on was mostly rumors. It was all they had, and as screwed up as it was, it all made sense.

If it helped to bring out the monster of Pennington, the thing that was keeping the souls at the hospital confined to that place, trapped in an afterlife filled with more torture, so be it. They'd use whatever was necessary to draw the lost souls away from him and set them free. Set Tessa free.

Luke brought his hand to his chin. He rubbed the stubble. "The woman who's been visiting Tessa in her dreams is Francis Walker. A woman strong enough to fight the evil bastard in death. She needs our help as much as Tessa does."

Trey, Liam and Clay nodded.

Luke stood and paced the floor. "She's been trying to communicate what happened there. She's probably connecting to Tess because of the baby. At first, I thought it was Francis who had taken over Tess and had her in a trance the other night because Tess said the two of them locked eyes. But it wasn't. It was Pennington. He was bringing her to the place where he'd done all of his evil deeds. He stayed quiet during our investigation of the hospital because he was out looking for Tess. He probably has control of all the other spirits. Tessa said there were dozens of people in her dream, all trapped. Francis was the one who led me to the file that had his name on it before it everything went quiet. She's the one I saw in the flash on my phone camera. She's guiding us."

"Sounds like you boys need to talk to Francis." Clay sat back and took a long swig of his whiskey.

"How do we do that?" Trey asked.

Luke looked up. For the first time in days, the excitement of paranormal investigating took hold. His heart raced, and his mind spun with information from past investigations and everything they'd learned over the years. "Liam, we need Dave."

"I'll call him. What are your thoughts?"

With a smirk he couldn't help concealing if he tried, the plan played out in Luke's mind like a movie. It would work. It had to work. Pennington was devious, but they had years of experience investigating the worst of humankind who haunted the living. They had the knowledge and the expertise to carry out experiments.

"We're gonna use his own crime against him. Give him a taste of his own medicine. Let's create a trap and hold the son of a bitch hostage."

Twenty-Five

Crashing waves echoed and carried in on the breeze that entered the room through the open sliding door. Luke always chose that room when visiting Liam's parents. Though all of the bedrooms opened to a wrap-around porch, it was the only one with unobstructed views of the ocean.

The salty air was refreshing, and for the first time in days, Luke felt lighter. The threat wasn't gone, but the plan had already been set in motion. Dave would meet them for their next investigation, and with his assistance, they'd hopefully be able to help the lost souls at the hospital cross over and send Pennington to hell.

Liam's parents had left that afternoon for vacation. Trey and Lexi left for home, and Emily and Liam returned to San Francisco.

Clay and Janet gave Luke and Tessa permission to stay at their house until they felt it was safe to return to Luke's place, so they now had the house to themselves, and Luke finally felt like he could breathe and think.

Tessa stood off to the side, her cheeks rosy from their conversation. She wore a fluffy robe that stopped just below her knees. Her petite feet were bare, toes painted in the perfect shade of red that hinted at black.

A stirring burst to life when Luke's eyes rested on the high arches of her feet. He loved placing kisses there, then working his way to her calves and her inner thighs, always keeping her guessing where he'd place his lips next.

Tessa huffed out a breath. "I'm going to be there, damn it. That fucker doesn't get to have any control over me." Her words sliced like shards of glass, and fuck how he loved her edges—smooth at first glance, but when tilted, throwing her off her axis, he saw all of her sharp angles.

He'd expected her to fight back when he stated she wouldn't be present at the investigation. Still, there was no way in hell he'd allow her to be anywhere near that place.

Despite her stubbornness, his dick always twitched at the sight of her. Somehow her heated response had him craving her. He remained relaxed. Normally he'd find himself agitated being in a conflict. He worried she wasn't going to back down.

Deep down, he also knew that victims of hauntings needed to take charge. They needed to set their own boundaries and make it clear themselves that the entities had no more control over them.

He also knew her presence was needed to draw Pennington out. It was a realization that gutted him. Her request was valid but pulled at his emotions. It wasn't just Tessa's life at stake. It was also their child's.

"Come here." Luke held out his hand. He hadn't even gotten as far as telling her the full plan before she insisted she be there.

The room was more than comfortable. A large, four-poster bed dominated the space. Curtains billowed in the breeze off the ocean, their light fabric moving effortlessly. The evening light was a fiery glow of orange. A cloudless sky, and sunset kissing the horizon, made a picturesque backdrop.

Tessa walked to him. He guided her to stand in front of the large window, folded her in his arms, and they stared out onto the ocean. "You know water is one of the most powerful forces on earth? It gives us life, generates oxygen, regulates the climate. At first glance, out there..." He lifted his arm and pointed toward the sea. "With the sound and the breeze, one might think the water is harmless, but the slightest thing can set it off. A storm. An earthquake..."

"Luke?" Tessa turned and faced him.

"It can destroy, but it can also be used to navigate, and it can be manipulated, used to our benefit. If you know what you're doing."

Her stare held so many questions. Worry and fear—everything swam in her deep emerald eyes. Luke lowered his voice, not wanting his words to even be carried on the wind that blew through the room.

With the full explanation of his plan, she stepped to the bed. After sitting on the lofty mattress, she stared out the window. "This has never been tried before. Has it?"

"That's the beauty of this job. We can try anything we think will work, but we're working with forces we don't fully understand. There are no guarantees."

"It's dangerous." She didn't need him to confirm that. Anyone who could follow along would know.

"There's an old pool on the ground floor. It was added in the sixties and used when the place was a retirement home. The current owners have already restored and filled it. They wanted it completed first so they could use the area for functions and start bringing in revenue. It's all ready to go."

"You really think it will work?"

"I'm confident we'll at least be able to make contact. Maybe even free the people you've seen in your dream, the patients held captive. And Francis. If we can do that, he won't have power over anyone. There won't be any reason for him to be there. I think one of the reasons he's hung around is to try and hide what he did. But we found it. Now he's powerless. Dave can help remove him from this plane of existence."

"I have to do this," she told him. "I know you don't want me to, but I have to."

"I know you do, and as much as I hate the idea, you're right. You have to show him he's lost. Still, as soon as we have him, you leave the building, and if anything happens before that moment, we pull the plug and try something else."

"Okay. I'm ready to be done with all of this shit."

Luke stepped closer to her, took her hand and pulled her into a standing position. Worry was still evident in her expression. "So what's got you concerned right this moment?"

"I'm still scared he'll find me here and do what he did before, put me in danger again. Since everyone left, I've been more uneasy."

Luke hummed. With one hand, he pulled the tie that held her robe closed. It opened, but he left it in place on her shoulders, only revealing a hint of her nakedness. Then, bringing the end of the belt up, he said with a smirk, "I could tie you to the bed. Make sure you don't go anywhere."

She laughed. It was a sound of pure delight that shot straight to his groin. "You would do something like that."

"I would. And you'd thoroughly enjoy it."

He bent to take her lips. Slow and steady, he dragged out the move and observed her eyes on him the entire time. Heated passion swirled around them. The coolness of the evening was no longer palpable. He didn't feel an ounce of shame for the desire driven by pure greedy need within him.

Her breaths became shallow pants, and when she snaked her fingers through his hair, his spine tingled.

He pressed his cheek to hers. "I've got you. Trust me. I'm going to put a stop to this."

"I know. I do trust you." Her answer was a whisper.

When he slid her robe from her shoulders, she stopped him. "We can't. Not here at Liam's parents' place."

"You don't need to worry. Those two love birds are as unconventional as it gets. I'll let Emily or Liam fill you in, but Clay and Janet literally got married the minute they met."

"Really?"

"Yeah. We'll wash the sheets before we leave."

She gasped when his fingers caressed her nipple. Then he cupped her breast. When her head fell back, her sweet scent hit him. It was fresh, unlike anything he'd ever smelled before, but if the ocean air were sweet and carried flower petals on its wind, that's what she smelled like.

Her skin pebbled when he stroked her silky flesh, and when her hand dipped under his shirt and touched his bare skin, his cock grew harder, painfully pressing against his jeans. He assisted her and pulled his shirt over his head in a swift motion. Her hands fumbled with his button and zipper. Her need was just as intense as his, and knowing it brought out the animal in him.

In the warm glow of the setting sun, her eyes turned a shade he'd never seen before. Gold streaks burst within them, and the glassiness that came over them revealed his reflection.

When she spoke, her voice was pure seduction. "I want you, now."

He loved hearing her say what she wanted. What she needed. "Turn around."

His requests were never demanding. Over time, they'd learned each other's rhythms. His directions and her eagerness to comply transformed into a beautiful dance. One that only two lovers so passionately connected could perform.

With her back to him, he pulled her against his chest. The touch of their skin ignited a fuse that burst into flames, and there was no putting out the fire. He'd die before he ever attempted to douse the blaze.

Her hand snaked behind her and brushed against the bulge in his jeans. "Is there something you're searching for?" He ended the question with a nip at her ear that earned him a soft moan. His arm inched its way up. Stopping at her nipple again, where he gently pulled and kneaded the protruding bud. He eased her mischievous hand back in front of her, placing it at the apex of her thighs, easing a finger into her soft heat. He moved his opposite arm farther up, placing his index finger at her lips. She opened for him, and he took full advantage by dipping inside. Her tongue swirled, her mouth just as silky as the folds between her legs. He salivated, thinking of everything he intended to do to her that night.

She rocked her hips, arched her back, and pressed her head into his chest. When he removed his finger from her mouth, he went back to her nipple and coated it in the wetness she left behind, tightening the bud more when the cool air hit the moisture.

Between her legs, his thumb stroked her ever-hardening clit. "On the bed, now." He couldn't help the roughness in his tone. His voice strained in his throat, matching the tightness in his pants. Once on the bed, he flipped her over, exposing her to his view. He eased his jeans down and knelt in front of her. She propped herself on her elbows. A glint in her eyes revealed her playful side, and he had every intention of fulfilling whatever fantasy she had brewing.

"I want to watch this time," she told him in a provocative tone.

His lips stretched, and he returned the playful stare, but instead of giving her what she wanted, he used his finger and touched every place between her slick folds, except the spot he knew she craved pressure the most. "Luke."

"What is it, darlin'? You need more?"

She nodded and panted, "Yes."

He used the tip of his tongue to give her the lightest lick. She tried to lift her ass off the bed to gain the friction she desperately craved, but he wasn't ready to give in just yet. His hands put firm pressure on her hips, keeping them in place.

In a playful voice, she said, "Is this the way you treat the one you..." Her voice trailed off. A flush of deep maroon bloomed in her chest and settled in her face.

Her gaze left his, and it killed him. He stood, leaned over her, placed his palm on her cheek, and said, "Make no mistake that what you're thinking is true."

Through thick lashes, her lust-filled eyes landed on him again.

"Let me show you how much. Keep your eyes on me. Don't close them."

They both resumed their previous positions, only this time, he inched two fingers inside of her, curling them, and watched the heated desire return to her expression. With his stare fixed on her, he licked her clit again and closed his lips over the bundle of nerves. She was already on the brink, and it took no more than a few moments before she was grinding against him. Her cries were musical tones of ecstasy. His fingers continued to thrust and ride the waves of her pleasure.

When she pushed his head back, he slowed his movements. He watched her breathing, her breasts rising and falling with her pants. A flush painted her body, and it stirred his urgency.

He lay next to her, and when she shifted, he brought her to him, settling her to straddle his hips. He was impossibly hard. When she closed her small fist around him, he sat halfway up as a groan escaped him. With a chuckle and a strained voice, he said, "Careful, you're gonna make me embarrass myself."

"You gonna lose control on me?" she asked in a devilish way.

He sat all the way up. Her hands ran down his hard frame as they shifted. His legs dangled over the side of the bed. "No. I'm going to lose control *in* you. I want to be buried deep inside of you. So deep that all you feel is me, filling every empty void."

He pushed her hand away, fisted his cock, and silently asked it to settle down. With a hand at her ass, he eased her up and then forward while placing the tip of himself at her center. He rubbed himself in her slick heat. "I want to be inside you for as long as possible, and as much as I love your pretty little hands on me, right now, this is what I want."

She seated herself onto him. They both moaned at the connection. Her tightness strangled him. She moved, rocking her hips back and forth. The motion sent delicious tingles down his back that instantly settled at the base of his spine. He latched onto her breasts, nipping and tugging, moving from one to the other while leaving desperate kisses across her chest.

He sneaked his thumb down. "Come again."

She whimpered. "I can't."

He eased his pressure. "You can." She was already pulsing around him. "I won't last long. Just one more time." He sped up his movements but kept his touch light.

Her legs shook, and when she threw her head back, he latched his mouth onto her neck, giving her a playful bite. That was all it took. He held her close while her body shook.

Before she could come down from the pleasurable high, he stood, lifting her in his arms, keeping their connection. He placed his knee on the bed. Then the other, and lay her beneath him.

The soft mattress under them cradled their bodies as they moved in unison. When he couldn't hold back any longer, he laced his fingers in Tessa's, bringing one of her arms above her head. His other arm snaked under her shoulder, cradled her head, and kissed her deeply.

This time, he didn't hold back. Didn't force himself to draw out the moments. He couldn't if he tried. The softness, the heat, the friction, it was all too much.

Like a tidal wave grows as it races toward the shore, the anticipation built to soaring heights. And with their lips sealed and bodies clinging to one another, he finally let go as the rush of passion crashed over them, again and again, until they both settled into a rhythmic breathing pattern, lulled by the sounds of the ocean outside.

Twenty-Six

Seances were only performed on TV, in dramatic light and with theatrical scripts.

So Tessa thought.

Never in a million years would she have imagined she'd be front and center taking part in one. Now, here she was, sitting at a circular table with Luke at her side, along with Trey, Liam and their psychic medium friend, Dave.

With Theo's and his grandmother's permission, the plan was to connect with Dr. Pennington in what used to be his home. Since Pennington seemed to travel back and forth, the team hoped that by having him travel, he'd be weakened for the second half of the plan at the old hospital.

"All of his memories, his thoughts, they're imprinted in this house." Dave sat in an almost trance-like state. "I'm seeing the attic."

"Is he here?" Luke asked.

Dave shook his head. "It's Francis. Did she spend time here?"

"We don't think so," Liam replied. "She was a patient at the hospital."

"Oh. I see now," Dave said in a whisper. "She's figured out how to follow him when he comes here. But why?"

The candle's flames danced in the still air. A strange chill charged with a current of static moved around the floor by their legs. Tessa pushed back with her feet. All of the small hairs on her body stood on end. The chair screeched on the wood floors, sending more shivers through her.

"This is Francis. She means us no harm."

Luke squeezed Tessa's hand.

Trey had the other in his grasp. "We can't break the circle."

"Francis," Liam called. "We're here to help you. Can we ask you some questions? Can you flicker the candle again? A flicker is for yes. Leave it still for no. Can you make it flicker if you understand?"

The candle's flame immediately danced.

"Good. Thank you. Can you tell us if Dr. Pennington is, in fact, the one wreaking havoc in this house?"

At the flame's answer of yes, Liam continued the questions.

Did you see something you weren't supposed to? Yes.

Was Dr. Pennington hurting the patients? Yes.

Did he hide you in a different ward and hold you captive?

The last question left the flame in a steady glow. "Did she leave?"

"No," Dave replied. "She's shifted her attention. She's showing me a memory."

Her ankles ached from the chains around them. The top floor was cold, dark, and quiet. Too quiet. Every now and then, she'd hear the whimpers of another woman, but nothing compared to the agonizing screams she had heard that night so many months ago.

She'd asked the doctor what had happened to the woman she'd seen in the operating room. That was the night he changed, right before her eyes. The man who once treated her with kindness and care turned into a raging creature she'd never seen before.

"How much did you see?" he demanded. The grip he had on her upper arms was painful. "Why were you up there?"

"I heard screaming. I thought I could help. I've been able to calm patients before," she answered. Somehow, she managed to push herself away and out of his grasp. Rubbing her arms where his fingers dug into her skin, she trembled. "What happened to her? I heard a baby cry."

"What happened to her is none of your business," he seethed.

"What happened to the baby?"

He remained quiet. Only stared at her with a hateful gaze she didn't understand. Hours ago, he was the Pennington she'd grown to love, then within a matter of minutes, he'd snapped, morphing into a different person. "You'll ask no more questions."

"Why?" she countered. "What I saw... What I heard was agony. She looked familiar. I saw her here in the hospital before you arrived. I thought she'd been discharged. Why was she on the fifth floor? How did she become pregnant?"

"I will not be questioned in my hospital."

Francis covered her ears against the boom in his voice. "What I do here is medically related. What people don't understand is it takes money to run a place and develop treatments that work. The group of individuals who own this hospital refuse to send funds sufficient enough to run a place like this and the families... Oh, my dear. The families, like your parents, only see these hospitals as a means to be rid of the ones who embarrass them. Unfit for society, they drop people like you here so they can forget about you."

His words stung. She'd always held on to the hope that her parents would return and take her away. As the years passed, and their visits became less frequent until they were non-existent, she accepted the fact that she may never leave this place. Until Pennington came along and promised her release.

She thought about what he had said so far. Everything she'd seen upstairs had to do with money?

She went numb as he continued. "They leave people like you and never give a thought as to what it takes to run a hospital. Becoming head doctor here was a dream. I'd be able to run tests and develop treatments. I'd go down in history books and change the world. That is until I realized the funding was nowhere near sufficient, so I had to devise a plan."

"A plan," she echoed.

"Yes. If the money wasn't coming in, I'd have to find a way to generate it myself. And, oh, how you and so many of the others were so gullible, believing everything I told you. And all I had to do was give you little glimmers of hope to gain your full trust."

Francis backed away, shaking her head. It couldn't be true. She may have been locked up in that place for years, but she wasn't completely naive. It was all making sense now, and she cursed herself for trusting him.

"You're selling the babies? That's how you're making your money? That's wicked. They're your own children!"

"There are plenty of people who pay good money for things they cannot attain on their own. They never even bat an eye at the offenses they take part in."

The ways of human nature nauseated Francis. She remembered the world being kind, and now, in an instant, everything she knew about the world had become twisted into barbed knots.

She was in a shrinking room, and the ropes were waiting to snag her. Each contorted loop was a pointed blade just waiting to cut its victim. How could things be so gnarled? So hideous and wrong?

"Did you really think I was going to release you, Francis?" Her name on his lips sickened her more. "You were just another way to help me achieve my plan. And if I'm not mistaken..." His eyes followed the length of her torso, landing on her stomach. A shock of realization shot through her. "My plan has worked."

She'd suspected it. The swell of her breasts had become more pronounced in recent weeks. She'd been sick from time to time, but she wasn't certain. She didn't dare ask one of the nurses for advice. She'd almost slipped and confided in Pearl the day before but decided against it for fear Pearl would be angry. That was a mistake. It was Dr. Pennington she needed to fear.

Francis felt dizzy, and the air went thin at the realization that struck her. All of those nights he'd snuck into her room and whispered sweet promises to her were all lies. They were nothing more than his manipulation to take advantage of her so that he could carry out his devious plan.

"You'll be caught. Someone will find out what you're doing."

"No. No, you see, the ones you pay and let in on the prize? They know to keep quiet. It's the only way the money keeps flowing." He reached out, but she flinched under his touch. "My good friend, the police chief, he's living well now. I suppose you're wondering why I'm sharing so much with you. I'm not worried, my dear. You're never getting out of here." He leaned into her ear, his hot breath molten against her skin. "No one is ever going to find out."

She dropped her hands from her stomach and turned to run. He caught her, slamming his fist against the door of his office and covering her mouth with his large palm. Her screams were muffled.

"You'll live out the rest of your days here. On the fifth floor. You'll help me accomplish what I've set out to do, and you'll do it quietly."

A painful sting on the side of her neck had her whimpering into the doctor's hand. Seconds later, her vision went blurry until finally, she was greeted with sleep.

Francis found herself in a small room that felt more like a prison than a hospital. Bars on the windows, a cot with a worn mattress and dingy blankets were all she had for comfort. The chains, just long enough to allow her to use the toilet and sink nearby, added to her despair.

The swell of her belly grew each day. It was a painful reminder of what she knew was to come. He'd take the baby from her, and she'd live the rest of her life a slave to his evilness. No one would ever know what took place behind these walls.

At that moment, she promised herself and her baby that once death took her, she'd find a way to seek revenge.

The doctor could hide his secrets, but secrets never stay buried forever.

Shadows of the past could wreak havoc on a soul. They always found a way back into the light.

Twenty-Seven

T essa listened as Dave described Francis' thoughts and feelings. Tessa's heart broke knowing what had happened to the woman. She'd known what Pennington had done, and now they all knew the stories were true. He really did have help from the city's chief of police.

"Is Francis stuck here?" Tessa asked.

"In this house? No," Dave replied with a shake of his head. "She stays at the hospital. She's telling me she only just learned how to travel back and forth. Pennington knows we are up to something. That's why he isn't here right now. It was the perfect time for her to sneak away." Dave tilted his head. "I think she's still looking after the patients, but she's also been looking for a way to get her story out.

"Pennington was really twisted," Dave went on to explain. "His energy is still present here. You were right.

I can feel that he's able to travel here, but only when there's a reason to. He's strongest at the hospital and keeps a tight hold on the souls trapped there. He was like a Jekyll and Hyde. He hid under his title. Outside of the hospital, his mask was that of a compassionate doctor who convinced everyone he wanted to cure the mentally ill, but behind closed doors, he had a sick obsession. He got a thrill out of the pain he subjected his patients to."

"What about the women he impregnated?" Luke asked. "They were all patients?"

Dave nodded. "He knew he could get away with it. The police chief was just as dark and twisted. They worked together." He paused, and his eyes scanned the room, falling on the area near the fireplace. "I'm picking up on memories he had while he lived here."

Luke turned to Tessa and stated, "Dave is claircognizant. He's able to pick up on information of a person and place."

"They're flooding into my head," Dave continued. "His mother had a child after him. I sense he hated his brother. He felt that the new baby had taken all of the attention away from him. Then she had another and another. Soon, it was as if he never existed. He was sent away."

"Where?" Trey spoke up.

After a moment, Dave stated, "To boarding school. He was forgotten."

"That's where his hatred for pregnant women comes from?" Liam asked with disgust.

Dave nodded. "He wasn't mentally well in life. Things that seem ridiculous to us will drive some people to do despicable things. It consumed him, and that's what drove him to his crimes."

"What about the police chief, Clark?" Trey asked.

"Probably just money-hungry." Dave's eyes scanned the room and landed on the area near the fireplace again. "Francis."

"I've been trying to put a stop to him for years," Francis said as her figure took shape in front of all of them. They all watched amazed as she formed out of thin air. "It was quiet for a long time, but then I felt the change. We all did. I knew he could go back and forth, so I decided to follow him one day, and that's when I met your friend."

"Tessa?" Liam asked.

Francis nodded. "There was nothing I could do once he found out about her. He'd already locked on her. All I could do was try to warn her."

"So, you came to her in the attic and in her dreams," Dave added.

"It was the safest way I could make contact with her. He found me in the attic. I was able to stop her fall then. That's why I moved to your dreams." She looked to Tessa. "He was weaker there and wouldn't be able to follow me as easily."

Dave dropped his head. "Someone else is coming through. She's keeping her distance, but she's showing me so many memories."

"Can you pick them out and focus on one?" Trey asked.

Dave shook his head. "No. She wants me to know everything. She's been trying to get back to him since she died, but he's been so resistant and blind to the truth of what took place. His own circumstances clouded his judgment."

Tessa sat forward. "What do you mean?"

"His stepfather is really the one to blame. He's the one who sent Pennington away to school and kept her away from him all those years." He paused, took a few deep breaths and continued. "It's his mother coming through. I don't even think Pennington was aware of when she died. He didn't find out until years later, and by then, he was grown."

Tessa bent her head. She could understand the pain. Understand the heartache. Still, that couldn't be used as an excuse for the atrocities the man committed.

Luke scoffed with disgust. "The guy had family issues, so he decided to take advantage of female patients and sell his own children in a scheme to generate money?"

Dave nodded. "She's showing me more. His stepfather was violent. Pennington got it in his head at a young age that he needed to prove he was worthy. That's what drove him. He planned to stop at nothing to make sure he was seen as nothing less than a respectable professional. That's why he had the Jekyll and Hide persona. On the outside, he was a perfect model citizen. But inside, he seethed. His rage festered and morphed into a hideous creature. When he died, he was still obsessed with his unfinished work at the hospital. That's why he stayed."

Dave paused, then asked, "It was the patients who murdered him?"

"Yes," Luke answered.

Dave nodded. "At death, he took control again."

"Wait!" Trey interrupted. "That book in the chest in the attic. The one with the dates and numbers. I know what it is. It's a damn ledger!"

When Tessa looked back at the fireplace, Francis had disappeared.

"Fucking hell," Liam cursed.

It was then that everyone sat back, their hands falling away and ending the séance.

"That sick fuck!" Luke seethed. "He was actually keeping a record of the babies he sold."

"We need to use that as a trigger object." Liam stood, and Trey followed. "We'll go grab the chest."

Tessa sat quietly, not able to absorb the conversation Luke was having with Dave. She barely noticed Liam and Trey walk back into the room carrying the chest they retrieved from the attic.

"They sold those babies," Tessa uttered as the words came to her. A faint whisper breathed in her ear. She placed her hand on the spot where the cold but gentle presence remained. Francis. Tessa wasn't frightened in that moment. She knew the story needed to be told. "Francis is here still."

Luke bent low and looked her in the eyes. "What is she saying?"

Tessa nodded. "I have to go to the hospital. I know where it all happened."

"We're all set up," Trey announced. "Let's go."

They headed for the door. Outside, a familiar face greeted them by the gate. The old woman and her dog, who passed by each day, stood waiting.

"Bonnie called me," the woman explained. "She said there have been some strange things going on here, and you all need information on old Dr. Pennington."

The group stood in shock as the woman spoke. Tessa noted the authority in her voice that she'd never picked up on before. "What's your name?"

"Tess, who is this?" Luke asked.

"We talk all the time. She always stops while she's walking Bruno." The dog wagged its tail at the sound of its name.

"My name is Alice. I used to work as a journalist for the local newspaper."

"Wait a minute." Trey took the lead. "Are you the anonymous reporter who ran the story on Pennington in the paper?"

Alice nodded. "That's correct," she said flatly. "Bonnie filled me in on the meeting you had with her. She called, knowing I was acquainted with her mother when she lived next door. Bonnie suspected but never asked her mother outright. I received all of the information from Pearl. After she was fired, she came to me knowing I worked for the paper, but she didn't want her name to be made public. I worked on getting more people who worked at the hospital to come forward, but it was hard. I had a couple of nurses admit they knew Pennington was committing crimes."

"Did you ever hear anything about him selling infants on the black market?" Luke asked.

Alice sighed. "Yes. I was able to track down sources who confirmed that those rumors were true. But in those days, being a woman, I didn't have my boss's permission to pursue the story. He forbade me from chasing any more leads. I was almost fired for running the anonymous story."

"So it's all true. All of the rumors. The information I received psychically. It's all accurate?" Dave asked.

"Every piece of it, no doubt."

"Is there a way to track down what happened to Francis' baby?" Tessa asked.

Alice had a look of defeat on her face as she shook her head. "It would take a large team and resources to track down those children. I regret not keeping my files, but I was afraid. In those days, it was easy to threaten someone's livelihood and get away with it. I destroyed all of my research for fear someone would use it against me."

"We understand," Liam said.

"Thank you, Alice." Tessa ran to the older woman and hugged her.

Alice pulled back and turned to continue toward her home. "Whatever you all are up to, please be safe. Bonnie says you're paranormal investigators. Hunting ghosts. If it's Pennington's ghost you're after, I hope you send him to hell." She walked off, using her cane to help her as she went.

The plan had been gone over, laid out, memorized, and now, it was time to follow through.

The seance was only a means to stir the activity in the hospital. They were hoping to draw the doctor away to relax the other spirits. Instead, it was Francis who visited them. No harm done, Luke assured Tessa. They'd pivot and make it work. Pennington was probably pissed the hell off and would respond to Luke's provoking more easily. This would give her and Dave the chance they needed to help free the spirits on the other side of the building.

She looked over at Luke. His skin glowed in the passing streetlights as they drove. When he parked the van in front of the hospital, he got out and ran around to help her. Dave stood off in the distance.

"Please be careful." Luke's words held a hint of emotion. "If you want to stop at any time, just let me know. You'll have your own walkie-talkie."

Tessa reached up, encircling her arms around the back of his neck. "I will." She placed a kiss on his lips. "It's going to be okay. I know it."

"Someone else is joining us. I thought we needed more help."

Before she could ask who, he tilted his head to the side. Her gaze followed, and Lexi and Emily appeared.

"You didn't think I was going to let my sister go on her first investigation by herself, now, did you?" Lexi raised an eyebrow as she spoke. Her thin eyeliner accentuated her sharp cat eyes.

Liam came up behind Emily and wrapped his arms around her waist. "These two are going to be in our command center inside. They'll be monitoring all of the cameras. If they see anything strange, they'll let us all know immediately."

"Are you guys sure?" Tessa asked.

Lexi adjusted her large shoulder bag. "Of course. Besides, it isn't like Em or I haven't done this sort of thing before. And this time, I won't be left alone. Em will stay with me. Plus, I've taken down a wicked witch. I think I can handle a pissed-off doctor."

"You better keep your ass in that command center," Trey insisted. "Don't you go snooping around the building." Trey pointed a finger at Lexi. It was a loving gesture, though his tone had a more serious note.

Lexi turned and walked away in silence.

"Lex?" Trey took off after her. "I'm serious. You stay put."

Knowing her sister, she was about to give him an earful.

"Emily, Are you sure. You don't need to do this." Tessa didn't want to mention that she knew about her pregnancy.

"Yes, of course. I do this from time to time for the team when they aren't on the road. It helps them out so they can focus more on the investigation and have all hands on deck at all times instead of one hanging back to monitor cameras."

Emily and Liam walked away. Tessa watched Liam pull her aside for what looked like a quiet, private moment.

Luke took her hand and walked her inside the hospital. It was the first time Tessa had been inside, other than in her dream. It was eerie and unsettling to know that it looked exactly like she'd dreamt it. Her sight fell on Trey and Lexi behind a glass-framed room.

"It's the old reception office," Luke explained. "Perfect place to set up monitors as there's a clear view of all of the corridors on this level, as well as the main staircase to the floors above."

"They'll be safe?"

"Yes. They will be. And if they really need to, they can get outside quickly through the main doors." he gestured with his thumb to the exit just steps behind them. "If a situation arises, we can all meet outside."

They entered the reception room. Two large computer monitors sat side by side. On their screens, camera feeds divided into frames were already illuminated.

Tessa took a relaxed pose, half sitting on the edge of the desk and propping herself against it, her palms flattened on the worn-out wood. She watched Luke as he loaded his vest, placing gadgets in the many pockets. She imagined his muscles flexing under his clothing. Only the skin of his tattooed wrists was visible, but she knew how each part of him looked when he moved. Blood rushed to her face. Heat burst in her core. Fuck, it was bad timing, but what she'd give to have him to herself for a few moments.

When he lifted his head, his eyes met hers, sending another rush of excitement through her. His tongue jutted out, slow and deliberate, licking his gorgeous lips as he flashed her a half grin. He knew he was driving her insane. The twinkle in his eye sparked, and he stared at her while setting a holster with a rigid bar attached to it down on the table. A small tablet sat connected to it.

She went to him, unable to keep her distance any longer. She needed to be closer to him, even if only just to talk.

His grin grew. "Here." He handed her a camera. Then walked behind her and buckled a holster around her waist. He pulled the adjustable strap so it fit properly. She didn't miss his hand resting on the small of her back while he loaded the belt. A flashlight and extra batteries went in. "This is a voice recorder." He held up the black device. "When it's on, it'll flash when it records a voice. That's how you'll know for sure you caught an EVP. You can play it back instantly. Here's your walkie. I already turned it to my channel. All you have to do is press and talk. I'll hear you."

"Got it."

He turned to the table and picked up the vest he'd set there moments before and put it on. "This holds the camera and device with the feed so I can keep my hands free."

She watched as he adjusted it. "That's quite the setup."

"Guys?"

Tessa turned toward Emily's voice. Liam and Trey moved closer. Luke held Tessa's hand in a tight, protective grip.

"She's aware of our plan," Dave said.

Everyone looked on while the frame of the camera that was filming a room at the end of one of the corridors on a floor above them struggled to keep the feed. Static took over every few seconds.

"It's time to move. The doctor is getting suspicious." Dave finished buckling a holster around his waist.

Tessa turned to Luke. "Go. We don't have much time."

Luke took her face in both of his hands. "Radio me immediately if something goes wrong."

"I will."

"Lexi and Em, that interference you're seeing is Francis. She has others with her. It's the influx of a lot of energy."

Lexi turned and faced all of them. "Okay, but where's the asshole?"

Emily reached out and placed a hand on her friend's shoulder.

"He's hiding," Dave confirmed. "It's where he stays most of the time. There's a basement?"

"Not really," Luke answered. "There's a lower level on the west side of the building. That's where the pool is."

"He knows we're up to something but thinks the other spirits are just hiding from him right now. We have to act fast before he leaves that area, and we can't lure him back there."

Luke's gaze traveled to land on Dave. There were no words uttered right away. The two men stared at each other for a long moment then Dave spoke. "I'll keep my eye on her. I promise."

"I think I should go with you." Lexi moved passed everyone and stood close to Tessa.

"I'd feel more comfortable with you being near her," Luke agreed. "Emily, will you be okay on your own?"

"Of course. It's nothing I haven't done for you guys before."

"This is more dangerous."

Emily held her hand up to Liam. "I stood up to a dead murderer. Faced him head-on. I can monitor these screens and keep an eye on everyone. Lexi should stay close to Tessa. It will help Luke focus on the task at hand."

"Alright," Liam blew out.

Tessa turned to Luke while Liam and Emily shared another quiet moment. "Go do what you do best. I'll be with Lex and Dave, and I'll be okay." She threw her arms around him.

He held her tight, and Tessa let the warmth seep from him and into her soul.

"I'll get him."

"I know."

He let go and followed his team to one end of the building while Tessa walked behind Dave as he led her and Lexi to the room where, if all went as planned, they'd set the trapped souls Pennington kept imprisoned free.

Twenty-Eight

Despite the fact that Lexi had sworn she'd never investigate again or use her powers, she found herself eager to see what would unfold. Hopefully, she wouldn't have a run-in with "The Doctor," as everyone kept referring to him.

She was, however, anticipating the possible encounter with the resident ghostly patients. Not that she didn't want to take pleasure in telling Dr. Pennington off for tormenting her sister and conducting unthinkable crimes. Her top priority was sticking by Tessa and making sure she was safe and rid of the attachment the doctor had on her once and for all.

The distraction of the evil spirit making an appearance was not something Lexi was interested in dealing with at the moment. She'd leave that to the guys. Her job was keeping Tessa safe.

The hallway vibrated with an energy she'd never felt before. Her skin itched with unease as they walked past the presence of individuals. Invisible to most, yet their auras were palpable to her and to Dave, calling out from beyond a thin shroud that cloaked their world.

Lexi concentrated on shielding herself from any negativity the spirits might send her way. She was there to help, but they didn't yet know that.

Her attention landed on her sister, where Tessa stood staring at a closed door in front of her. "Tess. What is it?"

Silently, Tessa reached out and opened the door. She walked through, and Lexi and Dave followed her inside. The room was barren, the walls covered in moisture and scarred with dark streaks from years of dripping water. The ceiling peeled away in places.

"Oh, God."

Lexi directed her attention to Tessa, who now stood frozen in the center of the room they'd just walked into. "What's wrong?"

"This is the same room as my dream."

"Are you sure?"

Tessa walked to a far corner in silence and crouched down. When Lexi made it to her side, she crouched next to her sister. The sight on the concrete floor confirmed what her sister had seen in her dream. Rows of holes littered the floor they stood on at the far end of the room. "Plumbing."

"This is where Francis died. She drowned in this room," Tessa whispered.

"This room was filled with bathtubs for shock therapy," Dave added. He held his fingers to his head. His eyes were closed. "*Gahhh.* The sadness in here is so thick. People were left in tubs for days at a time."

"That's barbaric," Lexi shouted. "None of the workers here ever went to the authorities to report what was happening?"

Dave shook his head. "Lexi, I'm getting tons of visions. Can you radio the guys? I want them to hear what I'm about to say."

Like a dark abyss in the middle of a glass enclosure, the pool room sat as an extension of a wing on the back side of the building. Pillars shot up, forming arches above that resembled Roman architecture. Luke could see why the owners wanted that area of the hospital renovated first. It was an impressive sight that would make a great venue for a multitude of events. Though the lack of light turned the water into an eerie sight.

A closer look at the pool's edge revealed the new tiles were an array of alternating dark blue hues, lending to the water's mysteriousness beneath. The moon's light reflected through the clear glass ceiling and was the only natural source of illumination in the space.

Using the substantial amount of conductive water in the room, the team engineered an experiment. It's said that water acts as a passageway for spirits, aiding the energy needed to fuel and help them take shape. So, Luke figured, all they needed was a way to draw

Pennington out into the open, and they could then trap him.

Two tall copper wires attached to a battery stood nearby at a safe distance from the water. Beside it lay a row of black tourmaline wands. They'd created Jacob's Ladder. The battery would charge the coils. They hoped it would entice Pennington, act like a high for him to stick around the pool and give him the extra energy he needed to fully manifest. Once close enough to the trap, the crystal wands would draw in his negative energy, trapping him in the room, giving Dave the time he needed to free the spirits on the other side of the building.

Lexi's voice coming through the walkie-talkie gave Luke a jolt. Immediately, his thoughts shifted to Tessa.

Trey held down the button on his walkie. "Copy that, Lex. Is everyone okay?"

"We're all fine." The rest of Lexi's words morphed into an echo while Luke's heart slowed its pace. "Dave is having a vision. I'm standing right next to him. He wants you guys to listen to what he has to say."

Dave's words came through the walkie. "Francis is here with us. She has others with her."

"So, we're on track," Liam whispered.

"She's shown me that the rumors of how she died are true. He performed a lobotomy on her, and afterward, she was put into a hydrotherapy shock bath where she drowned."

The three friends looked at each other. Even with the alleged knowledge of what happened, it was still a punch to the gut to learn that it was all true.

Luke bounced his shoulders in an attempt to ease his frustration. It was getting harder to keep his temper under control.

A rumble of a growl interrupted Trey.

The guys' heads raised, and they looked in the direction of the far end of the room. It was pitch-black, and something ominous was present.

"Dave, we'll check in with you soon. I think we have company."

"Copy that," he confirmed. "Keep your guard up."

"We always do," Luke answered.

His mood switched. Reminding himself that Dave was capable of judging dangerous situations and he'd keep Tessa out of harm's way. Luke went from anxious to confident. It was time he allowed his skills as an investigator to take center stage and put a stop to Pennington.

He had to admit the experiment they'd set up excited him. Now, it was time to put trust in their knowledge and capabilities. "Fuck. I'm pumped all of a sudden."

Trey nodded in agreement. "It's gonna work."

Liam pulled a small remote control from the pocket of his vest. With the touch of a button, he switched it on, sending life to the battery where they'd attached a power switch. The trigger objects in the chest from the attic, including the ledger and all of the papers that lay inside of it for decades, were near. They even added the file of Dr. Pennington that Luke found during their last investigation of the hospital.

"Go ahead, Luke. I know your itching to start."

He chuckled at Liam's statement. His friend knew him well. Luke had an affinity for provoking troublesome spirits, and he enjoyed every minute. Of course, he only provoked those spirits that needed to be forced to come forward so they could get answers and help the people who had called them in. Luke didn't believe in aiding anyone, not even ghosts, with excuses.

With his camera running and held out in front of him, he shouted, "Doctor Pennington!" Luke moved with caution around the electrical current.

"I have a box here." He stood next to the chest they'd brought from the attic. "I figured out where you used to live. Not too far from here. There are photos of you inside, and guess what." He paused and glanced at his teammates. The moon shining through the glass above provided some faint light, allowing him to see without the aid of the camera's viewfinder. "We also have a photo of you and the police chief, Clark. You were friends, weren't you?"

"Whoa," Liam and Trey stated in unison.

"I feel it, too," Luke said as a sharp chill cut through the air around them. His eyes stayed locked on the tablet screen connected to the vest he wore. "A figure appeared on the screen across the pool, but it's gone now," he told his friends, then went back to speaking to Pennington. "That got your attention. I know what you did. I know the awful crimes you committed."

"Motion detector." Trey indicated to the device lighting up on the other side of the pool. Then, the next one illuminated. A few yards after, the next one lit up, following a path that led straight to them.

Luke took a few steps backward, unsure of what was approaching. "Something is looming over me."

"Trey, get the thermal on him," Liam instructed.

His friend adjusted the thermal camera in his hands. "There's a strange temperature signature all around you."

"Yeah?"

"You're engulfed in a purple haze. It looks like it's pulsing in and out."

"Shit. My head." Luke squeezed the spot where his nose met between his eyes.

The Jacob's Ladder sparked furiously. The current moved rapidly like it was being pulled in his direction.

"Luke, get away from there." Liam insisted.

"Fuck, I can't move."

He was pulled to the left by his friend's grasp just as a hideous growl emanated from behind him. The experiment swayed back and forth. The bastard was trying to move it.

"Damn, It felt like an ice pick was being driven into my skull."

The realization of what he said hit him. *Shit.* The fucker was making him feel what he put his patients through.

"You're mad because we found you out, Dr. Pennington. It's a shame you ever held that title. You were no doctor," Liam spit out in a harsh tone. "You were a madman. It was you who should've been locked up all along. I'm only glad they finally caught you. Figured out what you were doing to the women admitted here. Now you're keeping watch, making sure no one ever finds out what you did. But you should know your secrets are already out. Those crimes have followed you into a different plane of existence. You can't ever escape them. They're stuck on you. Your legacy is now that of a greedy lunatic."

Trey stepped next to Liam. "Did they finally do to you what you did to the patients here, Doctor? Did you suffer that same fate? That same hideous procedure you performed on them—on people who didn't need them?"

Luke stood silent, still rubbing the spot that was now sore. His mind was clouded. He knew his friends sensed him struggling. They took command of the situation, taunting and provoking, doing what they could to keep Pennington right where he was and give Dave the time he needed.

Twenty-Nine

Emily sat in the reception area near the front of the building. Her nerves were on edge. She hadn't felt this unsure of anything since the night Lexi joined forces with a coven of witches to put a stop to a blazing wall of flames rushing for a small town while she stood and watched, not knowing if they'd make it out alive. Still, not even her own encounter with Banks had frightened her as much as this. For some reason, as she sat and watched everyone on the monitors, she felt a sense of unease that left her feeling uncomfortably ill.

She strained her eyes to focus on the screens in front of her. Breathing deeply through her nose, she tried to distract herself and pull her attention away from the nausea that struck her.

Blinking a few times, she thought her mind was playing tricks on her as she watched a black fog creep across the pool room where Liam and the guys were. Clear as day on the camera, a dark mist hovered around the edge of the pool. She watched as the guys moved back in unison.

She grabbed the walkie sitting next to her, and in a shaky voice, she radioed, "Liam. Come in."

"I'm here, Em."

"There's a black mass on my screen, and it's heading toward you guys. I watched it move from one side of the room over to where you're standing. It seems to be hovering."

"Copy that. We're getting a lot of activity in here now. Keep us posted on anything else–"

Static took over the channel. Emily's heart dropped. On the screen, she saw Liam trying to get his message across and Trey and Luke using their walkies. Most likely trying to reach Lexi and Tessa.

An explosion echoed through the halls, sending Emily into a momentary panic. She checked the monitor again and caught the sight of Liam unplugging the Jacob's Ladder from the battery. They would never end an experiment early unless something was wrong.

That's it. She pushed the chair away, pulled her jacket on, snatched up her cell phone and walkie and made her way to the door of the small, enclosed office. She'd promised Liam she'd wait outside if she became too uncomfortable. She'd continue to try and reach him on either the walkie or his phone, but she needed to keep herself and their baby safe.

Her hand went to her belly. No longer flat or soft. The slight roundness had hardened over the last week, giving her just a hint of a bump that was still hidden under her clothes.

She swung her head to the right, then the left, while using her flashlight to make sure there were no obstacles in her way. When her eyes couldn't decipher any dangers, she continued forward. One foot in front of the other, she walked down the few stone stairs that led to the front doors of the hospital. There she lifted her head and stopped in her tracks.

Her mind wanted to be convinced she wasn't seeing what was in front of her, but her heart knew it was real. A woman stood in solid form. Her blonde curls were disheveled. Piercing blue eyes pleaded as she motioned in a frantic "come here" gesture with her hand.

Emily walked to her, but her voice stuck in her throat. When she reached the door, she pushed it open. The woman still next to her helped her out into the night air. When she turned back toward the front steps, the woman said, "Stay away. You aren't safe here." Her eyes drifted down, landing on Emily's stomach. Emily instinctively covered her bump.

"What about Tessa?"

"I'll keep doing what I can. Stay out here until it's safe."

"When will that be?" Emily asked.

"You'll know." The woman stepped back and faded away into the darkness.

Emily stared in awe. A part of her wanted to run back inside, but she heeded the words of the woman. The one who had somehow managed to bring a team strong enough and knowledgeable enough together to fight the evil that was still hovering over the decrepit location. Emily knew without the woman's clues and risking herself on the other side, they wouldn't have gotten as far as they had.

"Francis."

Thirty

"There are so many people in here," Lexi whispered.

Tessa felt the presence of something around her, but she was too afraid to say it out loud. Dealing with the spirit world was new to her, and it still felt unreal.

"Yes. And they're scared," Dave validated. "I can feel Pennington. He's with the guys, but he knows we're up to something."

"Does he know what we have planned?" Tessa asked.

"Not the specifics. He's occupied for now. He wants to taunt the team. He thinks he can scare them, then move on to us. We need to be careful. He's very unpredictable."

Lexi moved to stand closer to Tessa. She wrapped an arm through hers, locking elbows and holding her close.

All of a sudden, Tessa's anxiety spiked. She rode a wave of anticipation that sent her into a nosedive, straight into uncharted waters. "Lex, I need to tell you something." Why she felt the sudden urge to share at that moment was a mystery to her, but when Dave looked up and locked eyes with them, Tessa knew it would have to wait.

"We need to begin now, Dave informed them. "Lexi, I want you to keep envisioning a protective light surrounding us. I'll guide as many spirits as I can away from here and hopefully cross them over."

"I can do that." She faced Tessa. "We'll talk as soon as this is all over."

"Okay, Sis."

Dave spoke to the spirits that surrounded them. His voice was calm and hypnotizing. It carried a gentleness as he told those who were trapped they were free and they needed to move toward the light.

Lexi stood, eyes closed, her features relaxed as she focused on what Dave had asked her to do. Tessa watched in awe as her sister assisted. Never in a million years did she imagine Lexi would partake in a paranormal investigation. But it seemed a lot had changed over the last year and a half.

Tessa's insides fluttered at the idea. So much more was about to change, and she wanted nothing more than to shout it out and let her sister know. Why her brain had decided to push aside her selfishness and share her news at that precise moment, Tessa had no idea. But the task at hand kept her quiet. She'd share as soon as the night was over. When they were safe. When they were rid of Pennington.

"It's working," Dave announced in his quiet voice. "They're moving. Keep focusing."

"Okay," Lexi answered.

Tessa focused her camera on the room. Nothing visual to her had happened yet, and aside from the room feeling statically charged, there was no noticeable change from what she could tell.

She panned the room. The static night vision cast the view in an eerie gray tone on the camera screen. She walked around while filming, unsure of why she felt the need to leave her sister's side.

At the door, she stopped. Peeking out into the hallway, she used the camera to view through the darkness and stepped into the black void. Instantly, she regretted it.

No longer was she in the same area of the hospital where she'd begun. Whatever complex power was at work in the place had instantly transported her to another part of the building. She ran through the unfamiliar hallway, unsure of where she was headed, with one goal in mind. Find Luke, and get out.

Paint peeled in long strips. Walls were eaten away by mold and time. Her feet splashed on the wet ground echoing around her. Her lungs wheezed as she cried out for Luke, but the sound only bounced off the solid walls, piercing her ears when no one answered back.

She kept running, trying to make sense of the layout and remember the way to the front of the building, but no matter how hard she tried, she only kept finding herself back in the same spot where she began. The longer she ran, the more confused she became.

She tried once more, taking off in a sprint. This time, she started out going right instead of left. A deep, cold chill gripped her wrist, stopping her in her tracks. She flinched and pulled away.

"*Shh.*"

She looked into the eyes of Francis. They shone with the same fear Tessa felt coursing through her body.

"What's happening?" Tessa asked in a hushed tone.

"He's escaped the room where your friends were. He brought you here. We don't have much time."

"What?" Tessa asked, still in a state of utter confusion.

"Tessa?" Luke's voice echoed in the distance.

Without thinking, she ran toward his call, ignoring Francis' plea to stop. She couldn't. She had to find Luke.

She pushed through a set of doors and burst into a full run. A stairway she hadn't come across before appeared, and she took them down, only stopping when she entered a large room where pillars stretched to a glass ceiling. Moonlight glistened on the surface of the pool, so still, it acted as a dark mirror reflecting the glass above.

"Tessa, stop!" Francis' voice called from somewhere behind her. "It's not safe."

Tessa looked around the room. The experiment that Luke had explained lay toppled over on the other side of the pool. The device he'd described had been tossed a few yards from where the battery sat. Her heart sank, and a queasy sensation took over. *What happened to the guys?*

With caution, she moved toward the experiment. A walkie-talkie lay in a puddle. She tried switching it on, but the water must have broken it. She reached to her waist and pulled out her own walkie. When she pressed the button, the light didn't come on. She tried again. Nothing. It was useless.

"Luke," she called again, and to her relief, he answered back.

She watched as the team, along with Lexi and Dave, hurried toward her. With relief, her heart slowed, and she relaxed. Just as the group reached the door, it swung, slamming against the doorjamb in a massive thud that sent a violent shockwave through the space. A moment later, the opposite door behind her slammed too. She screamed at the impacting sound.

Luke banged relentlessly. His fists reverberated on the metal, his calls for her muffled behind the heavy door.

"I'm okay," she shouted, her voice shaky with fear. She reached for the flashlight attached to her waist belt. It glowed in a dim yellow hue, indicating to her that the batteries were weak. Luke mentioned to her that ghosts liked to drain batteries. It seemed Pennington was feeding on every electronic device she had on her.

"We're going to find a way in. Just hang on," Luke shouted from the other side of the barrier that she was now trapped behind.

A heavy feeling descended. The weight of dread thickened the air.

She was done with Pennington. The bastard had shown himself to her before, and now that she was completely alone, she was sure he'd do it again, but this time, she'd be ready to face him.

"What do you want?" Tessa demanded, fed up with playing cat and mouse. She wasn't going to be his entertainment in a sick game. "I'm not running anymore, so come out and show yourself. Or are you too much of a coward?"

She scanned the area, looking for any sign of him. "You spent your time taking advantage of those who were weaker than you when you were alive. Using your authority to overpower them." Tessa turned in a slow circle as she spoke, hoping to capture a glimpse of Pennington. Her camera still worked, though the battery was draining quickly.

"You raped the female patients and sold the babies. You're a sick fuck. You showed your face to me once before. Why don't you do it again!" She spoke the words before she could decide if she truly wanted to speak them out loud. But it was too late. She held the camera up again, and when she turned to her left, she froze.

Standing in front of her was the man she'd seen in the hallway that fateful night, his eyes as evil as she remembered. Tessa was certain if she stared long enough, she'd get a glimpse of hell. Her blood ran cold.

She remembered what he'd done to her in the house. Recalled the images Dave described during the seance and what he'd done to Francis. And now, she was face to face with the demon. He was as solid as any living being. And she was alone.

Thirty-One

Luke's fists turned numb from his relentless pounding, so he threw all his strength against the heavy, metal double doors. He ignored everyone around him, his only goal breaking into the room and getting to Tessa.

He was so close. So close to having her back in his arms. How could he have been so stupid to agree to her staying for this part of the investigation? His entire world stood on the other side of that door, and a ghost hell-bent on tearing it all away from him was with her.

"He's shut us out," a familiar voice called out.

Chills ran down Luke's spine. He felt the hands of his friends on his shoulders. He turned, glimpsing everyone present, staring at him in silence. His eyes followed their line of sight. When he landed on what had captured their attention, shock hit him.

Francis stood. But not in the transparent form she took back at Tessa's house. She was solid now, and clear as day in front of everyone again.

"Is there another way in?" Dave asked, seeming not as shocked as everyone else.

"He's locked that entrance too.

"We have to get in there," Luke pleaded. "Please."

"Luke." Lexi took hold of his forearms and squeezed. "Tessa is smart, and she's strong. She's going to be okay."

He stared at Tessa's sister, struggling with how to tell her that it was more than Tessa in danger. He ran his hands over his head. He heard Tessa's faint voice from behind the door, but he couldn't make out every word. It sounded like she was conducting her own EVP session.

He brought his hands to the front of his face in a prayer motion. Lexi's eyes stayed locked on him like a hunter about to pounce on its prey.

"Why do I feel like I don't know the entire story?" she asked.

"Lex," Trey cooed as he walked up and placed his hands on her shoulders.

Emily appeared, running toward them, her flashlight bouncing with her steps. Liam caught her as she ran into his arms. "What happened?" he demanded.

Emily looked over and smiled at Francis.

"I told you to wait outside. It isn't safe for you in here," Francis said.

Emily turned to Liam. "I headed outside when our walkies stopped working, and I ran into Francis. But when you didn't answer your cell, I came back in to see if the monitors were working again. They were, and I saw all of you gathered here, so I came. Your walkie still isn't working, so I couldn't tell you. The static camera's feed by the pool is up again. I saw Tessa, but her walkie isn't working either. She was a safe distance from the water when I left the headquarters." Emily's last statement was directed to Luke.

Lexi stepped forward, hands out in front of her. "Wait." She turned to Francis. "Why isn't Emily safe in this place. What about the rest of us?"

"Lexi, listen," Emily began.

Luke knew he had to be the one to say it. His eyes landed on Trey, who gave him a nod. He stood in front of Lexi and placed his hands on her shoulders to get her full attention. "Lex. Tessa is pregnant."

There was no beating around the bush. No hesitating. Just straight to the point. The moment of silence ticked loudly, but Luke didn't have time to argue with anyone. He straightened and dropped his hands from her shoulders but didn't miss the speechless surprise that washed over her face. He watched Lexi turn to Emily. Her mouth still hung open, and her eyes widened even more.

"Are you...?" Lexi asked in astonishment.

Emily nodded.

Luke watched Trey shoot a surprised look at Liam. It took a second for the information to sink in. His friend and his wife were expecting a baby too. What should have been a joyous moment was ruined because an asshole ghost had a vendetta against pregnant women.

"We need to find a way in there. Now." His statement was more of a demand that he directed toward his teammates. "Emily, you need to go where it's safe."

Liam stepped in and spoke to his wife and her best friend. "We'll talk about everything when this is over. Right now, we need to get you safe so we can focus on getting to Tessa. I want both of you to go back to HQ. Stay there. If anything else happens, anything at all, go outside and don't come back in here." His gaze landed on Emily with intensity, and she agreed.

Lexi looked at Luke in silence. "I'll get to her. I promise," he said.

Emily took her friend's hand and headed down the hallway, disappearing into the darkness.

As soon as they were out of sight, Trey asked Francis, "Can you get in the room? Can you open the door?"

"I can try. If he's distracted enough, I can sneak in."

"She's still talking to him. Try now," Liam insisted.

Francis nodded and faded away. Dave walked to the door and placed his hand on it. "Tessa is facing Pennington. She's talking to him."

"Fuck." Luke seethed.

"Francis is inside. He's distracted by Tessa. He has so much hatred. A hatred for women. Pregnant ones especially."

"Why?" Liam asked.

Dave closed his eyes. "He wants to continue doing what he was doing in life. He feels wronged. All he was doing was trying to fund his research. When Francis questioned him, that threw him off. He thought he had her under his control. He had given her more freedom. It was his way of gaining her trust. Still, she wouldn't back down. That's when his world started falling apart. She had no right butting into his business. He was a doctor. He had a right to conduct his work."

Dave pulled his hand away from the door and shook his shoulders as if trying to erase the images and thoughts from his mind. "Fuck. Doesn't matter how long I've been doing this job. I still can't believe how sick some people are. His only motivation in life was to become famous for inventing treatments. That's how he wanted to be remembered. It's all he cared about. It didn't matter if the treatments harbored any improvements for the patients. Only if he claimed they did."

"We need a plan," Liam said.

"I'm heading straight for Tess once these doors open."

Liam put a hand on Luke's shoulder. "Get her outside. Take her home. Trey, Dave and I will stay here." Liam turned to their psychic friend next. "Can we cross him over, so he can't hurt anyone else?"

"We can try, but it won't be easy."

"After the situation with Banks, I think we can handle it," Liam argued.

Just then, the door in front of them vibrated. Francis was working from the other side. Luke rushed and pressed the push bar. His friends joined him. It took all four of them to push against the energy that blocked them.

Once the door finally burst free of the otherworldly restraint, Luke looked up. Tessa stood on the other side of the pool, her camera held out in front of her. She spoke to Pennington, whose apparition faced her.

Time stood still. Pennington turned his head. Eyes ablaze with disgust, he stared at Luke. It was at that moment he knew he had to act fast. He turned and broke into a full run.

He barely felt his feet hit the ground as he rounded the end of the rectangular pool. Tessa spun so that her back now faced Pennington. Her gaze fell on Luke. He watched as her hair lifted and flew around her head as if the wind were picking it up. Her arms raised above her head, and her feet left the ground.

No matter how fast Luke ran, he couldn't move fast enough. Tessa levitated. In the blink of an eye, she was hovering over the water. Luke yelled, but it was too late. She hit the surface with brutal force. The sound of her connecting with the water was loud enough to break bones.

He didn't see Francis attack the evil that had kept her captive and stolen her life. Nor was he aware of the glass above shattering into millions of shards as Pennington let out a thunderous roar.

Luke dove into the deep end of the pool without a second thought. The moon's light was no longer visible, and he swam blindly in bleak water that now held the most precious things in the world to him.

Thirty-Two

L iam watched Francis attack Pennington, but his ghostly form threw her aside like petals on the wind. Liam and Trey grasped each other's shoulders as they worried for their friend and for Tessa.

The former domed ceiling above lay in millions of shards at their feet. The majority of those shards ended up in the pool. Pennington's fury directed each piece like a missile homed in on its target.

Both Liam and Trey made a move to jump in the pool, but Dave stepped in front of them. "It's too dangerous," he shouted. He motioned with his head in the direction where Pennington stood in the shadows. Their flashlights cast just enough light, but where the doctor lurked, the light wouldn't penetrate.

A vibration grew and shook the room. The three of them were lifted from the ground and thrown out into the hallway. They landed with a thud against the hard, stone floor.

Groaning, Liam rolled. "Is everyone okay?"

Confirmations came from both Trey and Dave. Liam got to all fours and pushed to his feet. They were lucky no one was seriously injured. It wasn't the first time they'd been physically attacked, but every time it happened, it was a reminder of just how dangerous their job was.

"What do we do now? Luke needs us," Trey pleaded. "Dave, any ideas?"

"Liam, I think it's best you go and stay with Emily and Lexi. We've underestimated this bastard, and he's a hell of a lot stronger than we thought. I'm going to have to call on my spirit guides to help me out. Trey? I need you to stay behind. Can you open yourself up and direct Luke for me? I'll open up a doorway and see if I can communicate with this lunatic's mother. I don't think she was as terrible as he remembers. If I can link a pathway to the two of them, I may be able to move him out of here. But I can't do that and communicate with Luke at the same time. You have a bond with him and can patch into him easily."

Trey turned to Francis. She stood outside the door with them once again. "Can you get back in there and do what you did before?"

"I can try."

"Let's move." Liam picked up his flashlight that lay on the floor. "We've got this. Luke will hear you." He placed his hand on Trey's shoulder again.

"I know. Get to Emily, and tell Lexi to stay put."

Liam gave his friend a nod and took off down the dark hallway. Downstairs, in the front of the building, he found Emily and Lexi behind the glass of the reception-ist's office. Emily came running out. "What happened?"

He moved her back inside and shut the door. Before Lexi could say anything, he held his wife in front of him and looked her up and down. "Are you okay?"

"Yes. I'm fine."

"Liam. Where is Tessa?" Lexi demanded.

"What did you guys see before the cameras cut out."

"Nothing," Emily said. "When I got back here with Lex, the screen was blank again. I thought they became unplugged, and we were waiting for you guys to restore the feed."

So they hadn't seen Tessa's violent plunge into the pool. Or Luke jumping in after her. He was thankful for that, but he didn't have the words to tell Lexi what he'd seen. "Pennington pushed us out. Luke is locked in the pool room with Tess. I'm staying with the two of you while Dave and Trey work on connecting with Luke. Dave thinks he has some leverage to get Pennington to listen. Francis is with them too."

"Locked in? Liam, tell me you're going to get my sister out of there." For the first time since Tessa's ordeal began, Liam heard emotion grip Lexi.

"Trey is going to communicate with Luke while Dave does his work."

She nodded in understanding.

"They won't stop until they're both safe."

Thirty-Three

"My guides are showing me what's going on." Dave pressed one hand to the door. The other was stationary in mid-air, held out in front of him.

Trey could feel Luke's panic. Trey used his mind to direct his thoughts and speak to him. "We're with you, brother. Hang tight." He couldn't be sure if Luke heard him or not. He could have pressed harder but felt his friend needed to focus, so he eased back and kept himself in tune with the emotions Luke generated. If there was a change, he'd step in again.

He looked around and noticed Francis wasn't in sight.

"She's trying to sneak inside," Dave said, reading his thoughts.

Trey breathed a sigh of relief. They'd run into friendly spirits before, but never had they established an open communication where they relied on them to help guide and watch out for the team on the other side. "Luke is okay. Anxious but alive."

"Can you get a reading on Tessa?"

"No."

"She's alive," Dave said, releasing a long breath after a few moments. "But still in danger." He inhaled deeply. "Let's get to work."

Trey let out a relieved exhale. *Thank God.* But Dave was right. If everyone was going to walk out of that building alive, they were going to need to work quickly. Pennington was a ticking bomb with his finger on the detonator. There was no telling what his next move would be.

"What do you need me to do?"

Dave once again closed his eyes and took a wide stance. Trey had seen that posture before, and it always meant he was preparing for war. Trey mimicked the position. "I'm ready."

"Good. Shit's about to turn on him."

"What do you mean?"

"Luke and Tessa aren't alone. They have help. Our job is keeping Pennington away from them."

Trey drew his attention back to the closed door as Dave began a series of deep breaths. Trey knew better than to disturb his friend while he worked on grounding himself.

Some burning questions blazed at the surface, though. How the hell were they going to intercept Pennington? Also, who was with his teammate and pregnant girlfriend?

Thirty-Four

He never understood the gut-wrenching pain. Even when watching Liam and Trey desperate to get to Emily and Lexi, he never fully understood. Not until he broke the surface of the cold water.

His strong arms and legs pulled and pushed him. Sounds of rippling water whizzed past his ears as a muffled explosion burst above him, but he didn't dare look up to see what had happened. He focused straight ahead. He knew Tessa couldn't be far, yet searching in this sea of blackness was like looking for a thumbprint in wet sand.

He reached the bottom and righted himself, turning in circles with his hands out in front of him. *Where is she?*

The pressure of the water weighed on him. His lungs burned. He wasn't as good a swimmer as he was a runner. Determined not to give up, he inched along while he continued his search.

He dove in right where she'd hit the water, so why wasn't she right in front of him? His panic multiplied. If his own lungs were crying for air, he knew Tessa had to be fighting too. He found the bottom with his feet and pushed with all his strength to the surface. He would be of no good to her if he drowned.

Gasping, then gulping a lung full of fresh air, he yelled for Tessa but was only met with silence. He scanned the depths from above, hoping to locate her visually first, but the doors to the room were closed, and his friends were nowhere in sight. The son of a bitch had cornered them and shut out any light that could possibly leak into the chamber.

Luke dove again, but for some reason, this time, he held back.

Trey's voice came through. *"Trust your gut."*

Luke stopped in his tracks. His teammate couldn't assist him physically, but he was still with him.

He closed his eyes under the dark water and brought to mind the soft, billowy waves of her hair. Her bright green eyes. He envisioned her in his mind, beckoning her to call out to him. *Where are you, darlin'?*

Opening his eyes, Luke blinked against the water's distorted view, and a faint flash sparked in the distance. He swam to it without hesitation. In all of the surrounding blackness, it had to mean something.

He swam toward the opposite end of the pool. It gleamed bright like a firefly sparkling in the night. The closer he got, the more distant it seemed until he reached the shallow end. There, floating near the steps, a figure lay.

"Tessa!" He pumped his legs, fighting through the water. The moment he was within arm's reach of her, he grabbed hold of one of her arms. Relief hit him when he realized she was face up. Holding her to him, he carried her out of the pool. The cool night air chilled him. He went to the far wall that he could just barely see and sat with his back to the stone. Every thought imaginable went through his head. He didn't understand how he had missed her. She should have been right in front of him unless she'd somehow surfaced faster than he'd expected and swam to the other end of the pool. But how?

Nothing in the world except her opening her eyes could ease the worry. She was breathing, though, and that was enough for now.

"Open your eyes, Tess. Look at me."

The silence was loud. Anger and frustration took over. It was then that he heard his teammate. He knew Trey had some abilities but had never heard him in his head before, and he couldn't have been more thankful to hear him at that moment.

"We're right outside. We have a plan."

"Hurry," Luke said out loud.

For the first time in all his history of investigating, he had to stand down and let his team handle everything. He couldn't risk putting Tessa in more danger.

A cold wind blew through, and when Luke looked up, the stars shone brightly. They were clearer than they should have been, and he realized the glass ceiling was gone. That's where the wind was coming from. He clutched Tessa to him, tightening his hold. That's when dread filled him to his core. Across the room, someone watched.

Pennington.

Luke ground his teeth. He'd never been afraid of facing a spirit head-on before, and he tamped down the fear now. He replaced it with a pure drive to protect Tessa at all costs. He'd trade his soul to keep her safe.

The evil that had tormented her stepped out of the deepest shadows across the room. There he was.

"*I've got him in my sight. I've got Tess. We're against the wall directly across from the door. He's looking right at me, Trey.*" Luke hoped like hell his friend could hear his mind calling out.

"*We're coming.*"

Thank God. He had nowhere to run to take cover. He'd have to trust that his team would see him as soon as the doors opened. How they planned on busting into the room when an angry entity's rage had locked them out, he had no idea, but if Trey said they had a plan, he trusted it.

No sooner than the thought took hold in his mind, the door creaked open. Light from the overhead bulbs in the hallway flooded in through the smallest crack between the door and its metal frame. Luke heard grunting as his friends struggled past the otherworldly strength of Pennington.

The wind picked up again, but it was different this time. It didn't carry the scent of the outside world in with it. A hideous stench filled Luke's nose. With Tessa pressed against him, he braced for the impact he knew was coming.

A cyclone picked up, stealing the breath from his lungs. Blaring wind whistled as it rotated around the room's columns and walls. Droplets of water blew off the surface of the pool in a kind of reverse rain. Waves splashed onto the floor. Dave and Trey stood bracing themselves on a post.

Luke saw Dave's mouth moving but couldn't hear any words over the torrential whirlwind. He squinted and covered Tessa's face with his own, shielding them from the battering rain.

A light caught his attention. The same flickering that had drawn his attention in the pool and led him to Tessa. It grew, and a moment later, Luke realized it was floating toward him. It wasn't Pennington. It didn't possess the same vindictive aura. He wasn't certain it was harmless, of course, but he couldn't pull his gaze away. In awe, he stared until the flicker of light was only a few feet away. The closer it approached, the more he noticed the wind calmed around him and Tessa, just enough to make it bearable.

Tears flooded Luke's eyes when the image of his mother formed out of the tiny light. It could've just been a hallucination, but fuck, he wanted it to be real. Wanted it with every fiber of his being.

"Mom," he choked.

Her smile was just as warm as he remembered.

"This isn't real."

She reached out, and her ghostly hand stroked his cheek in a sensation that traveled through his skin and hugged him from the inside out.

"Luke, you have to let me go." The sound of her voice was a lullaby. A core memory deep inside of him. It struck a chord of greed. He could never let her go.

"I can't."

"You've been placing blame on yourself. You're carrying a burden that you had no control over. It's time to let all of that go. Don't let what happened to me hold you back from living your life."

"Mom, I'm so sorry."

"*Shh*. There's nothing to be sorry for."

"I should have been there," he admitted.

"What would you have done? My choices are not your fault. Nor are they your father's. They're mine and mine alone. I'm so sorry I left the way I did. I need you to know I'm okay. You've helped me, and I'm okay."

"How?"

His mother's beautiful electric blue gaze drifted to Tessa's calm face. "You gave me a reason to come back here and make sure everything turns out the way it should." She stroked Tessa's forehead, and for the first time since he pulled her from the water, Tessa made a sound. Not one of whimpering or discomfort but a soft, peaceful sound as if she were just sleeping. "She's going to be just fine, and so is the baby."

If there was one thing his mother never did, it was lie. He believed her and held on to the promise.

"How do I get her out of here?" From his peripheral vision, Luke knew there was a fight going on beyond the safe bubble that his mother had created around them, but he couldn't pull his sight away from her. He wouldn't. After all these years, he finally had her back in front of him, and he was going to soak up every last second he could get with her.

"You'll know when it's safe. They have help."

"Mom, I..." He struggled to find the words. How do you come up with the right words when you're trying to say your peace? There were no right words, Luke realized, so he said the one thing that meant the most to him. "I love you."

"I know." She smiled gently. "You tell me all the time."

"You hear me?"

"Always. But it's not me you have to tell tonight. You need to let go of your guilt. Don't carry what happened to me as a heaviness with you anymore. I'm okay."

He bowed his head, losing sight of what sat before him. He instantly regretted the decision and breathed a sigh when she still sat in front of him. "You were the light in the pool? You got her to safety before I could?"

His mother nodded.

"Thank you."

She leaned forward and placed a light kiss on his head. "I love you, Luke."

That broke him. Hearing the words from her after so many years—her voice still the sweet tone from his memories. All his years of searching and investigating had finally come to fruition. His goal had always been to talk to her one more time. Now, here he was, with her soft touch on his skin.

"We don't have much time, baby." She looked behind her and then back at him.

She blocked his view, and as much as he cared about his team, he didn't dare take his eyes off of her.

"I don't want to move her," he pleaded.

"She has a bump on the head. Nothing too serious, I promise. When I say, you get to your feet and run for the exit. Don't look back."

He hesitated for a moment. This was it. It was his final goodbye.

"I'm always with you, Luke. Don't worry about me."

A tremendous sound pierced his ears. The safety of the bubble his mother created was gone, but she still held on to him with her hand at the back of his neck, her forehead pressed to his. "Don't look back," she repeated. "Only look forward from now on. Promise me."

"I promise."

"Now go!"

With Tessa in his arms, he kept his word and stood. Luke ran against the wall of wind, not knowing how he gathered the strength to press through its force.

Each stride carried him closer to the only usable exit of the chamber. A quick glance revealed Pennington at the far end. Blinding light erupted from all directions.

Luke's brain didn't care to decipher Dave's shouted words, but Luke knew he was in the process of clearing the evil doctor from the building. Decades of pain, mistrust, and lies were about to be moved from one dimension to another. Where Luke thought Pennington was going, he didn't care. The only thing that mattered was the souls who'd been stuck in that place were free to move on, and Pennington was about to suffer the fate he was meant to receive.

The air moved like a cyclone while Luke focused only on reaching Trey at the door. His friend's hand grabbed his elbow, but a blast threw them to the side, once again hindering Luke's efforts to escape.

Luckily, he managed to twist in time to break the fall for Tessa. She landed on top of him with her hand pressed to his chest. She tried to lift her head.

Dave lay on the ground. He struggled to get to his feet. "Help him!" he shouted to Trey. His words were barely audible over the treacherous wind.

Panic set in as Pennington's ghost took a solid shape once more. With Dave's focus cut, he'd regained strength, and his sight was set on Luke and Tessa.

Luke rolled her to the side of him where he could shield her with his own body. She shifted, and her eyes fluttered open and locked on him in terror. She didn't need to turn to know that something wasn't right. The state of the atmosphere was enough to make anyone question their safety.

"It's going to be okay," he yelled. He tilted her head and held her still. He didn't want the sight of Pennington coming toward them to alarm her. In his peripheral vision, he saw Trey reach Dave, who was now back on two feet. The two men assumed their positions.

Tessa's eyes softened. No longer were they filled with alarm. She was relaxed and confident. "I know. I need to face him."

He shook his head. There was no way in hell he was allowing her to stand in front of the man who tried to kill her and their child.

"Luke! I have to. He's going to go to hell knowing that I won."

There they were. Those sharp edges that he loved so much, cutting to the surface, like the calm before the storm, and in that moment everything inside of him settled. "I love you." The words slipped from his lips in an easy stream.

Tessa's eyelids fluttered. Her mouth hung open after she gasped, and she fell silent. He didn't need her to repeat the words. The emotion that washed over her face the moment he said them told him everything he needed to know. Everything he already knew to be true.

"It's okay. I need you to know right now. I love you," Luke repeated. "You ready to get rid of this bastard?"

With a gentle nod, she pushed him, and he allowed her to sit up. He watched her for a moment, then he helped her stand. His arms tightened around her when she swayed, but she found her balance.

With his mouth close to her ear, he said, "You talk, but I'm staying right beside you." He stepped to the side and kept a firm hold on her with both arms wrapped around her waist.

They stood front to front, exercising their bond for one another on full display. Luke laced his fingers behind her back. He'd be damned if Pennington tried to rip her away from him again.

Thirty-Five

"You lost!" Tessa's words didn't waver. Gone was the shakiness she'd been feeling. The uncertainty. "Your wrath is not going to break us, and you sure as fuck are not taking my soul or our baby."

The evilness in his stare hadn't changed from the first night she'd seen him. It still held an intense bitterness, but now her fear had turned into pure motivation to beat the bastard.

She'd spent too long fighting for what she wanted. Fighting to live her life the way she needed. She'd broken away from her mother's suffocating grasp, and if she could overcome and beat Pennington, there was nothing she wouldn't be able to do.

"We know what happened," Luke interjected. "We know everything about you, the secrets you've been hiding. We found your record book. We know you were selling those infants. Taking your anger out on innocent people has turned you into a monster, and there will never be forgiveness for you. You're a coward. A real man would have moved on, not stayed behind holding a grudge."

Pennington let out a growl that shook the concrete walls.

Tessa's grip on Luke tightened. "I'm not afraid of you anymore."

Dave shouted, "The others have moved on. Your mother is here. She showed me what really happened when you were a boy. Your understanding of what took place is distorted."

Pennington paced like an angry carnivore being kept from its prey. Tessa relaxed when Dave confirm that he was able to help the other spirits cross over. Now they only had the doctor to deal with, and they had every intention of making sure he never harmed another person again.

From the corner of her eye, she caught movement. She focused and gasped when Francis and another woman, who she was sure was a spirit, came through a blown-out window that faced the outside. The two glided to Luke and Tessa and took their stance on either side of them.

"You won't be fighting alone," the spirit she didn't recognize said from behind her.

Luke stood in silence. Tessa noticed he appeared to be captivated by the beautiful woman. She turned her head more and noticed the woman's eyes were locked on Luke's in a bond that seemed eternal, like a mother's love.

"Luke?" her voice broke with emotion. Tessa looked up at the man whose arms held her in a vice against his body. Tears welled in his eye. "Your mom?" He squeezed her tight. She didn't need his words. The unbroken stares between them and the pure love flowing from his expression told her all she needed to know.

Dave began shouting commands that prompted Pennington to burst into a fit. Tessa jumped in Luke's hold, but he held her in a firm grasp. Pennington's raging temper was contained behind a field that surrounded him. Francis stood in front of them now, all of her focus on the man across the room. The man who kept her prisoner in life and in death. The man who committed unspeakable crimes was now held in a force field behind invisible bars.

Tessa heard Dave chanting and saw Trey standing close behind him. "What are they doing?" she asked Luke.

"They're opening a portal. Pennington doesn't have the strength this time to stop them. Dave is trying to cross him over."

"Where?"

"Who knows. Just away from here. Away from us."

Dave's commands echoed around them. A burst of light erupted from behind the entity he was trying to cross over.

Pennington looked back at everyone, for the first time, his expression was one of apprehension. All the energy he'd directed toward them shifted as the light surrounding him engulfed his body. Now, he was the victim of his own wrath as the shattered glass and debris around them formed a cyclone that encircled him. Gone was his sinful and vicious confidence. In that moment, Tessa realized it didn't matter how powerful you were, not in life or in death. There was a force beyond us—beyond any reasoning one could ever imagine. The laws of the universe never wavered. Cause and effect would always reign. It was outside of human control.

"Leave now!"

It was the last phrase audible from Dave before the entire room ignited in a blinding light, and a loud blast shook the ground. Tessa buried her face in Luke's chest, waiting for the wind to die down.

"It's okay," he whispered. "He's gone."

In a tentative peek, she opened her eyes to slits. Trey and Dave stood in the same place close by. The light that had pierced the room and taken Pennington still remained, only now it radiated with warmth, and Francis and the other woman glowed in its haze.

"Thank you," Francis said. "Thank you for listening."

"The others have all crossed over," Dave told her. "You helped them. You helped all of us. We should be thanking you."

She smiled and turned to Tessa. The two of them would forever have a bond that would link them eternally.

"Take care."

Tessa nodded. "We will."

The other woman stepped beside Francis.

"I'm not leaving you," she told them with a smile. "I'll always be near."

"You better be," Luke said with a tearful chuckle.

When they turned, the women's images disappeared, becoming one with the light as they walked side by side.

Thirty-Six

T essa lay against Luke, naked, her heated, silky skin gleaming in the sunlight filtering in through the window. It was morning and a rare, warm-spring day for the city.

His hand had a mind of its own. He stroked her arm, then down the side of her torso before snaking around to cradle the swell of her belly. He closed his eyes and silently thanked his mother. Thinking of that time four months prior always threatened to gut him. He didn't understand how a person could be tossed and hit the water as hard as Tessa had and not suffer any significant injuries. As far as he was concerned, his mother was truly a guardian angel. She saved both Tessa and their baby that night.

Tessa had only suffered a bump on her head and a minor concussion. She stayed in the hospital overnight under observation. After a doctor checked on their baby, she was cleared to go home. As hard as he tried, he couldn't stop the occasional thought from passing over him, always a reminder of the treasure he had by his side.

A moan escaped her lips. She stretched and brought her arm up behind her to wrap around the back of his neck. She pressed her ass to him, and he met her halfway, letting her feel his early morning desire grow between them.

She hummed when he cupped her breast. Its firm weight stirred the heat gathering in his cock. When she moved her arm, he missed the connection but was gratified at the feel of her touch inching between them. He thrust, filling her hand with what she searched for.

All the bad memories melted away in that moment.

He caressed his way down her body, landing at the apex of her thighs, where he teased and brought her to the brink.

They were ravenous for each other. Her hungry kisses deepened, and he gave into her want. She twisted so he could reach her easily. He broke away. The sounds of her heavy breaths matched the rhythm of her hips as she moved them in a delicious dance.

When she came, skin pink, lips parted, momentarily frozen in a state of pure euphoria, his heart burst into a million pieces. It happened every time, and he never grew old of the sight.

Her eyes opened, and that loving gaze of hers glued every one of those pieces back in its place where they waited to be split apart again and again. It was an addiction that he could never overcome.

"Good morning," she moaned in a voice still raspy with sleep.

"It's almost a good morning." He buried his head in her neck. She arched into him, and when he nipped her delicate skin, she gasped. "What have you done to me?" It was a question he asked her often. Not that he expected an answer, but it still amazed him to think the fates and the stars had sent her his way. A brooding tough guy like him with no interest in a family had been sent to his knees at the first sight of her, and he willingly accepted the destiny the universe laid out for him.

"I've never believed in fighting what's meant to be." He grasped his throbbing cock in his hand. Tessa tipped her ass, giving him full access from behind, and he rested himself just at her waiting hot and wet entrance. "I was always afraid fate would find me because I know you can't escape the gifts that the universe sends you. So I kept dodging, staying on defense, protecting my little corner of existence where I knew I was safe. I know now this is what the stars had lined up for me all along. They let me think I had the upper hand—knew how fucking stubborn I was. So they sat back and let me fall into my destiny on my own."

He pushed himself inside of her, feeling her tightness give way to his girth. He moaned with her. Then rocked in and out of her in a gentle rhythm that moved them both to the heights of ecstasy. "I waited for you all these years, and I didn't even know it."

"Luke."

His name in her breathy voice did him in. He wanted to go slow that morning. He had time before teaching the online masterclass for their investigation academy with his teammates later in the day. But the sight of her could not be ignored.

She lay completely open, in complete trust, and as he spoke, she relaxed into him more. They lay on their sides in a connection no one else in the world could possess. It was more than physical. It was emotional. Spiritual.

"I love you."

He froze, afraid his ears might've played a trick on him. He looked down at her, and the smile that stretched from ear to ear told him he'd heard correctly. It was the first time she'd said the words out loud. The sound would forever be burned into his memory.

"I was running too," she went on. "I never let myself dwell on that ache inside of me that wanted to find the other half of my soul. You're right. No one can escape fate. If something is truly meant to be, then it will always find a way. I love you. I'm not afraid to say it anymore."

"I'll never leave you, darlin'. Not in a million years could I ever let you go. I know reincarnation exists, and I'm spending every moment of my next life finding you again."

He resumed his thrusts, never taking his gaze from hers. Tessa's glassy eyes were windows into her soul, only open for him. Inside, an endless abundance of love existed.

How he was lucky enough to be a part of what she had to offer was beyond his comprehension, but he'd never fight it—wouldn't even dwell on it. He'd spend the rest of his days open to whatever the universe was willing to throw his way. Even the bad.

He knew better than anyone there was always light at the end of the tunnel.

Epilogue

Hospitals were always teeming with emotions. Most people associated the confines of their walls with death and sadness, but there was an element of joy to them too.

Lives were saved there, and in these buildings, a soul's passage to earthside took place.

Dave was reminded of this each time he entered a hospital for any reason, even more so that night. He didn't just walk through the halls and pass the living. Lost spirits also wandered the corridors. It was impossible to help every spirit he came across. Over the years, he'd learned how to protect his energy and block them out when he wasn't working. Otherwise, he'd be tormented constantly.

He entered through large, automatic glass doors that separated a wing and made his way to the maternity ward. In a dimly lit room, the entire Spirit Hunters team, including Lexi and a very pregnant Emily, gathered around Luke and Tessa, who'd just welcomed their baby into the world hours earlier.

The little bundle slept in Luke's large arms. He looked comfortable holding the tiny human. Fatherhood already agreed with him.

"Alright," Lexi said gently. She leaned over where Luke sat and marveled over the little wonder. "You two have kept us waiting long enough. Have you chosen a name?"

Luke smiled and looked over at Tessa in the bed. She cleared her throat and said. "Her name is Lilah Alexis Francine Collins."

"Really?" Lexi asked in surprise.

"That's right," Luke confirmed. "Lilah, after my mom."

"Alexis, for obvious reasons," Tessa added with a smile.

"And Francine," Luke continued. "Because without Francis' help all those months ago, we might not all be here today."

"That's a beautiful way to remember her. I'm sure she'd be honored," Dave offered.

While the team chatted in hushed voices, he sat quietly and watched everyone. He wasn't normally standoffish around the group of friends, but something nagged at him, pulling his attention relentlessly away until, finally, he couldn't ignore it any longer.

He allowed the knowledge to pass through him. At the realization of what was happening, Liam's phone buzzed.

His friend pulled it from his back pocket. Dave was already sitting forward, prepared for what his friend was going to say.

"It's Pop." He read the message, then looked at everyone. "Casey's in trouble."

Dave was on his feet before Liam had finished speaking. Trey followed.

Liam's eyes were ablaze. Dave had never seen his friend so angry. His intuition told him Casey was okay but in desperate need of help.

He didn't know what Liam's father had written in the text message about Liam's sister, but Dave was sure it would fire up his own temper after seeing Liam's response.

"Mike's gone too far. Pop says he and Mom are on their way to pick her and the kids up. They want our backup."

Trey stepped forward. "I'll drive you."

"Go," Lexi said. "Give me your keys. I'll take Em home and stay with her until you get back."

"What's going on?" Luke asked.

"No, man. You stay here with your family. Trey and I got this. We'll fill you in later. Take care of that baby and Tessa."

"Let me know if you need anything."

Trey and Liam hugged their friend and their women. Dave followed them into the hallway. Silent, and his head down, he felt the burning questions drift from Liam. He wished he could avoid this difficult conversation with his friend.

They all stopped at the elevator. Liam faced him with a serious expression. "You know what's been going on, don't you?" His friend pushed him against the wall, but Dave didn't fight back. "She's been through enough. How long have you been seeing her?"

Liam's baby sister was the little sister of the entire group. She'd gone off and married straight out of high school but didn't realize the boy who promised her the world was full of broken and empty promises.

"I'll explain later. She needs us. I can feel it."

"Come on, Liam." Trey eased the tension between them.

Dave could understand Liam wanting to protect Casey. She'd moved away so young and was forced to stay away for so long. No one was aware of the magnitude of the situation.

When she'd reached out to Dave at Liam and Emily's wedding, the bond the two of them formed years prior, under the radar of everyone, ignited once more. He'd been unable to sever their connection ever since, and he'd be dammed if he tried.

Her ex-husband, Mike, was going to be sorry he'd ever crossed any line that involved Casey.

Dave pushed himself off the wall that Liam had him up against and started for the hospital's exit. "Let's go. We can talk about this another time. I know where she is. I'll meet you there."

His next stop was Casey's, and it would be the last time he'd leave her in that hellhole. It was also the last time he'd leave her, ever again.

Want More Temperance Dawn

Thank you so much for reading! If you enjoyed the book, please leave a review on Amazon and/or Goodreads. It is greatly appreciated.
Be sure to sign up for my newsletter at www.temperancedawn.com and follow me on social media to stay up to date on all the latest.
I love hearing from all my readers. Check out the Linktree below for all the important links. Thanks again for reading!
https://linktr.ee/temperancedawn

Acknowledgements

To all of my readers,

I would not be able to do this job without you. Thank you for picking up this book. Thank you for taking a chance on me. Thank you for helping make my dream come true. You've allowed me to have the coolest job in the world. For that, I am eternally grateful. You all are the best.

Torri, Burnt By Hades, Piper, and Gina,

You ladies are the best. Thank you for always being there. I love you guys.

J,

I love you.

Also by Temperance Dawn

Spirit Hunters Series
Haunting Emily
Haunting Lexi
Haunting Tessa
Book Four (TBA)
Spring River Series
A Haunting At Spring River Chateau

About the Author

Temperance has combined her love of romance with the paranormal world. She writes stories with strong characters who overcome fear and encounter the spiritual unknown. Her stories mostly center around ghosts and hauntings, but she enjoys dabbling with tales of Vampires too!

She loves all things both dark and gothic, and feminine and frilly. Can you say afternoon tea, followed by a cemetery stroll?

Temperance is a wife and mom to two rambunctious, beautiful kids. She recently moved across the country with her family and is enjoying her new life in the southern United States.